DEAD WEIGHT

DEAD WEIGHT

Susan Rogers Cooper

This first world edition published 2012
in Great Britain and in the USA by
SEVERN HOUSE PUBLISHERS LTD of
9–15 High Street, Sutton, Surrey, England, SM1 1DF.
Trade paperback edition first published
in Great Britain and the USA 2013 by
SEVERN HOUSE PUBLISHERS LTD.

British Library Cataloguing in Publication Data

Cooper, Susan Rogers.
  Dead weight.
  1. Pugh, E. J. (Fictitious character)--Fiction. 2. Women
  novelists--Fiction. 3. Women private investigators--
  United States--Fiction. 4. Detective and mystery stories.
  I. Title
  813.6-dc23

ISBN-13: 978-0-7278-8195-3 (cased)
ISBN-13: 978-1-84751-452-3 (trade paper)

All Severn House titles are printed on acid-free paper.

Severn House Publishers support The Forest Stewardship Council [FSC],
the leading international forest certification organisation. All our titles that
are printed on Greenpeace-approved FSC-certified paper carry the FSC logo.

Typeset by Palimpsest Book Production Ltd.,
Falkirk, Stirlingshire, Scotland.
Printed and bound in Great Britain by
MPG Books Ltd., Bodmin, Cornwall.

To Marian Harper Law, my granddaughter

ACKNOWLEDGMENTS

I'd like to thank all the people who have started the various twelve-step programs, and all those who have been helped through the years by this concept. I'd personally like to thank my agent, Vicky Bijur, for her help and advice, and the intrepid Joan Hess for her counsel.

ONE

As I was heading to the bedroom to get ready, Willis, my husband, met me at the door, his index finger stiffly pointing to the ceiling. 'Have you seen Ridley Hamilton's front lawn?' he asked me sternly.

'No—'

'You ask me, how can Ridley Hamilton's front lawn be green in this, the worst drought in Texas history?' he said, index finger still stiff and pointed.

'I don't think it's the worst in his—'

'I'll tell you why!' he said, his voice getting loud. Then there was silence. Finally he said, 'Aren't you going to ask me why?'

I sighed. 'Why is Ridley Hamilton's front lawn green in this, the worst drought in Texas history?' I asked.

'He cheats!'

'Ah,' I said, trying to move around him to the bedroom. Unfortunately, he followed me. I wondered if he was losing all the blood from his index finger that was still stiffly pointed ceiling-ward.

'Don't "ah" me, missy!' he said.

'Then don't call me mis—'

'Two hours a week!' Willis almost shouted. 'Two frigging hours a week is all we're allowed to water both the front and the back lawn. I looked over his fence!' Willis said, having moved straight into shouting mode. 'The backyard's green, too!'

'Honey, I have to—'

'I can barely keep the shrubs and the perennials alive! Forget about the annuals and the lawn! Have you seen our lawn?'

'Of cour—'

'Dead, E.J. It's dead! And I follow mandatory restrictions! How can my lawn be dead if I'm following mandatory restrictions and Ridley Hamilton's yard be lively and green if he's following mandatory restrictions?'

'Well—'

'Because he's not!' Willis said, now thrusting his finger to the ceiling. Luckily the ceiling in our bedroom is vaulted; otherwise he might have poked a hole.

'You know what?' I said, taking him by the arms and turning him toward the door of the bedroom.

'What?' he said, moving but looking over his shoulder at me.

'I think you should go next door and tell Luna about this,' I declared. Luna is a homicide detective with the Codderville Police Department. We live in Black Cat Ridge, a wholly made town/subdivision developed in the mid-eighties, which is right across the Colorado River from the much older town of Codderville where my husband was raised. Although she lives here, Black Cat Ridge is not Luna's jurisdiction, but it would get Willis out of the house so I could get ready.

'You know, you're right!' he said. 'Maybe she'll let me borrow her gun!' and he moved fast out of our bedroom. Seconds later I heard the front door slam.

I sighed and began to prepare myself for the upcoming ordeal. I'd recently bought a full-length mirror for the back of the closet door. It was a gift to myself for losing thirty-five pounds through the aptly-named 'Weigh In', my weight-loss group. I followed that with a trip to the hairdresser where my shoulder-length mass of red and gray curls was colored as close to the original red as possible, and all of it was cut into what they call a bob, which is shorter in the back then comes down longer over the ears. It's usually done on straight hair and looks sleek and cool. As my hair is kinky-curly, it was a little different. I think it was the first do my hair ever liked, because I was looking Good, and that capital 'G' is on purpose! The first article of clothing I bought was a little black dress; unfortunately, it was for a memorial service, which I was getting ready for as I stared at my reflection.

I'm in my forties and looked better at that moment than I had since my late twenties. I may have had to energize my hair color, but my eyes were still a fairly brilliant green, if I do say so myself, and my smile was still just as straight as when the orthodontist sent me home for the last time. And my body, well, it was definitely in fighting condition, if you know what I mean. I thought I might attempt seducing my husband when I got home later. If the kids were out. If we weren't too tired. If there wasn't anything really good on TV.

The black dress was knee-length and with cap sleeves, as befit a Saturday in July in central Texas. A normal July, that is; this one, however, any clothing at all was too much. The memorial service was for a woman I barely knew. She'd been in my weight-loss group, but I'd rarely talked with her. My neighbour Trisha McClure, however, who lived across the street, knew the woman much better. They were in a MADD group (Mothers Against Drunk Driving) together and had bonded when picketing the capital in Austin over drunk-driving laws.

The deceased was Berta Harris, a thirty-something woman with dark brown hair, brown eyes and a body that was neither heavy nor light. If anything, I'd say she'd been maybe ten pounds over her ideal weight. We'd both been going to Weigh In for six months and I'd never seen her take off a pound. She'd lived somewhere in Black Cat Ridge and the memorial service was being held at the Episcopal Church of Black Cat Ridge. It was going to start in another twenty minutes. I ran into the bathroom and applied lipstick. Yes, I was going all out. I figured a lot of the Weigh In crowd were going to be there, and I was eager to show off my new figure.

Now that my eighteen-year-old son Graham was driving and my fifteen-year-old daughters would all be eligible to take driver's ed this summer, my husband Willis and I decided, with some heavy pushing on my part, that it was time for me to get rid of the old minivan and buy me my own vehicle, one just meant for me. Willis had always had his own car, the one he took to work but was never used for family. My car, whatever it was at the time (station wagon, minivan, SUV) was always the family car. Instances of us going anywhere as a family had become fewer and farther between, and now, if we *did* venture out as a family, we usually took two cars where ever we went – Willis and me in one, Graham and the girls in another. So I was pushing for a two-seater. Willis had finally gotten his huge pickup truck with the oversized tires that took two steps for me to get into, so now it was time for my sports

car – one of those cute Audis, or one of the new Z's. I was
punch drunk with excitement about it. Whatever it was would
have a top that came off, I can guarantee you that.

But at this moment I was still driving a minivan, so I went
into the garage, crawled in, and buzzed across the street to
pick up Trisha. I'm five foot eleven inches. Trisha was one of
those women who always made me feel like the fifty-foot
woman. A petite five foot two, she couldn't possibly weigh
more than a hundred pounds, and her blonde hair was either
natural or the best bleach job ever. She was also incredibly
sweet. She had two little girls, ages five and three, who both
looked just like her, and a husband as big as mine who doted
on her. The McClures had moved in across the street about
a year and a half ago. We were friendly but this would be the
first time Trisha had been in my car. I threw out some of
the trash. Trisha came out of her house to meet me, wearing
a black suit that looked as good on her as my black dress
looked on me. Well, almost as good.

She jumped in the minivan, pulling herself up the step with
the help of the 'sissy' bar above the door. 'God, can you
believe this heat? I think it's already reached a hundred!' she
said.

'And it's only eleven o'clock,' I muttered, turning up the
air conditioning as I pulled the car away from the curb. 'How
well did you know Berta?' I asked, speaking of the woman
whose memorial service we were about to attend.

'Not really that well. Other than that rally in Austin last
month, we didn't talk that much. But Austin was a lot of fun.
There's nothing like a good protest to get the juices flowing.
We all went back to the hotel and got drunk afterwards. And
no,' she said, shooting me a look, 'no one was driving! We
all stayed the night in the hotel!'

'I can't imagine Berta drunk,' I said. 'She was always so . . .'
I struggled for the right word, but Trisha beat me to it.

'Depressed?' she filled in.

'Exactly.'

'Well, let me tell you, she was a depressed drunk too. Three
drinks in and she burst into tears.' That's when she sighed
heavily. 'We all have our own reasons for being members of

MADD. I joined because my dad was a drunk and I was always terrified that he was going to kill himself or someone else. He never did it with a car, but he died of liver failure, so I guess he did kill himself.'

'I'm sorry, Trisha,' I said. 'I didn't know.'

'I don't talk about it much, but it's no big secret. It happened a long time ago and MADD is just the way I deal with it. My brother has his own way – he drinks.'

I patted her hand and she went on: 'But that night when we got drunk, Berta told us about her little boy who was hit by a drunk driver. It happened ten or so years ago, but that's something you never get over.'

I shuddered at the thought. 'God, the poor woman. She was in the weight-loss group because her mother was obese and died from complications of diabetes,' I said.

'I didn't know about that,' Trisha said. 'And now this.'

'What happened anyway?' I asked.

'I don't really know,' she said as we pulled into the parking lot of the church. 'She was in the hospital for something, and the woman who called me – someone from MADD – just said it was complications.'

'Lot of that going around,' I said, while trying to find a place to park. The church had kept almost all of the trees that had originally been in the space designated for a parking lot, and there were so many of them that actual parking spaces were at a premium. It was a very eco-friendly and pretty parking lot, what with all the cars having to find space on the street. I finally found a spot and we parked and headed into the church.

The pews were three-quarters full when we got there, and by the time the service started there was standing room only. I saw several people I knew, some sitting, some standing against the walls. The pastor did a bit of sermon and then the eulogies began. The first was a woman from my Weigh In group, whose tearful goodbye seemed to set a tone. After her was a man from 'an anonymous group' he said, leaving it at that, but his eulogy seemed to indicate that Berta had been a drinker at one point in her life. Next was a woman from Trisha's MADD group, who tearfully told the story of Berta's young son's death and how they would be reunited at last. There was a speaker from a support group for those who had lost their spouses, one from a support group for abused women, one from a support group for family members of institutionalized patients, one from a victims' rights organization, and another from a group of wives of prison inmates. There weren't any family members or friends other than those from these groups. But by all accounts, and the eulogies, it appeared as if Berta Harris had outlived all her family and probably most of her friends.

Berta had been cremated so there was to be no graveside service; instead, we went directly to the rec room of the church where there was punch and cookies. I couldn't help thinking about the services I'd gone to with my mother-in-law at her little Baptist Church in Codderville, where after the service there'd be refreshments – either at the deceased's home or at the church, and everyone would bring their best dish. Fourteen different salads, five of them coleslaw, three green bean casseroles and four broccoli-rice casseroles, a ham, fried chicken, and occasionally a whole turkey. And, oh my God, the desserts . . . As a soon-to-be graduate of Weigh In, that was not something I should be contemplating. But punch and cookies? Come on, people. Is that anyway to send someone off to their maker?

Out of curiosity I made my way amongst the different groups represented and began to get a bio of Berta Harris. Her mother was an obese woman who died of complications of diabetes while addicted to meth; her father was an alcoholic who beat her mother and then shot and killed her when Berta was in her teens; her husband of fifteen years recently died in a car wreck, not unlike her ten-year-old son; her brother, a paranoid schizophrenic, had been hospitalized for several years; and she'd been married to a man who had held her at gunpoint for several hours one dark and stormy night – he was currently incarcerated.

There were so many holes in this bio it was beginning to resemble Swiss cheese. One thing no one knew was how Berta Harris died. Trisha had said she'd been told Berta had been hospitalized and died of 'complications.' Of what, she didn't know. Why she was hospitalized she wasn't told.

The anonymous guy, who was with a group of people swilling coffee like it was going out of style, and who all introduced themselves by first name only, said he'd heard she'd died of a heart attack while on the toilet, Elvis-style.

A woman from RIPS (Relatives of Institutionalized People's Support group) had been told Berta died of anaphylactic shock from a bee sting while on a trip to Six Flags in Dallas.

A woman from WII (Wives of Imprisoned Inmates – not to be confused with the gaming system, or World War II for that matter) said she'd heard she'd died of a heart attack while on a conjugal visit with her husband.

So, that was two for heart attack, one anaphylactic shock, and one hospital complications. I asked my weight-loss sponsor what she thought, in hopes of a consensus of some sort.

'Oh, it was awful!' Consuelo Rivera said. 'She got car-jacked! But her sleeve got caught in the door and she was dragged to death!'

No consensus.

'Who told you this?' I asked her.

Consuelo shrugged her shoulders. 'I don't remember her name. A woman called me at home, after eleven at night, woke me up! Then she tells me this, and I swear, I didn't sleep another wink! And this happened right here in Black Cat Ridge! What is this world coming to, E.J.?'

I shook my head and patted her arm before I walked away, mumbling to myself. Something was up, and it wasn't just my blood pressure.

'Do you know where Berta lived?' I asked Trisha as we left the church parking lot.

'Yeah, I drove her home after the Austin trip. Um, over on Weed Willow, I think,' she said.

'Mind if we go by there?' I asked, turning the opposite direction from where we both lived.

'I guess not,' Trisha said. 'What's up, E.J.?'

'Were you paying attention to those eulogies?' I asked her.

'More or less,' she said, looking away from me, which I thought might mean she'd been making a mental grocery list while people from the various self-help groups poured their collective hearts out.

I told her what I'd pieced together from the eulogies, and answers to questions.

Trisha shrugged. 'So you think Berta just liked joining groups? Maybe she was lonely.'

That pissed me off. There was a very good chance Trisha was right. What other reasons would Berta have for joining twelve-step programs? And was she lying about her history to get in these groups? It just all seemed fishy to me.

'How come all the inconsistencies with the cause of death?' I asked Trisha.

'Huh?' was Trisha's response, so I told her what I'd found out.

She looked at me and her eyes got huge; 'Oh, jeez, E.J., is this going to be one of your cases? Do you think Berta was murdered? Are we going to go to her house and see if the killer's there rifling through her stuff? Looking for, what? Diamonds? Microfilm! You think Berta was a spy? Can we stop by my house real quick? Tom has a handgun—'

I patted Trisha's knee. 'Calm down,' I said, not wanting to contemplate Trisha with a gun. 'I'm not sure what I think at this point, just that something's not right. I just want to go by her house and see what's up.'

I found Weed Willow Lane and drove down it. Trisha pointed out Berta's house. There was a For Sale sign in the front yard. Luckily the sign was for a real estate agency owned by a woman I'd known since my girls were in grammar school. We'd both been on different teacher's committees over the years, and even into high school where Kerry was currently president of the PTA. She was a serious go-getter and it usually just made me tired to watch her, but I liked her all the same. Kerry Killian had her own agency in one of the two shopping centers in Black Cat Ridge. There was the white rock shopping center, and there was the faux redwood shopping center. Kerry was in the faux redwood center. Both centers had grocery store anchors, with smaller stores surrounding. Kerry was stuck between Bijoux's Frozen Yogurt and Cat's Eye Sports Equipment. Trisha and I dropped in and found Kerry on the phone talking to a client. This was the first time I'd been in Kerry's office. There was an ornate French-looking desk in the center of the room, totally cleared except for a few tasteful nick-nacks. A computer was stationed behind her desk on a matching credenza. Four ornate chairs with damask-looking upholstery surrounded a golden metal and glass claw-foot table, and a settee with matching upholstery sat in front of her desk. Everything was in shades of gold and cream.

My girls were going into their junior year of high school, which meant I'd first met Kerry Killian, mother of twin boys in the same class as my girls, at least ten years ago. She looked exactly the same, down to the clothes. Medium height, dark brown hair in a ponytail with short bangs up front, Betty Page style, big blue eyes, and wearing a white tennis skirt showing off terrifically shaped and tanned legs, a white Polo shirt with a yellow sweater tied around her neck, and white tennis shoes with big yellow pom-poms hanging out the back from those little short socks.

'Yes, I want to get them in this house, too, Astrid, but they've got to come up with a down— Oh, honey, listen, someone just came in. Let me run the numbers again and I'll call you back, 'k? Great, bye.'

'E.J.! Hi! It's great to see you!' She moved into my space and gave me a hug, which I'd known she would do. Kerry was a big hugger and, having read a book on the benefits of hugging, gave great bear hugs. At least, she always had until today. Today's hug was actually painful.

The word 'spunk' has gone into disuse mainly due to Kerry Killian's overuse of the symptom.

'Hi, Kerry. This is my neighbor, Trisha McClure—'

She simultaneously grabbed Trisha's hand to pump while saying, 'Now Luna didn't go and sell her house and not contact me, did she? I'll spank her, I swear!' she said and laughed heartily.

'No, no. Trisha lives across the street,' I said.

She eyed Trisha. 'In the Stanleys' house or the Masons'?'

'The Masons',' Trisha said quietly.

'Rita Mansaur, right? She was your agent!' Kerry declared.

'Well, yes, she was,' Trisha admitted, seemingly a little frightened regarding the consequences of her admittance.

Kerry looked very serious for a moment. 'She's good,' she finally said. 'She's doing mostly commercial now. This was, like, almost two years ago, right?'

'Yes,' Trisha said.

Kerry nodded and kept nodding. 'She's into commercial now. Not homes. You probably bought her last house.' Kerry burst into laughter. 'Isn't that hysterical!'

I decided to jump in before things got even more bizarre. 'Kerry, we're here about Berta Harris's house on Weed Willow. I saw your sign.'

'Of course you did! How could you miss it? Yes, Berta decided to sell and move back to Jacksonville, Florida.'

'Ah, when did she decide this?' I asked, exchanging glances with Trisha.

'A week ago,' Kerry said.

I looked at Trisha. 'What was the day she, you know . . .'

'Tuesday,' Trisha answered.

'Of last week?' I asked.

Trisha nodded.

'What day last week did you sign her up?' I asked Kerry.

She tilted her head like a curious bird and then smiled brightly. 'I'll have to check my calendar!'

I was getting a little worried about Kerry. She had always been perky, but this was more manic than perky.

She leaned on her desk, one calf raised with tennied toes pointed, like a girl in the movies getting her first screen kiss, and poised one finger against her check. Then she looked up and smiled. 'Wednesday!' she declared.

Trisha and I looked at each other again. Neat trick, I thought, for a woman to sell her house the day after she died. And why didn't Kerry know Berta was dead? My hackles were on red alert. Something was more than fishy here.

'Are you thinking of buying?' Kerry asked, coming back around the desk. 'Berta's asking a song for the place, I swear to God! A song! You could buy it for the kids, E.J.! Just think, they'd be right down the street!'

I only contemplated the idea for a moment, then said, 'No,

neither of us is interested, Kerry. We're just wondering about Berta.'

Kerry's smile was so huge it hurt the muscles of my face just to look at it. 'Berta's just fine,' she said.

'Kerry,' I said, laying a hand on her arm. 'Berta's memorial service was today. She's been cremated.'

'Oh,' Kerry said, the painful smile not budging. 'Well, that's interesting.'

Trisha and I exchanged looks again, and I patted Kerry's arm. 'Thanks, Kerry,' I said. 'If you need to talk, about anything, just call.'

'Okie dokie,' Kerry said, following us to the door. As Trisha headed for my minivan, Kerry grabbed my arm. When I turned, her smile was gone. 'Be careful, E.J. Stay out of it.' Before I could even take in what she'd said she was back in her office, the door closed, and her back to me.

MEGAN

It's not easy being Megan Pugh. First of all, from kindergarten on, you get 'Pee-ewe Pugh' as a nickname. And I was burdened with Graham – my older brother. He should be committed. Then, just when I think things might be going OK, my parents adopt Bess. Don't get me wrong, I love Bess like a sister. Which is the problem. Who wants a sister? I have dreams of being an only child. I'd make a good one. I could totally handle a life that's all about me. My parents and grandparents doting on me. It wouldn't matter what grades I got, or if I stayed out too late, or if I ditched school. They'd just be damn happy to have me. Our precious child. No such luck.

So finally, ten years go by with a brother *and* a sister, and I'm beginning to adjust, when, whammo, I get another sister – Alicia. This one is just as needy as Bess, but newer. Well, I don't mean she's newer; well, she is newer, but I mean her neediness is fresher. She was a foster kid and had this mean foster mother who, like, made her take care of the little kids and she had only one outfit that she had to wear *every* day! I kid you not! And it was fun at first, buying her new clothes and fixing her hair and make-up and stuff, but you can only do that for so long, and besides, she's like a size three and I'm like a nine so I can't borrow anything, so what's the point? Bess can wear a size one or a size three so they can trade off clothes, and I'm stuck with just my own wardrobe, which truly sucks because my *mother* buys my clothes. If she'd just give me her credit card and drop me off at the mall it wouldn't be so bad, but she wants to make a *girls* day out of it, which means Bess and Alicia and me, with Mom leading the way. Gag me.

So I came up with a plan. With Mom and Mrs McClure across the street spending so much time together, I figured Mrs McClure would need, like, a part-time nanny. Who better than me? Not a living soul, that's who! And with the money she gives me, I can buy my own clothes! Get Graham to drop me off at the mall, and then it'll be a *fait accompli*, as they say in French class! Not a darn thing Mom can say about it. As long as I don't get anything too cool, like body piercings or tattoos. Seriously, I'd love a tatt of a dolphin on my ankle, but Mom would totally see that. I'll have to settle for my butt. She wouldn't see that – she gave up bathing me like a year ago. *Kidding!*

So that's what I do. I, like, walk across the street after Mom dropped Mrs McClure at home and then took off – gawd knows where – probably the grocery store, she goes there every day! I walk up to the door and hear all this yelling. I almost turn around, but it's Mrs McClure yelling at the kids, and I think, cool! She *really* needs a part-time nanny! So I ring the bell and after way too long a wait, Mrs McClure opens it real fast and starts to say, 'What?' in a mean voice then sees who it is – namely me.

Mrs McClure then smiles. 'Sorry, Megan, the girls are driving me crazy. What can I do for you, honey?'

I'm taller than she is so it's kinda funny her having to look up while talking *down* to me, if you catch my drift. 'Hi, Mrs McClure. I'm here about the girls. I know you and my mom are hanging out a lot, and I thought you could use a part-time nanny.'

She looked interested. 'How much?' she asked.

Oh, jeez, I hadn't thought that far ahead. Which my

counselor at school seems to think is a problem, but I believe in spontaneity. 'I'm not sure. Whatever you think is fair.'

'Fair would be having perfect children, but somehow that didn't work out. Come in, come in. Let's get a calculator and discuss it.'

'Do Kerry and Ken have enough money for her to be hospitalized for exhaustion, or will it just be Prozac and Jack Daniels?' my husband asked me as he stared at the interior of our refrigerator.

'This isn't a laughing matter,' I told him. 'Close the door.'

'I'm hungry,' he said, door still open.

'You've seen what's in there. Now close the door and make your decision.'

Willis closed the door and turned and looked at me. 'I'm not Graham!' he said.

I smiled. 'Then don't act like him.'

'I want food,' he said, reopening the refrigerator door.

'As opposed to what?' I asked. We'd had dinner less than an hour ago, so he couldn't actually be hungry. My feeling was he was just bored. 'Talk to me about this mess with Berta Harris instead of eating. You're getting a gut.'

He shut the door and looked at his stomach. He pulled in his gut and said, 'I am not.' He walked stiffly to where I sat in the family room, his gut still being held in.

'I don't suppose you can talk and walk *and* hold your gut in all at the same time?' I asked.

His tummy bulged out. 'No,' he said, flopping down on the couch next to me. 'I want something sweet.'

'Like what?' I asked, checking the cable guide on the TV for anything interesting.

'Lemon meringue pie,' he said.

I refused to dignify that with a response.

'Oh, so now you're all down on anything good because you lost a couple of pounds—' he started.

'Thirty-five, thank you! And you don't need pie.'

'I do need pie,' he whined.

'How about sex instead?' I offered.

'We really don't have any pie?' he asked.

I hit him on the head with the remote control and he laughingly shoved me down on the couch. 'You ever had sex with a hungry man?' he whispered in my ear.

'No, but I've had plenty of sex with an idiot,' I said.

Much later I brought up the day's festivities yet again. 'So Berta belonged to all these twelve-step programs, and I think maybe she lied to at least some if not all of them about her reasons for being there, and somebody called all these programs and gave conflicting accounts of how she – Berta – died. And then Kerry – that was just bizarre.'

'Kerry's always been bizarre,' Willis said, his head in my lap.

'No, you just don't like perky.'

His whole body shuddered. 'There's that,' he said.

'She knows something, Willis! I can feel it.'

My husband sat up and turned to face me. 'Don't,' he said. 'Do not get mixed up in something. No dead bodies, E.J. I'm serious. Not one more!'

'What? I'm supposed to ignore all this? Berta may have been murdered—'

'I know Kerry's a nutcase, and this Berta woman sounds like she was one too. Stay out of it.'

'Is that an order?' I asked, glaring at him.

He sighed and laid his head back in my lap. 'No, of course not. I'm not allowed to give you orders. It's a very heartfelt request.'

The doorbell rang. Willis pulled himself off me. 'I'll get it,' he said, dejected. I turned on a show I wanted to watch while he was gone.

Even over the noise of the TV I could hear voices at the front door. Willis and another man. I muted the TV and tuned in to their conversation.

'—and I don't know what to do with her,' the one who wasn't my husband said.

'Come on in the living room and sit down, Ken,' Willis said.

Ken, I thought. We knew two Kens, the barber who cut Willis's hair every other Tuesday, and Kerry Killian's husband Ken. Was it too much of a coincidence that Ken Killian would show up the same day I had an impromptu meeting with his wife?

'Ah, where's . . .' Ken asked.

'E.J.? In the family room. She can't hear us in the living room,' Willis said.

Like hell, I thought. All I had to do was go into the dining room and stand between the buffet and the corner cabinet and I could hear just fine. Now explaining what I was doing in that position might be a bit of a problem, but one I was willing to face at a later date. I jumped up and got in position.

'I don't know, Willis. She's jumpy as a cat. She's looking out the window constantly, and when I ask her what's going on she just gives me this really phony smile and says, "Oh, nothing!" I figured with what you've had to put up with E.J. and all her dead bodies, you'd know what I should do.'

I almost humphed out loud, but decided to keep my opinions to myself – at least for the time being.

'I'm not sure they're the same thing,' Willis, my hero, said. 'With E.J. it's just willfulness. Doing whatever she wants to do despite the family's needs.'

OK, nookie on the couch was definitely a thing of the past.

'But when she gets in that state, when she's tearing around trying to find out what's going on, what can you do to stop her?' he asked.

'It's like disciplining a child,' my soon-to-be former husband said. 'One time one thing might work, the next time you have to try something else. But the main thing is, try to keep communications open. Try getting her into a dialog and see if you can find out what's going on—'

OK, Dr Phil. Show's over. I left my hidy-hole and headed to our bedroom, where the door would be locked to intruders.

'Why's Dad on the couch?' a voice said, waking me up from a wonderful dream in which George Clooney was nibbling on my neck.

'Huh?' I opened one eye to see my son standing there with a screwdriver in his hand – the kid knows no boundaries.

'You overslept. I need breakfast. The girls are in the bathroom fighting over crap and I'm hungry.'

I closed my eye. 'Then fix yourself something. And something for the girls, too, 'k?'

'Calendar says you've got that thing at the school for teacher appreciation today at nine,' Graham said. 'And since you have to get up anyway, why don't you make French toast?'

Although it was July, Graham was still in school. Summer school. He and three of his best friends were caught doing something stupid at the school two days before graduation and none of them were allowed to graduate. Now all four were in summer school taking a course called 'Establishing Boundaries for a Worry-Free Environment.' In other words, throw cherry bombs in the girls' toilets again and you still won't graduate. Today was a thank-you ceremony for the teacher who gave up her summer to babysit. Thursday night was a small graduation ceremony for the four boys – paid for by – you guessed it – the parents.

I opened both my eyes and looked at the clock. Twenty to eight. The class started at 8:05 a.m. I threw my legs off the bed and let that motion lead me to an upright position. From there I wandered into the kitchen. I pulled out three boxes of cereal, both the whole and one percent milks, the pitcher of O.J. and one of grape juice, a container of already cleaned and cut strawberries, and a banana, and threw them all on the counter just as the girls came downstairs.

'Dry cereal again?' Megan whined.

I was tempted to pour the milk (either whole or one percent, I had no preference) straight into the boxes of cereal, but knew that would mean me going to the store to replace them.

'Either eat dry cereal or learn to cook,' I said and wandered back into the bedroom. Willis was already in the suite, in the bathroom, door open, doing his morning toilet.

'You shouldn't have locked the bedroom door,' he said through a mouthful of toothpaste.

'You shouldn't have said those things about me to Ken!' I said, looking in the dresser for clean underwear.

'They're true,' he said nonchalantly, then spat.

'They are not!' I protested. 'And if you think you can manipulate me like you told Ken, you are terribly mistaken!' I yelled. I'd been up half the night crying over the betrayal.

He rinsed his mouth and turned to me, his chest hairs all sexy-looking. 'I don't think I can manipulate you, but I think

Ken can manipulate Kerry in her present condition. I was just giving him advice.'

'Oh,' I said and smiled at him. Then I frowned. 'You jerk! You're trying to manipulate me right now!'

'Ah, honey,' he said, coming close and cupping the back of my neck with his big sexy hand.

I jerked back. 'You're doing it again! Get away from me!'

'Now, baby doll—' he said and laughed.

I ran into the closet and closed the door until I heard his truck leave.

I decided this was yet another opportunity to dress up in my new skinny clothes. I was going to take every opportunity to show off my new body before it returned to the body from hell. I wore a red-print dress, the hem of which came to the middle of my knees, and whose square-cut bodice showed just a mere hint of cleavage.

There were five women in the teachers' lounge, two members of the three-member committee for teacher presents, the same committee that ruled during the school year, and the mothers of the other miscreants. I sat with the other mothers.

The one woman conspicuously absent from the committee was Kerry Killian.

'Where's Kerry?' I asked of the room in general, before I even noticed the swollen eyes and the Kleenex in the hands of the committee members.

'You haven't heard, E.J.?' asked Arlene Clutcher, the woman who always knew everything before anyone else. There was speculation she was sleeping with the chief of the small Black Cat Ridge police department.

'Kerry was killed last night,' Arlene said, and had the grace to look upset. 'She was murdered.'

TWO

'**B**ut I didn't find the body!' I yelled at my husband.
'Yeah, but I bet you want to worm your way into the investigation, don't you?' Willis yelled at me.

'Of course not!' I yelled back. 'I can't help it if Luna asks for my help!'

'But she hasn't!'

'There are things – like the whole Berta Harris business – she needs to know about!'

'Stay out of it!' he yelled.

'Stop yelling at me!' I yelled.

Our faces were mere inches from each other's and spittle was dampening them. And then the doorbell rang.

'I'll get it,' Willis growled at me. I was right behind him when he opened the door. I think I was the only one pleased to see our next-door neighbor Elena Luna, newly appointed lieutenant with the Codderville Police Department, standing there.

'Hey, Willis,' she said, then leaning around him, 'hey, E.J.'

Willis said nothing. I said, 'Elena, please come in.'

Willis turned and growled at me then stomped off to the garage to do something manly to take his mind off whatever had him so pissed off.

'Can I get you a Coke?' I asked her. 'Or a beer?'

'I'm on a diet. Some ice water, please?'

We went into the kitchen where I got a glass down from the cabinet, filled it with ice, then water, and handed it to her. We wandered to the kitchen table and sat down.

'Did I inspire you?' I asked, indicating my svelte new body.

She inspected me for a moment then said, 'Well, the girls still look good.'

Thrusting out my chest, I said, 'They always do.' Then, 'So, what's up?'

'George Perkins' – that's the Black Cat Ridge police chief

– 'asked me to step in on the Kerry Killian case. I know you knew her. What can you tell me?'

I sighed. Thank God she asked and I didn't have to go next door and convince her to listen to me. This wasn't my fault, I can tell Willis. She *asked*, for God's sake! So then I told her all about Berta Harris and the weirdness that had gone on.

'So you think Berta Harris was murdered?' she said.

'It's beginning to look that way. Something fishy is going on! And I really believe the two murders are connected,' I said. Sometimes Luna needs a little help getting started in the right direction.

'Did Killian really tell you to beware?' Luna asked me out of nowhere.

'Well, those weren't her exact words,' I said. 'It was more like, "be careful," and maybe "stay out of it."'

Luna hooted with laughter. 'That last part I can believe.'

'Can you do an autopsy on cremains?' I asked.

The look she gave me made me wish I hadn't actually asked the question aloud. 'I didn't think so,' I said, answering it for myself.

She picked up her cell phone. 'Look,' she said, 'I'll call the M.E.'s office, see who wrote the death certificate and if there was an autopsy done before she was cremated.'

'I think the Berta was short for Roberta, but maybe check both ways?'

Luna raised an eyebrow. 'Gee, I never would have thought of that,' she said in a monotone. Getting ahold of someone on the other end, she said, 'Check death certificates issued in the county for the last three weeks under the name of Berta or Roberta Harris, or any Harris for that matter, and call me back. Asap. Need a cause of death.'

Looking at me, she said, 'I take it Willis is pissed off because you're involved in another murder case.'

'I'm not involved!' I protested.

'Good,' she said. 'I'm going to take you at your word. I'm going now and I don't expect to hear from you at all. Got it?'

'Just some quick questions—'

'Nope,' she said, standing up. 'You're not involved, remember.'

'Just questions any friend would ask—'

Luna sighed and turned toward me, one hand on her hip. 'What?'

'When was Kerry killed? Where was she killed? How was she killed? Any clues at the scene—'

'Stop!' she said forcefully, her hand up like she was a Supreme doing 'Stop in the Name of Love.' 'Sometime between six p.m. and ten p.m. When her husband started looking for her. At her office. A gunshot between the eyes.'

'Caliber?' I asked.

'Jesus, Pugh, get a grip. You're not a cop, OK? You know as much now as her husband does, which is more than you should. And I know I'm talking to the hand, but you need to stay out of this. I'll look into what you told me about Berta Harris but you have to stay out of this.'

'Will you at least let me know what you find out about Berta?'

She sighed as she stood up. 'I knew I shouldn't have come over here. Yes, I'll let you know. But only about Harris! Got it?'

'Got it!' I said enthusiastically as she walked out the door.

I went to the kitchen to look for something in the freezer to try to defrost for dinner.

But then I thought of Kerry's twin sons. The same age as my girls – fifteen going on sixteen. Kerry ran her home like she did her office – a place for everything and everything in its place. I wasn't sure if Ken and the boys – Keith and Kenneth, Jr – would be able to survive without her.

But beyond all that, she had been loved. Her boys idolized her and her husband grinned whenever he saw her. Willis sometimes does that and I know what it means. It means love. It means I know your panties have a hole in them and you threw the dirty dishes in the oven when Graham's counselor came over, and when you scolded the girls you were really laughing inside at their ingenuity. It means I know you lied about spending that money at the mall and you know I peek at you in the shower. It means I know you forgive me for what I said to your father back in 'eighty-nine, and that first dinner you made for me wasn't really all that bad. It means after twenty-something years of marriage, I would still follow you across the quad and try to get the nerve to talk to you in the book store. It means I love you.

Something had been going on with Kerry. Ken knew that. He'd come to Willis for help. Fat lot of good that did him – seeking advice from Mr Don't Get Involved. Ken had said she'd been nervous, jumping at shadows, staring out the window. Looking for what? I wondered. When Trisha and I saw her she was perky to the point of manic. What was going on with her, and did it have anything to do with Berta Harris's murder? Because now I was convinced Berta had been murdered. And I was also convinced something had been going on between Berta and Kerry. Had she and Berta Harris been involved in something together? Something illegal? Fraud? Robbery? Drugs? Kerry could have been using her real estate office to launder money, or to fence stolen property, or to make drug deals. But why? Ken was a corporate attorney who headed up his firm's office in Austin. He commuted three days a week and played golf the other four. They couldn't be hurting for money. Kerry was a volunteer at just about everything Black Cat Ridge had to offer, and still had time for a couple of charities in Codderville. The woman knew how to organize a day, I can tell you that. OK, had known. Jeez, it was hard to believe Kerry Killian was dead. She'd been a force to be reckoned with. Like a hurricane churning in the Gulf of Mexico.

I felt my eyes well up with tears and headed to my bedroom. Twenty minutes later I was awakened by my three daughters. For the uninitiated, let me explain the circumstances by which Willis and I have ended up with, count 'em, three daughters. I'm going to explain this in order of their appearance in our home: Megan arrived in our apartment in Houston one sunny February morning, two days after a ten-hour labor and five-degree episiotomy. She weighed eight pounds, four ounces, and was fourteen inches long. Our second daughter, Elizabeth, now called Bess, we acquired four years later when her birth parents, our best friends, Roy and Terry Lester and their two older children, were murdered in their house next door to

ours. We legally adopted her about two years later. Our third
daughter, Alicia, we took in last year as a foster child. We
were thinking of starting adoption proceedings, but then Willis
suggested we put that off for a while. When I asked him why,
he said for me to check out the way our son Graham looked
at her. When I finally noticed, I had to agree. It would be
much less complicated for everyone if they were not legally
brother and sister. So far I don't think Alicia has a clue, or
the other girls for that matter, and I'd just as soon leave it
at that.

Anyway, they woke me up by jumping on the king-sized
bed and all going 'Mom!' at the same time.

I sat up. 'What?' I asked in a not-very-kind voice.

Then I saw the tears in Bess's eyes, the shock in Alicia's
and the 'wait until I tell you this' look in Megan's.

'What's up?' I asked.

'Keith and Kenny's mom got killed!' Megan said. 'Murdered!
Strangled in her own home! Bludgeoned to death! Then hung
from their second-floor balcony!'

Bess elbowed Megan. 'That's not what happened,' she said,
sniffing back tears. 'Or at least, I don't think so. That sounds
like overkill.'

Then Bess and Megan looked at each and both had to cover
their mouths to keep from laughing out loud. I think maybe
my children have been around a little too many dead bodies
in their relatively short lives.

'God, y'all, stop it!' Alicia said. 'This isn't funny!' Being
new to the family, Alicia still had appropriate feelings.

Then my door burst open again and Graham, my soon-to-
graduate son, came rushing in. He saw where Alicia was sitting
and moved to the other side of the bed to sit down. Not too
obvious, kid.

'I take it they told you about Keith and Ken's mom?' Graham
asked.

'Yes, and Luna was over earlier. So I had heard.'

'We've got to do something for those boys,' Alicia said.

'Like what?' Megan asked. 'Make them cookies?' she said,
her tone sarcastic.

'Actually,' I said, 'that's a good idea. That's what people

do when there's been a death. Make food, take it to the family . . .'

'Did people do that when the Lesters died?' Bess asked, speaking of her birth family.

I smiled. 'They sure did. I think we ended up with three of those sweet potato casseroles with the marshmallows on top. They stayed in the fridge for a week before I ended up throwing them out.'

'That sounds good,' Graham said. 'I could go for some marshmallows right now.'

Ignoring my son, I said to the girls, 'I think we should start work on this right now. Let's see what we have in the fridge and pantry, then make a grocery list, and since I'm sure Graham's going to refuse to help us cook he can go to the grocery store and get the stuff we need. Oh, and pick up one of those rotisserie chickens so I won't have to worry about dinner.'

With that, the girls and I jumped off the bed and headed into the kitchen.

Trisha and her girls showed up about the time Graham got back from the store, so it ended up with Trisha and me doing most of the cooking while the girls babysat/played with Trisha's girls. Alicia, the sane one, helped with the cooking. We made a batch of brownies, and a green salad. Trisha ran to her house and brought back stuff to make a from-scratch lasagna and her famous church supper potato casserole. I stayed downwind of all of it as much as possible.

MEGAN

I have nothing against Alicia; she's a perfectly nice girl, if not just a little creepy – all that hair last year practically covering her face. She looks better this year with the make-over me and Bess gave her, but Bess and I had this thing – it's not like we were BFFs or anything, not since we were, like, kids, but we had a workable relationship. Sorta me and Bess against the world kinda thing. Now Alicia's in the mix and I feel left out.

Not that I really care. They were babysitting Mrs McClure's girls, so I took that moment to scoot into the living room and text my new BFFs, Azalea and D'Wanda, who are twins.

Fraternal not identical. Azalea's hair is longer and her feet are bigger, and D'Wanda has a mole behind her left ear. Other than that, it's hard to tell them apart. They're African American and cheerleaders and very popular, and they think hanging with me will help their rep. I'm not sure about that, but me hanging with them has certainly helped mine. Anyway, I texted them about Keith and Kenny's mom getting killed. Azalea and D'Wanda were in the twin club at school with Keith and Kenny, so they knew them. D'Wanda even had a crush on Keith in sixth grade. Anyway, she thinks it was Keith.

I did my texting thing and was getting ready to go back and help with the babysitting when I got a text back. 'UR sik. No way. Details! D.'

So I shot off details as I knew them, but before I even hit send, I was getting another text. 'R the boys OK? Horrible! What can we do? A.'

Another difference: Azalea tends to get mushy about things, whereas D'Wanda's like me – anything out of the ordinary in this horribly boring place is fun! Even if it is sad, ya know?

I sent a reply then headed back into the kitchen where Mom and Mrs McClure were busy baking away for Mr Killian and the twins.

'Mom,' I said, all sweetness and light – it fools her every time, 'did Mrs McClure tell you about the deal we came to?'

'Deal?' Mom asked. 'What deal?'

'I'm going to babysit for her when y'all need to go do something!' I told her, all smiles like the thought of spending 'quality' time with Mrs McClure's bratty kids was somehow going to be fun.

Mom looked at Mrs McClure, who nodded her head. 'Yes, we did, but I didn't realize, Megan,' she said, turning to me, 'that you hadn't discussed this with your mother.'

OK, Biotch with a capital bitch! 'Mom usually doesn't have a problem with me babysitting, especially when it's someone we know,' I said, not losing the smile.

My mom shrugged her shoulders. 'It's OK with me,' she said, 'if it's OK with Mrs McClure.'

'I'm tickled to have her,' Mrs McClure said. 'I think Megan is very mature for her age and I know the girls just love her.'

I smiled brightly, wiggled my fingers at them and went over to where Bess and Alicia were watching Mrs McClure's girls.

'"Megan's so mature!"' Bess mimicked in a sing-song voice. '"The girls just love her!"' Turning to the little girls playing with Barbies on the floor, Bess said, 'Don't you two just love old Megan here?'

The two little girls – sorry, I forget their names – looked at each other then back at Bess, and shrugged. 'Ha!' I said. 'Good enough!'

Without even communicating our decision, Trisha and I told my girls to watch her girls and we were off to the Killian household together.

Once in the car, I told Trisha, 'You keep the guys busy while I check out the house, see what I can find.'

'I don't know, E.J.,' she said, shaking her head. 'They just lost Kerry. Isn't this kinda mean?'

'Finding her killer is mean? I don't think so.' I said it, but I didn't believe it. Rummaging through their house the night after their wife/mother was killed was an awful thing to do. But let's face it, that wasn't going to stop me. 'All you have to do is talk to them, the kids. I'll do all the heavy lifting,' I said.

Kerry's house was one of the nicer ones on her street. Being a real estate agent gave her first crack at the better deals, and rumor was she and Ken had gotten this two-and-a-half story, five bedroom with formals for a song. It was also on two lots backing up to the green belt. Primo property. I pulled into the driveway where the twins were shooting hoops with the basket attached to the front of the detached garage. One held the ball (I could never tell them apart) while the other took a couple of steps toward us.

'Hey, Miz Pugh,' he said.

'Hi,' I said, avoiding calling him by name. Instead I held up the dishes I was carrying. 'We brought y'all some supper.'

'Cool,' the one with the ball said. He threw it into the open garage and headed for the back door. 'Come on this way. I'm starving.'

We followed both boys into the kitchen. I'd always loved Kerry's kitchen – huge, country-style, with black and white tile floors, whitewashed cabinets with glass doors showing how perfectly organized her kitchen was, shiny red accessories and a big Coca-Cola clock bringing the color scheme together. Ken, Sr sat at the black lacquered kitchen table, his head in his hands.

'Dad,' one of the boys said softly. 'Miz Pugh's here with some food.'

Ken, Sr dug the palms of his hands into his eyes, looking like a lost little boy, then raised his eyes to us. 'Hey, E.J,' he said, trying to stand. I shooed him back down. 'Thanks for this,' he said, his hand encompassing the dishes of food laid out on the countertops.

'You boys sit down,' Trisha said as she opened the cabinets to get down plates.

'Who wants what to drink?' I asked, going to the refrigerator.

One boy said, 'Milk,' while the other said, 'Water.' Ken, Sr didn't answer, so I fixed him ice water as well.

We served them dinner. The boys ate ravenously as only teenaged boys can. Ken, Sr pushed his food around the plate.

Trisha and I were leaning against the sink, watching, when I caught her eye, indicating I was heading out of the room. She nodded her head and I stepped out.

Kerry's house was beautifully decorated, but you could still tell teenaged boys lived there. In the formal dining room with its Shaker-style table and buffet, two backpacks adorned the table top while jackets rode the backs of chairs. Peeking into the living room, beautifully decorated in an eclectic style, I saw a baseball bat on a chair and a soda can leaving a ring on the coffee table.

Knowing I didn't have much time, I left all that for a look in the master bedroom, definitely a woman's bedroom, white on white, with lace and pillows galore. Seeing a romance novel on a side table, I went to that side of the bed first. Her table had three drawers, the top one a small drawer containing a china box with nail file, cuticle scissors, and hair clips, a newish edition of a tabloid magazine, rolled up and bound with a pink ribbon, two ballpoint pens and a small tablet stolen from a Holiday Inn.

The first large drawer beneath the small one held hand lotion, a couple of bottles of prescription medicine (Tylenol II and penicillin), and two more romance novels. The second and last drawer, deeper still, held one of those mesh bags for delicate washing filled with socks for all occasions – Halloween, Thanksgiving, Christmas, Easter, the Fourth of July, etc., although wearing socks on the fourth in central Texas seems masochistic – some designer scarves, and underneath all that a nice-sized (and manly shaped) vibrator. My first thought was, *You go, girl.*

But that thought was pushed out of my head when I heard Ken's voice. 'You're looking in the wrong place.'

I swung around to see Ken and both boys standing in the doorway to the master bedroom, Trisha behind them, jumping up and down in some sort of warning frenzy. I hoped she realized it wasn't working.

'Ken – I'm sorry. I was looking for the bathroom—'

'Save it, E.J. I know what you're looking for. I was hoping that was the real reason you came over. The food's great, and we thank you for it, but—'

'We know what you do, Miz Pugh,' one of the boys said.

'And we'll help you anyway we can,' the other one said.

'I'd rather the boys stayed out of it—' Ken started, while both boys interrupted with 'Dad!'

He looked at his sons and tousled the hair of the one closest to him. 'I know you want to find out who did this, guys, but E.J.'s a pro at this. We'll leave it to her.' Looking back at me, he said, 'We know the police are going to be looking into it, but I also know that you can go places and do things the police can't. I'll pay you any amount of money you want to find out who did this to Kerry and why.'

I moved to Ken, Sr and hugged him. Stepping back, I said, 'I won't take your money, Ken, that's an absolute. And I'm not a pro. I'm a bumbling amateur who doesn't know what the hell she's doing half the time. But Kerry was my friend and I'll do whatever I can to find out what happened. Just don't tell Willis.'

THREE

Father and sons sat on the taupe tuxedo sofa in Kerry's living room while Trisha and I took our places in high-backed, armless, tightly-stuffed chairs covered in black, white and taupe-striped silk. The coffee table, with the new ring on it, was a galley door from an old ship, and had been covered in glass – so the ring was no problem.

'If you're sure you want to do this—' I started.

Ken interrupted me. 'I'm sure. Ask any questions. Our lives are an open book.'

'OK,' I said and looked at Trisha. She shrugged. So I asked what I thought was an important question. 'Did you know Berta Harris?'

Ken frowned. 'Berta Harris? Do you think she has something to do with this?'

'No, not at all. We had her memorial service yesterday morning. I'm just wondering if you knew her.'

'She's dead?' Ken said, standing up from the sofa. 'How? Was she murdered too?'

I stood up and went to Ken, taking him by the arms and encouraging him to sit back down.

'Ken, you need to calm down or this isn't going to work. She may have been murdered, but there's no proof yet. It's all very confusing.' I then went on to tell him about my encounter with Kerry and how she'd acted about the news of Berta's death. I ended with, 'How did you and Kerry know her?'

Ken shrugged. 'I didn't, not really. I came home from work early one day because I had the flu and Berta was in the living room. I had no idea who she was. But when she saw me she looked terrified. Then Kerry came downstairs and saw me and *she* looked terrified. And I asked them what the hell was going on, but then Kerry just laughed and said I'd startled her. Then she introduced me to the Harris woman, said she was a client, and then she walked her to the door. But the thing is, she tried to hide it but I saw that she handed the woman a wad of cash. I don't know how much.'

'Did you ask Kerry about it later?' Trisha asked.

Ken shook his head. 'No. I figured it must have been a refund or something. Maybe the woman gave her cash to hold a house before she made a bid or something. I don't know. Real estate is not my thing.'

'Did you ever see Berta Harris again?' I asked.

'No.'

'Did Kerry ever mention her again?' I asked.

'No,' Ken said.

One of the boys said, 'I heard Mom talking to her on the phone once. It seemed like she was trying to calm her down or something. I know she said "Berta" because I remember thinking that was a weird name.'

'Do you know what she was calming her down about?' I asked.

The boy shrugged. 'Naw, and I didn't ask. Mom's always on the phone with somebody.' Then his head dropped. 'I mean, was.'

I stood up and Trisha followed suit. 'Ken, I'm going to keep looking into this, but I can't promise I'll do better than the police. Just tell them everything, including what you just told me. I did mention to Lieutenant Luna what I just told y'all about Berta Harris, so she might ask you about it.' As we headed to the door, I thought of something else. 'Oh, and, ah, don't mention to Lieutenant Luna that I'm, um, looking into this, OK?'

Ken nodded. 'Don't tell Lieutenant Luna and don't tell Willis.'

'You got it,' I said and hugged him goodbye.

'So now what?' Trisha asked as we got in the minivan. I so wished I already had my new two-seater. It would be so much cooler doing this in a sports car with the top down. My hair blowing in the breeze – forget it. It would be a tangled mess.

'Now we go back to Berta's house,' I said, and held up a key card I'd found in Kerry's top drawer. 'I think this will get us into the lockbox on the door.'

Trisha grinned. 'Way cool,' she said, taking me back to
tenth grade. God, if I only had my sports car!

The sign was still up in Berta Harris's yard on Weed Willow.
I pulled into the driveway of the single-story house like I
owned the place and we got out. 'Walk confidently. We belong
here, in case the neighbors wonder. We're with the new real
estate company representing the property. Ah, Black Cat
Realty.'

'Is there a Black Cat Realty?' Trisha asked.

'We're new,' I told her.

'Roger.'

So I marched confidently up to the front door and tried to
stick the card key into the lock, but it wasn't that kind of lock.
You had to punch in numbers, not a card key. My confidence
was ebbing when, just for kicks and giggles, I turned the knob.
The door opened.

Trisha and I looked at each other and I wondered if I was
the only one thinking about running back to the minivan
and buying a nice conservative sedan. I took a deep breath and
opened the door. Behind me, Trisha pushed and I found myself
in Berta Harris' foyer. To the left was a small formal dining
room with nothing in it. Directly in front was a large
living room with a fireplace and a glass wall looking into a
sun room with a patio and pool beyond. It was also empty
of furniture. A wet bar was just to the left of the fireplace
and between that and the dining room was an opening that
led to a large kitchen and family room, with the fireplace
from the living room doing double duty in the family room.
The kitchen had a breakfast area at the front of the house that
was surrounded on one side by a large bow window. There
was a card table and one folding chair set there. In the family
room was a broken-down recliner and a fourteen-inch
television sitting on a TV tray. Beyond that, towards the back
of the house, was a hallway that led to a door to the laundry
room and the attached garage at the back of the house (there
was an alley entrance), another door that led to a bath with
a large shower, and yet another door leading to a room set
up as an office. There were built-in bookcases with nothing
in them, and a folding chair in front of the built-in computer

center with a laptop sitting there. Another door in the office led to the sunroom.

On the other side of the living room were two doorways – one an actual door, the other an entrance to a hallway. The hallway led to two empty bedrooms with a shared bath in between. The door in the living room led to the master suite, a large bedroom with his and her bathrooms and separate walk-in closets. There was an air mattress on the floor with a blanket thrown on top, and a box with clothes. The bathroom held a few toiletries in the female half (you could tell which was which because the female half had the giant sunken tub. What man wants that, right?). The tub, however, held something else.

Blood.

Not a great deal, but enough to shake up Trisha and myself. Not only that, but the tinted glass window that was one wall of the tub and looked out at the landscaped garden and pool of the backyard had been broken out. And not just a little break – a great big one. The only way I knew the window had been tinted was by the tiny shards still clinging to the window frame.

'Don't touch anything,' I told Trisha. 'Let's just back out. We need to call the police.'

We moved into the living room where I dialed Luna's private number at the police department.

'What part of "stay out of this" did you not understand?' Luna said, not even pretending to glare at me.

'We were just driving by—'

'Her bathtub?'

'You know Kerry didn't have a partner, and Ken asked me if I'd check Berta's house to see if there was anything on next of kin. He wanted to notify Berta's family.'

'Did he give you a key?' Luna asked.

'The door was open,' I said, not for the first time.

'So that takes breaking off the table. Now let's talk about entering,' she said, giving me a look.

'Ken said we could!' I said, knowing how childish that sounded but unable to stop myself.

'Ken had no right to say you could, if he really did, which I don't believe for a moment. Meanwhile, we have break— Sorry, entering without permission and vandalism.'

'This is all on me, Luna. Trisha had nothing to do with it,' I said.

She turned and looked at Trisha. 'And I thought you were sane,' she said, sadly shaking her head.

'We could have called you from a payphone,' Trisha said, 'and you would have never known it was us. But instead we do our civic duty and this is the way we're treated?'

I was frantically making hand signals behind Luna's back, but Trisha either didn't see them or was ignoring them.

'Civic duty,' Luna repeated. She turned to me and smiled. It was a big smile. A big, phony smile. 'Civic duty! My, my. Is that what we're calling it? Civvv-ick dooo-ty. Hum. Kinda just rolls off the tongue, doesn't it? Civvvvvv-ick dooooo-ty. Is that what you've been doing all this time, Pugh? Exercising your civic duty?'

'Luna—' I started.

'Falling over dead bodies all the time – that's your civic duty?'

'I did not fall over anyone or anything this time!' I protested.

'Yet you felt a need to extend your civic duty to breaking and en— I'm sorry,' she said, oh so sarcastically, 'I just mean *entering* the former Berta Harris's home.'

'I think we're forgetting the main thing here!' Trisha said, little hands on little hips as she glared up at Luna. 'There is blood in the bathtub and the glass wall of the tub is shattered! Someone did break in here but it wasn't us.'

'And how do I know that?' Luna demanded, her face getting red. 'So you broke the back window to get in and do whatever it is you did, then lied about the front door being open! Martinez!' she shouted at the other plain clothes cop in the room.

'Yeah, Lu?' he asked.

'You think maybe these two here,' she said, pointing at us, 'broke that tinted window, entered this home and then lied about the door being open?'

'Well, now, Lu,' Martinez said, scratching his head, 'that

could very well be! Ma'am, I think you done solved this case!'

Luna smiled brightly at him. 'Thanks, Martinez, you got your cuffs?'

'You betcha!' he said, pulling out his handcuffs and heading toward me.

I backed away, saying, 'No, oh no, get away from me!'

As I was being read my rights and Luna was cuffing Trisha, I heard Trisha say, 'I have small children! My husband's an attorney!'

And then we were stuffed into the backs of separate squad cars. It was going to be a long night.

I have never had any desire to run for office. Good thing. With my record, it could be problematic. I've never been actually tried for anything, have never even been before a judge, but I have been arrested a few times. OK, maybe more than a few. But the charges have always been dropped. Of course, not before Willis became involved. This time I didn't call him to rescue me. I called my son Graham. OK, I agree, not a motherly thing to do. But having bailed him out of jail two months ago for dropping cherry bombs in the girls' bathroom, I thought it was more or less tit for tat, so to speak.

Unfortunately, Willis was the one who showed up. Graham and I were going to have some serious words. But the first thing my husband (and I use that term loosely) said was, 'Don't blame Graham.' He used his head to point at Trisha. 'Tom called me.' Tom was Trisha's husband.

'Is he mad?' Trisha asked.

'Concerned,' Willis said. 'But I'm afraid he's not going to let you play with E.J. anymore.'

'Willis—' I started.

'Trisha, please explain to your friend that I'm talking to you, not her.'

Trisha looked at me and opened her mouth to speak. I just said, 'Don't.' So she didn't.

'I have bail money for both of you, although Lieutenant Luna is going to let you go, Trisha. Your friend, however, is another story.'

'I can go?' Trisha asked, jumping to her tiny little feet. 'Right now?'

'Yep,' my husband said. He moved aside while a guard unlocked our cage and escorted Trisha out.

Looking back at me, she said, 'Sorry, E.J.'

I shrugged. 'Not your fault. Enjoy your freedom.' I looked after her as she was escorted out of the jail wing. And for a while after she was no longer visible. It beat looking at Willis.

'You're going before a judge in the morning,' Willis said. 'This time Luna's serious. There will be actual bail set; we may have to put the house up as collateral. You'll have an actual record. You may end up going to prison. Have you reached your goal yet? Is this the ultimate thrill? Have you been all you can be?'

I didn't look at him.

'Answer me, damn it!' he said in a very loud tone.

Finally I turned to face him. 'I did not do what Luna has accused me of. I'm innocent.'

'You didn't go in Berta Harris's house?' he asked in a sarcastic tone.

'Of course I went in her house! I just didn't break the window to get in! The door was open!'

'What difference does that make?' he yelled at me.

'I. Did. Not. Break. And. Enter!' I yelled succinctly. 'I just entered!'

'Are you saying the window was broken by someone else?' he yelled.

'Yes!' I yelled back. 'I'm saying the window was broken by someone else! And that's the truth!'

There was silence for a moment. Then he yelled, 'I'll be right back!' and left.

It was a quiet ride home. Until I said, 'Can you swing by Berta's house? My car's still there.'

'Your car was towed to impound. That's a hundred dollars we could have used towards Graham's education.'

I laughed. 'A hundred dollars one way or another will have no effect on Graham's education. Stop trying to make me feel guilty for something I didn't do. So where's the impound?'

'It closes at six. It's now nine o'clock. I lost two hours of work, plus the hundred dollars plus the doctor bills for this ulcer you're giving me!'

'You gonna yell at me some more?' I asked, rubbing his thigh.

'Jeez, don't tell me yelling at you turns you on now.'

'That would be unfortunate,' I said. 'I'd stay horny constantly.'

'I don't yell at you that much,' he said, his voice softening.

'Yeah, you do,' I said.

'You yell back,' he said.

'I know,' I said.

'The kids are all home,' he said.

'Too bad we don't have the minivan,' I said.

'I sorta know the guy who runs the impound,' Willis said. 'Maybe I can get him to open it.'

I continued to rub his thigh. 'That's the best idea I've heard all night.'

An hour later I was following Willis's truck home in my minivan. It was true that I was slightly turned on, not so much by the yelling, more by being out of jail. Willis never needed to know that the real reason I wanted the minivan out of impound was to protect Berta Harris's laptop. I'd moved it from her office to the van while waiting for the police to show up. Somehow, I think it might have hurt his feelings.

'So what's on it?' Trisha asked. We were sitting in my office under the stairs while Megan watched *Sesame Street* with Trisha's two daughters.

'Nothing yet,' I answered. I was trying to peruse Berta Harris's laptop but was having no luck. I can write a book on a computer, find the internet, and turn it on and off. Other than that, computers are not my friend.

'Let me try,' Trisha said, shooing me out of my chair. She found a few more things than I did – mainly Berta's email account. Her password had been simple: her first name.

There were emails to and from Kerry Killian.

The latest one from Kerry had a long history of former

emails to and from. We scrolled to the bottom to the start of
the message, which began in early November of the previous
year, and ended about a month ago:

Berta: I'm scared. I heard someone walking on the
          sidewalk in front of the house! What am I
          supposed to do?

Kerry: Bert, honey, sidewalks are public property,
          remember? It's OK if someone walks on it.
          You need to just calm down. Drink some warm
          milk and get some sleep, OK, sweetie?

Berta: OK, I slept OK last night. I took one of those
          sleeping pills you gave me. They're the only
          thing that helps. Sometimes I feel like I'm
          coming out of my skin. I don't think your plan
          is working! Nothing is coming to me. I went
          to a new group last night, MADD, but I don't
          think I hurt anyone while driving drunk. I sure
          didn't feel guilty when I went there. Nervous,
          but not guilty.

Kerry: Great! That's something else we can mark off
          the list! Have you checked your weight?
          Gained a few more pounds?

Berta: Up to 145. Yea!

Kerry: You betcha yea! I'm proud of you.

That one ended. I looked at Trisha. '"Up to 145? Yea"?
Since when do women go "yea" over gaining weight?'

Trisha shrugged. 'Not in my lifetime,' she said.

'She joined MADD to see if she felt guilty?' I pondered.

'Yeah, to see if she'd run over somebody while drinking,'
Trisha said, wrinkling her pretty brow. 'That doesn't make
sense,' she said.

'No, you're right, it doesn't. None of this makes sense.
Kerry seems very close to her from these emails, yet Ken
barely knew of her existence. What's that all about?'

Again the shrug.

'Can you get anything else?' I asked.

'There's older email threads,' Trisha said.

We looked and they were all basically the same. Berta frightened or upset, Kerry trying to settle her down. Berta conceded she probably wasn't an alcoholic because she didn't crave liquor, but she might keep going to AA because she thought one of the guys there was, as she put it, 'super hunky cute.' She liked going to Weigh In because she discovered lots of new places to go eat where she could, as she put it, 'pig out like a real oinker.' None of this made a lick of sense, and Trisha and I were about to give up when I heard Graham and the girls come in from various summertime activities.

'Graham!' I yelled.

'What?' he yelled back.

'Get a snack and come to my office. I need your superior tech skills!'

'Whatever,' he yelled back.

'He's good?' Trisha asked.

'Yeah, got a couple of hundred bucks last year for changing the grades of half the football team. Of course, he got caught, and we made him pay the money back. But still.' My turn to shrug.

'It does show skill,' Trisha conceded.

'That's all I'm saying.'

Graham wandered into my office with an apple between his teeth and a bagel in his hand. 'Waa?'

'We got the emails off here, but what else can we get that will tell us something about the owner?' I asked.

Graham took the apple out of his mouth. 'Who does this laptop belong to?' he asked.

'Does that really matter?'

'Is it stolen?'

'That doesn't concern you. I just need you to—'

'Does Dad know about this?' Graham asked, hands on hips.

I stood up. 'You are *not* playing that card, young man! How much stuff do I have on you that I haven't told your dad? Or Luna next door, for that matter?'

'So,' he said, leaning over the laptop. 'You want to see the history of where the owner's been on the internet?'

'Yes, that would be lovely,' I said.

'Ma'am,' my respectful son said to Trisha, sliding her out of the chair and himself into it. He fiddled for a while, said, '*Voila!*' and turned to me. 'We're even.' He stuck out his hand and I shook it.

'Even,' I said.

He stuck the apple back in his mouth, picked up the bagel and left my office.

'You have a strange relationship with your family,' Trisha said.

I sat down in my office chair. 'True, but it works for us.'

FOUR

With only a fourteen-inch TV and a couple of chairs, I didn't blame Berta Harris for spending inordinate amounts of time on the computer. Her user history was long and varied. Everything from Tour Excursions of Madagascar to brain maladjustments, with even weirder stuff in between, like symptoms of rickets, Bollywood movie posters, the history of venereal disease – you name it, Berta Harris looked it up. That didn't seem to get us anywhere.

'Should we give this to the police now?' Trisha asked, indicating Berta Harris's laptop.

'And how are we supposed to do that? "Oh, Luna, I forgot this was in my van. How did it get there? Gee, I guess the guy who broke in must have waited around and put it there."' I gave her a look.

'Don't get snippy with me! Remember, I'm a volunteer!' Trisha said, hands on hips and lines forming between her brows. Did I really want to be responsible for giving Trisha McClure wrinkles?

'Sorry, Trisha,' I said and sighed. 'I'm worried about the same thing. And I obviously don't have a good answer.'

'What if we take it back to Berta's house and, like, I don't know, put it in her backyard? Under a bush or something? Like the thief dropped it? After we wipe our fingerprints, of course,' she suggested.

I had to admit it was better than anything I'd been able to think of. I wouldn't admit it to Trisha, but the scenario I'd offered so sarcastically, about approaching Luna with the story of the thief putting the laptop in my car, had been the best one I'd come up with.

So we made plans to sneak out that night after our families were asleep and take the laptop back. And maybe make an anonymous call from a pay phone (if we could find one), telling the cops that the laptop had been spotted.

The evening went as expected. Whenever I have nefarious plans, I can always count on my family to screw things up for me. Megan and Graham got into a fight that got very close to the physical, on Megan's part, at least. This lasted until eleven, causing everyone to stay up way past their bedtime. Then we had to have a cooling-off period, which involved all three girls, three spoons, and a half gallon of Blue Bell peaches and cream ice cream. Graham convinced his father he needed a light beer. I know, I should have said no, but I've decided to pick heavier battles to come, rather than one light beer in the living room. When I finally got everyone into their own bedrooms and myself into mine, Willis wanted to discuss the kids' fight, the origins of which I knew nothing. So I had to act like I was interested for another half hour. Trisha's plan had been to stay in her living room until I called to tell her that the coast was clear. I woke her up at one-thirty. She'd fallen asleep on her couch.

Unfortunately, as we headed outside, we discovered it was, and I'm serious here, a dark and stormy night. Black clouds had rolled in to cover the moon, and lightning flashed in their depths. I hoped it wouldn't get too close because close thunder could wake up Willis, who might notice I wasn't in bed. Of course, with all the talk of drought, he might be so excited about the possibility of rain that he wouldn't notice I was missing. If I was a really good wife and mother, I'd wake the whole family up so they could share the wonder of wetness (which we hadn't seen in these parts for several months) with me. Thank God I'm not that good a wife and mother.

We parked the minivan three houses down from Berta's house and, both wearing black, slinked our way to Berta's back-yard, feeling lucky that the rain hadn't started yet. Just as we put the laptop under a nice droopy bush, I glanced at the house and saw a light. It wasn't a steady light either; the light was moving, like someone with a flashlight moving from place to place.

I grabbed Trisha's arm. 'Look!' I whispered.

She turned, and saw what I saw. We squatted there with our arms in a fireman's square, like we were going to carry someone out of a burning building. Finally we let go and I whispered to Trisha, 'Should we go check it out?'

'No!' she whispered loudly.

'Yeah, I think so too,' I whispered as I duck-walked toward the back door of Berta's home.

The sliding glass door was open and I went inside. Someone was in the family room going through papers on a table next to Berta's stuffed recliner. I turned my flashlight over and, using the smaller side, stuck it in the small of the person's back.

'Put your hands up slowly,' I said.

The person screamed. A very feminine scream. She whirled around and hit my supposedly gun-toting arm with her flashlight, fortunately not very hard; I used my own flashlight, still clutched tightly in my hand, to hit her back. We were standing there in the dark – her flashlight bulb broke with her first blow against my arm – whaling away at each with our flashlights when the overhead light came on.

'E.J.?' said the person with the feminine scream.

'Berta?' I said.

Trisha stood by the overhead light switch, the laptop under one arm. 'I think I'm confused,' she said.

'You and me both,' I agreed.

'Trisha?' Berta said. 'What are you two doing here? Is that my laptop?'

'What are *you* doing here?' I asked. 'You're supposed to be dead. Trisha, why'd you bring that in?' I asked, indicating the laptop.

Berta sank to the floor.

Trisha sank down next to her and I followed suit. 'It was starting to rain. I thought that might ruin it,' she said, setting down the laptop.

Berta picked it up and hugged it to her chest. 'This is the only reason I came back.'

'My first question,' Trisha said, 'is why were you happy to gain weight?'

'Yeah!' I said. '"Yea! I'm up to 145 pounds!" What's that all about?'

Berta was shaking her head and looking confused.

'Your emails to Kerry.'

'Oh!' she said, and I could almost see the light bulb shining over her head.

Then she sighed. 'It's a very long story,' she said. 'Besides, y'all have no right to be looking at my laptop!'

'We've got the time,' I said, giving her a harsh look. 'But before that why the hell did you have a memorial service for yourself? That's just creepy.'

'Yeah!' Trisha said, imitating my look, as best a blue-eyed blonde with dimples could.

'Do you know about Kerry?' I asked.

Berta lowered her head and nodded, tears beginning to fall in her lap.

'I'm sorry,' I said. 'I know y'all were friends.'

'Best friends,' Berta whispered. 'My only friend. I don't know what I'm going to do without her,' she said. Then she looked up at me. 'I mean, really. I have no idea what to do without her!' And then she began to bawl. And bawl. And bawl. And as she did, she just got louder. And louder. And louder.

I finally put my arms around her, more to get her to shut up than because of any feelings of sympathy (bitchy, but I was still pissed), since she still hadn't told me what was going on, and said, 'You have me. And Trisha. You can count on us. We're going to help you.'

Sometimes I say the dumbest things.

'Someone's trying to kill me,' Berta finally said. 'I think they killed Kerry to find out where I was. Maybe they tortured her; I don't know.'

'What do you mean someone's trying to kill you?' I asked.

'Have you seen my bathroom?' she asked.

'The broken window, yes,' I said.

'Someone threw one of those small electric space heaters through the glass while I was taking a bath about two weeks ago. I guess the dumbass didn't realize how short the cord was. It was unplugged when it came through. But the glass cut me. I fell out of the tub and grabbed my robe and my purse and ran to my car.' Her voice became shrill, the words coming out in short staccato sentences. 'I drove to Kerry's office. I had a key. I went in there and called her. She had a couch in her private office. I stayed there that night.'

'Why would someone be trying to kill you?' I asked. Berta

was the least likely-looking murder victim I could imagine. Short and pudgy, she had dark hair and brown eyes and was totally bland. I thought.

'Well, you see, that's the whole problem. Someone's been trying to kill me for nine or so months now.'

Trisha and I exchanged a look. Maybe we had a paranoid on our hands here. 'That's a long time,' I said.

Berta nodded her head vigorously.

My plan was to sneak Berta into my house to my office under the stairs where I had a nice easy chair she could sleep in, not to be accosted by my husband as I walked in the door of my own home. Unfortunately, that's exactly what happened.

By the time we left Berta's house, the deluge had begun. Rain that heavy wasn't necessarily a good thing during drought conditions. It hadn't rained in so long that the ground was hard as a rock and what we really needed was long, soaking rain, not the kind of heavy rain that would just cause run-off. It was in situations like this that we got flash floods – creeks and rivers overflowing, low-water crossings getting so deep a car could be swept away. Two or three times a year citizens would be lost when they tried to ford a low-water crossing, not knowing it was running deep and fast.

The three of us ran to the minivan with Berta still clinging to her laptop, which was shielded from the downpour by her body. We were drenched by the time we got to it. The lightning was still ripping the sky and the thunder was right on top of it, meaning the lightning was close. The tires of my car sang on the wet pavement as we made our way through Black Cat Ridge.

I pulled into Trisha's driveway to get her as close to her house as possible, then pulled the minivan into my drive. As my vehicle was older than Willis's new truck, he got the one side of the garage that was clean enough to park in, and I got the driveway. Berta and I jumped out of the minivan and headed to the back door of my house, which lead to the kitchen, both of us dripping water on my semi-clean floor.

Willis was sitting at the kitchen table with a cup of coffee in front of him. Elena Luna sat next to him, a steaming cup in front of her. God, having a serious sense of humor, took that moment to unleash a very close lightning bolt that managed to knock out the lights. Berta and I stood there in the darkness as the immediate crash of thunder shook the house. Willis and Luna also sat there in the darkness – even with the drama of the storm that fact was not lost on me. No one said anything.

I finally managed to get my wits about me and felt my way to my junk drawer where I had emergency candles and matches. There were also little holders in there that I'd found at the dollar store, and I used a lit candle to find them. I stuck the candles in the holders, lit them all, and placed them around the kitchen, the last one in the middle of the table. All this was done in total silence. Except of course, for the raging of the storm. All the other raging was being kept bottled up, for the moment anyway.

I took a chair and indicated with a nod of my head to Berta that she do likewise. We sat at the other end of the table from Willis and Luna. Three of us just stared at each other. Berta looked at the table top.

Nodding her head at Berta, Luna said, 'Who's this?'

'Berta Harris,' I said.

'The one who's funeral you went to?' Luna said.

'Memorial service,' I said. 'She was cremated – well, pretended to be cremated rather than in a coffin, which would be buried, which would make it a funeral.'

Luna shot me a look so I stopped talking. Then she said, 'This is the one you asked Kerry Killian about and she told you to stay out of it?' Luna said.

'Right,' I said.

Berta's head shot up. 'You asked Kerry about me?' she whispered, her voice shaking.

I turned to look at her. 'Yes,' I said.

'When?'

'Right after your memorial. The afternoon before she died.'

'You mean,' Berta whispered, 'before she was murdered.'

'Right,' I said.

'What is it?' Luna asked Berta.

Berta shook her head and tears began to trickle down her cheeks. 'I didn't tell Kerry about the memorial service. I did all that myself. She put a For Sale sign in my yard to make it look like I'd moved. She thought that would be enough. But I knew they wouldn't leave me alone until they thought I was dead.'

'Who is "they?"' Luna asked.

But I interrupted. 'How did you do all that? Your memorial service?'

Luna shot me another look, but Berta perked up a bit and began to talk. 'Oh, it was easy! I called the church and told them about my friend who died here but was from out of town and wanted a memorial service here as well. And they said sure and I sent them a check. And then I just ordered flowers and had handouts made. Then I emailed all the groups, except one who I had to call. I disguised my voice.'

'Why did they have conflicting stories of how you died?' I asked.

Berta had the grace to blush. 'Well, I got kind of bored with the whole thing and so I got a little inventive.'

'I'll say,' I said, laughing. 'Being dragged by a car—'

'Enough!' Luna fairly shouted. 'You said someone tried to kill you. Who was it?'

Berta lifted her head again where it had drifted back to stare at the table top, and looked at Luna. 'I don't know,' she said succinctly.

'You don't know?' Luna repeated.

'No, I don't know.'

'Why don't you know?' Luna asked.

'Why don't I know?' Berta repeated. She looked totally confused. Then she said, with a little aggression, 'Because I don't! Jeez!'

The powers that be took that moment to turn the lights back on. We all blinked at the bright light. And, for the first time, I noticed Willis was staring straight at me.

'What?' I said. OK, also a little aggressively.

'You just do whatever you want whenever you want to do it, don't you?' he said. 'It doesn't mean a thing to you what I say or what I want.'

'You're not the boss of me,' I said.

'OK,' Luna said, 'you kids need to let the grown-ups talk now.'

I glared at her.

'Why do you think someone is trying to kill you?' Luna asked Berta.

'Did you *see* my bathroom?' Berta asked, more aggressively.

'Besides that. Did you steal something from someone? Witness a crime? Sleep with someone's husband? Threaten to tell a lover's wife on him? What did *you* do that would make someone *else* try to kill you?'

Berta shook her head. 'I don't know,' she said.

Luna sighed. 'Did you steal something?' she asked slowly.

'I don't know.'

'Witness a crime?'

'I don't know.'

'Sleep with someone's husband?'

'I don't know.'

Luna literally threw up her arms. 'What the hell does that mean? How can you not know if you stole something, or witnessed something?'

There was a taut silence that was finally broken when Berta said, 'Because I don't know anything. I don't even know my own name.'

The story went something like this: Berta woke up in Codderville Memorial Hospital last October. A nurse saw she was awake and sent for the doctor. The doctor was dealing with an emergency and it took him over an hour to get to her. During that hour Berta managed to find out where she was and realized that she knew only one thing about herself – that she was in deep doo-doo. She didn't know from whence the doo-doo was coming, only that it was. And she knew she couldn't trust anyone. So when the doctor told her that she didn't have any I.D. on her and they needed to know her name, she noted the following: the doctor's name was Robert Simms and he was wearing a Harris tweed jacket. *Voila*, Berta Harris. She made up an out-of-town address and said she couldn't remember her social security number. They told her she'd been found unconscious on the side of the road. She had two broken fingers, bruises and abrasions, and a cut on the back of her head that needed four stitches. Dr Simms told her she needed to stay at least one more night, possibly two.

After he left, she (known to us as 'Berta') got gingerly out of bed and headed to the closet, only to discover there were no clothes hanging here. Nothing, not even dirty underwear. All she had was the hospital gown, opened to the back, with only her butt to show the world. It was at this point, Berta said, that she fell to the floor and began to bawl. She was discovered only moments later by a hospital volunteer. You guessed it, Kerry 'I'll Volunteer for Anything' Killian.

As Kerry got Berta back in bed, Berta tearfully told her the truth as she then knew it. That is: she'd woken up with no knowledge of herself or her surroundings, only knowing that she was in trouble. Berta said Kerry believed her right off the bat, and helped her leave the hospital by smuggling in some scrubs and a pair of slippers, then sticking Berta in her car until her shift was over, then driving her back to Black Cat Ridge.

As a realtor, Kerry had access to houses before they went on the market, and she had actually bought one to flip. It was to this house that she took Berta – the house we had been in earlier. The two decided the first thing to do was to hide Berta for a month or so, during which time she should change her appearance: dye her hair, get contacts in another color, and gain weight. (Which answered another question.)

Meanwhile, Berta read up on amnesia, and discovered that it was often caused by the combination of a bump on the head and a severe emotional trauma. The stitches proved the bump on the head, and she started hitting twelve-step programs like AA and Gamblers Anonymous, and other groups like MADD and Weigh In, to discover her emotional trauma.

'So far, I haven't come up with it,' Berta said. 'And then, there I was, just soaking in the tub, and that electric space heater came flying through the window.' She hiccupped a sob. 'They found me.'

'Who found you?' Luna demanded.

Berta's tears dried up immediately. 'Haven't you been listening?' she demanded rather loudly.

'Hey!' Willis said, just as loudly. 'The kids are asleep!'

'Great!' Berta blasted back. 'At least you know you have kids! I could have some out there some place starving because Mama forgot to bring home the bacon!' Then she burst into serious tears.

I put my arm around her shoulders and muttered variations of 'There, there' in her ear, while simultaneously shooting daggers with my eyes at both Willis and Luna.

'So the boy who died by a drunk driver—' I whispered in Berta's ear.

'Made him up,' she whispered back.

Willis sighed heavily. 'Well, at least we got some rain,' he said lamely.

'Oh, that's your big concern!' I hissed at him. 'A friend murdered, another friend in serious trouble here, and you're still going on about the stupid drought?'

'Stupid? Do you have any idea of the repercussions of a twenty-year drought?' he yelled at me.

'It's been less than a year!' I yelled back.

'It's just the beginning! They're predicting a possible twenty-year drought!'

'Who's predicting?'

'I don't know!' he yelled. 'Somebody!'

'Somebody?' I yelled back. 'OK, well I'm predicting a possibility of snow by morning!'

'E.J.—' he started.

'Jesus, will the two of you put a sock in it?' Luna said. 'Ms Harris.'

Berta wiped her face with her hands while I went in search of a box of Kleenex. Finding one on the kitchen counter, I brought it back and sat down. Berta wiped her face, blew her nose, and then looked up at Luna. 'Yes?' she said.

'I think you need to come with me to the station—'

Berta jumped up and headed for the back door, yelling 'Noooooooooooo—' as she went.

I caught her with the door knob in her hand. 'Berta, wait,' I said.

Luna was already standing. She came around to where Berta and I stood by the door. 'OK,' Luna said, 'no station. I can see you're frightened of that. And I can understand. Police stations are scary places—'

'My God, haven't you been listening?' Berta whispered. 'I can't come out of hiding! I certainly can't go into Codderville! That's where all this started. The people who are after me are in Codderville—'

'But you were in Black Cat Ridge when your bathroom window was broken,' Luna said softly.

Berta sank into the nearest chair. 'Oh my goodness. Yes, yes, I was.'

'We need to get you somewhere safe,' Luna said.

'New York City?' Berta suggested. 'Lots of people there.'

'I was thinking more like lock-up. We could keep you safe, make you comfortable—'

'Hey!' I interjected. 'I've been in your lock-up. There's nothing comfortable about that place!'

'Pugh—' Luna started.

'She should just stay here,' Willis said, surprising everyone, I think even himself.

'Willis! I thought you were on my side!' Luna said.

'Come on, Elena,' my husband said. 'I wouldn't want anyone having to stay in your lock-up. Ms Harris hasn't done anything that I can see. Are you arresting her for something?'

We all turned to stare at Luna.

'No, of course not,' she said, not all that convincingly.

'What do you think she's done?' I demanded.

There was a long pause. 'We have questions about Mrs Killian's death,' Luna finally said.

Berta grabbed my arm. 'I don't know anything about that!' she said. 'I heard about it on the TV at this bar I went to when I couldn't get ahold of her.' She teared up again. 'My God, she was helping me! She was my only friend! Why would I kill her?'

'I thought possibly we could discuss that,' Luna said.

'Give me one reason, one shred of evidence to indicate Berta had anything to do with Kerry's death!' I demanded.

'I believe we can start with the fact that we have no idea

who this woman is!' Luna said. 'We have no idea where she came from, and we only have her word about her relationship with Kerry Killian!'

'Why would I lie?' Berta demanded.

'I don't know,' Luna said. 'But I intend to find out.' And then she began to read Berta her rights.

FIVE

Willis made an emergency call to Tom McClure, Trisha's husband, who was a criminal attorney. Since it was the middle of the night, he of course woke him up. I had to wonder if Trisha had actually gone to sleep yet, but I let that slide.

Willis and Tom made arrangements for Tom to go into Codderville the next morning and see about getting Berta out on her own recognizance, or have Willis and me post bail. There went my new two-seater.

Finally, around five a.m., we were able to fall into bed. Even though he had eventually managed to get on my side in the stand-off with Luna, he still wasn't speaking to me. Which was OK since I was too tired for a coherent answer.

By eight, Willis was up and getting dressed for work.

'Honey, come back to bed,' I said. 'You didn't get any sleep!'

'And whose fault is that?' he said, pulling on a Polo shirt. Every day is casual Friday in Willis-world.

'Screw you,' I said, and nestled under the covers and closed my eyes.

The next time they opened it was to the noise in the kitchen, just beyond my bedroom door. I gingerly got out of bed and waddled to the door to take a peek.

Graham was dressed and ready for his summer job (working concession at the Movies Six in Codderville), and just sitting down to a bowl of cold cereal. Bess was warming a bran muffin (she actually eats them like they taste good – you can certainly tell she's not my biological child), and dressed for her summer job (working retail at a dress shop in the white rock mall here in Black Cat Ridge). Alicia was drinking orange juice and eating an apple (again, not my biological child, obviously), and dressed for her summer job (interning at the D.A.'s office in Codderville), while Megan was just sitting down to a platter of eggs, bacon and two donuts, and still wearing her nightclothes (yes, my biological child).

'Too much noise,' I said through the crack in the door.

Graham looked up. 'You sick?' he inquired, milk and cornflakes visible when he spoke.

'Yes!' I said and slammed the door.

I awoke again at the ringing of the phone. I ignored it. Five minutes later Megan came into the room.

'Mom, that was Mrs McClure. She wants me over there and she's coming over here. I have to get dressed and I would suggest you do the same,' my darling daughter said.

'Excuse me?' I said, in my most haughty mother-getting-uppity voice.

'It's just a suggestion!' she said and left the room in a huff.

I was not in a good mood. I require a full eight hours of sleep to become, once again, a human being. Give me less than that and the result is not pretty. I was sitting on the edge of the bed contemplating my feet when I heard Megan shout out from the front door, 'Mom, I'm leaving!'

I nodded my agreement and thought again of standing up. Before that thought could go from my brain to my feet, the doorbell rang, I heard the door open and Trisha say, 'E.J., you in your room? I'm coming back!'

And she followed the word with the deed. I looked up to see her standing at the door to my bedroom. 'What happened to you?' she asked.

And well she might. Standing before me was a cute little woman, blonde hair curled and combed, face painted and plucked, and clothes just so. Standing before her was a not-so-cute bigger woman, with newly colored red hair standing straight up in every direction, face still wrinkled from the sheet creases, and only one button functioning on ten-year-old flannel pajamas.

'Willis and Luna were waiting for Berta and me when we walked in last night,' I told her.

'Oh, shit!' she said, and came to sit down on the bed. 'What happened?'

'It wasn't pretty,' I said. 'Bottom line, Luna arrested her

and she's now in lock-up. Your husband is supposed to be trying to get her out.'

'He is?' she said, eyebrows arched.

'He didn't tell you?' I asked.

'Tom doesn't tell me about his clients. He considers even their identify privileged.'

I contemplated the thought of a man keeping his mouth shut. Amazing.

'E.J.?' Trisha said, breaking my reverie.

'Huh?'

Trisha sighed and turned toward the door. 'I'll make coffee,' she said.

'Huh?'

The coffee was strong and hot and it made the agony of putting on clothes worth it. I took the cup in two hands and sat down at the kitchen table, only then realizing that I'd put on my 'big' jeans – from before I lost the thirty-five pounds – and not my 'new' jeans. As I sat, the butt of the jeans slid down and I ended up sitting on my panties. I was actually quite proud of that.

In a halting, slightly confused and roundabout diatribe, I told Trisha what we'd learned about Berta Harris the night before.

'So what do we do now?' Trisha asked.

'Umm,' I said.

'E.J., that's not an answer,' Trisha said.

'I don't know,' I said, holding the coffee mug tightly. 'What time is it?'

'Ten o'clock,' she said.

'What's the temp?'

Trisha shook her head. 'You don't want to know.'

'How bad?' I asked. Along with the drought, we'd been having record-breaking high temps with so far this summer thirty days of plus-one-hundred-degrees temperatures.

'Ninety-two,' she said quietly.

I said a very bad word.

Trisha stood up. 'Come on, let's go to the police station. See what Tom's doing about getting Berta out of jail.'

She grabbed an arm and pulled. I reluctantly stood up.

MEGAN

I saw Mom and Mrs McClure pull out of the driveway in
Mrs McClure's car, one of those Toyota hybrids that are really
cute and, you know, save the earth and stuff. As soon as they
were gone, I set the girls (Tabitha and Tamara, btw) down in
front of the TV to watch *Sponge Bob*, and walked casually
into Mrs McClure's bedroom. In the original book written for
babysitters everywhere, it is not only OK but a downright
requirement that you check out the lady of the house's jewelry
box and underwear drawer. You don't actually *take* anything,
for gawd's sake – it's just what one does.

Mrs McClure had a dressing table with a rolling stool in
front of it that was padded and had a ruffled skirt. It was rose
colored to match the walls and bedspread. On top of it was
an obvious jewelry box and two smaller Asian-looking round
china boxes, and some perfume and cologne bottles. I only
sprayed a couple of the cologne bottles because I didn't want
her to smell it and think I'd been riffling through her stuff.
The smaller of the two china boxes held costume jewelry
earrings. Some really cute, some old-lady-looking. The larger
box held an assortment of junk: fingernail stuff – emery files,
cuticle sticks, scissors, etc. – key rings, and an ornate, old-
fashioned key attached to a bejeweled key ring. The jewelry
box – the big wooden one – looked like a miniature hutch or
whatever you call that thing in the dining room that holds
china and stuff. The two doors on either side of the piece held
necklaces – long ones with pendants, and short ones with
pearls and diamonds and stuff. This box, I think, was where
she kept the good stuff. The top you lifted up and it showed
a velvet ring holder thingy with some really, *really* nice rings
– like diamonds and rubies and stuff. Real expensive. Under
that top part were drawers that held bracelets – one tennis
bracelet with so many diamonds it made me almost swoon!
– and pins and stuff. My mother's jewelry was nothing like
this! She had a diamond in her engagement ring, but it was
way less than a karat. I know these things. I think I was born
with this knowledge.

Then I moved to her dresser and found her underwear

drawer. OMG! Mrs McClure was a slut! There was a teddy with the nipple holes cut out, and panties with the crotch cut out, and – yes, you guessed it! – handcuffs with pink rabbit fur trim! Not only was she a slut, she killed a bunny to further her erotic fantasies! I was flabbergasted. I got on the phone immediately to Azalea and D'Wanda. There was no way I was keeping *this* to myself!

We picked the wrong day to visit the Codderville Police Department. It seems, I gathered from bits and pieces I over-heard while waiting for Luna, that CPD had raided a meth lab at the crack of dawn this morning and now had in custody eight guys who were actually there to cook the meth, plus ten women and seventeen children who were asleep in various parts of the house. All except the men were milling about while CPD officials tried to figure out if the women were culpable and, if so, what to do with the children. And the children were what you'd expect from kids raised in a meth house: slightly, but not by much, better behaved than my own.

After an hour of sitting on our butts on a waiting area bench, Luna stuck her head out of a door I knew led to the homicide division and crooked a finger at me. Trisha and I followed like good puppy dogs.

Lt Luna had been upgraded from a desk to an actual office. It was a little smaller than my under-the-stairs-closet-turned-office at home, and, relatively speaking, as or more crowded than the bullpen out front. Luna sat in a big chair behind her desk. There were two visitor's chairs – in a room that could barely house one – in which sat Tom McClure and Berta Harris. I hugged Berta while Trisha stayed outside, then traded places so Trisha could hug her and glare at her husband.

'How was I supposed to know she was a friend of yours?' Tom demanded. Well, actually, it was more pleading than demanding.

'Are you releasing her?' I demanded of Luna.

'And why should I?' Luna demanded back.

'Because she's innocent!' I said rather loudly. I had pushed my way back into the office and was caught between Luna's desk and the wall.

Berta leaned forward and patted my hand. 'It's OK, E.J. I think we're working things out,' she said.

I patted her back. 'Just don't trust her!'

Luna gave me a vaguely hurt look and I felt vaguely guilty.

Finally Tom spoke up. At first he tried to stand to speak, but realizing the futility of that gesture, he fell back in his chair and said, 'Lieutenant Luna and I have worked out a plan.'

'Hi, E.J.,' came a voice from outside the office. I turned to see Ken Killian, Sr, Kerry's husband.

'Ken!' I exclaimed. 'What are you doing here?'

'Berta called me. She told me everything she knows. I believe her. What about you?' he asked, obviously seriously wanting to know.

I nodded. 'Yes,' I said. 'I believe her.'

'Well, isn't that nice,' Luna said. 'Now that we have Pugh's *approval*, may we please move forward?'

Everyone, including Trisha and myself, nodded.

'So Berta will be staying at Mr Killian's house—'

'What?' I said, turning quickly to Ken. 'Ken, are you sure?'

'We have a guest room—'

'*And* she will report in daily,' Luna continued, 'to me. If she misses a day, we'll find her and she'll be locked up again.'

'Why?' I demanded.

Luna stood up and leaned on her desk, glaring directly at me. She had more room to stand behind her desk. '*Because* we still don't know *who* this woman is! Or what connection she has to Kerry Killian's death.' She looked out the door at Ken. 'Sorry, Mr Killian. At your request, Pugh, I had Martinez look up Berta Harris's death certificate, and surprise, surprise, there wasn't one! Since she made up the name and she isn't dead!' This time she shot a look at Berta. Berta shrugged her shoulders. 'For all we know, this woman could be a mass murderer! An escapee from an asylum! We just don't know! I could put an ankle bracelet on her, Pugh – would that work better for you?'

I held up my hands in surrender. 'No, no, this is fine,' I said. 'Just fine. May we leave now, Lieutenant?' I asked sweetly.

'Please,' she said, standing tall. 'Please leave. I'm begging you all.'

We worked our way out of her office then headed through the bullpen, where some of the children had found the crime scene tape and were cordoning off the area near the water fountain.

Five minutes later we were sitting down to ice tea at a diner in Codderville. It was close to the police station and one I'd never been to before. Molly's Munchies. A brave name, I thought, for something so close to the police station. And it was true to its word. The entire establishment smelled like patchouli and was decorated in Grateful Dead posters and Indian-print bedspreads. It looked and smelled like my dorm room in my freshman year of college. The food items were vegetarian, heavy on the tofu. I'd be coming back, if only to bask in the ambience.

'Is your husband still mad?' Berta asked me once we'd been seated.

'He'll get over it,' I assured her. He always did, I'll give him that. Mostly he was worried for me, but when it involved the kids, like last year, he was happy I knew a little something about what to do.

'So have you gotten any new memories?' Trisha asked Berta.

She shook her head. 'No, none at all. It's like I was born in that hospital. The day I woke up. If Kerry hadn't found me . . .' Her voice trailed off. We were silent, all of us getting real busy putting things in our iced tea – the offerings were packets of raw sugar, a bottle of locally grown honey, and that new 'natural' artificial sweetener, Truvia – anything to keep from having to deal with Berta's pain. Finally Berta said, 'It's my fault she's dead.'

Ken covered Berta's hand with his own. 'No, it's not. It's the fault of whoever shot her. You didn't do that. If she hadn't helped you she would never have been able to live with herself. Kerry was a helper. It's what she did. The fact that she never told me about you says a lot about my wife,' Ken said, tears floating in his eyes. 'We were very close, and she didn't even tell me about you. That's how far she went in protecting you.' He shook his head. 'She didn't suspect me or anything, I'm not saying that. But I could have dropped a word or a hint that someone else might have carried to someone else, and so on. Kerry always said a secret wasn't a secret if you told someone.'

Berta was nodding, her head down. I saw Ken squeeze her hand then place his own back on his side of the table.

'Maybe if we drive around Codderville you might recognize something. Obviously you don't really know anything or anyone in Black Cat Ridge,' I said.

Berta's head sprang up. 'No! This is where I was found! This is where the person who wants to kill me is!'

'She's right, E.J.,' Trisha said. 'We shouldn't take the chance.'

'But how else are we going to find out anything?' I asked.

'I'm with Trisha on this,' Tom said. 'I really don't want my client putting herself in harm's way.'

'I disagree,' Ken said. 'I think E.J.'s right. If Berta stays here we'll never know anything. We'll never know who Berta really is, or who killed my wife.'

'I don't mean any disrespect, Ken,' Tom said. 'We just met, and I didn't know Kerry. But aren't you thinking more about finding the murderer than you are about Berta's well-being?'

'No,' Berta said. 'Tom, don't. He has every reason in the world to want to find out who killed Kerry. I don't think either he or E.J. want to see me hurt. I'm just a big old scared-e-cat.'

'No one's saying that—' I started.

'I am,' Berta said. 'I'm scared of my own shadow. I leaned on Kerry for everything! She not only paid for my groceries, she went to the store and got them and brought them to me – I was too afraid to leave the house. The first time I ventured out was when we decided to try the twelve-step groups.'

'You say when you woke up you knew you were in trouble, right?' I asked.

'Well, I was alone for quite a while before they discovered I was awake. It was like, well, I was lying there, all bandaged up, with a little buzz from the painkillers, and I didn't know why any of this was happening, and I started asking myself why I might be there, and it didn't take long to discover that I had no idea about that or who I was.'

'But you realized you were in trouble?' I persisted.

'It was a feeling, at first. And as time moved on it became a certainty. Then the doctor came in and told me I'd been hit by a car, a hit-and-run driver,' Berta said.

'Who has paper and a pen?' I asked the group in general. Tom the lawyer pulled his briefcase to the tabletop and pulled out a legal pad and pen.

I started a list called 'facts,' putting down 'hit by a hit-and-run driver' in the number one slot. 'So you knew you were in trouble. What else did you know?' Berta looked at me like I was special. 'Do you have a favorite color? Do you prefer regular or Diet Coke? Or do you like Pepsi? Or Dr Pepper?'

'Diet Coke,' Berta said. 'And blue. And I love Mexican food, but I'm not crazy about Chinese. I prefer Reeboks to Nikes and I don't like sandals, which sucks in this weather. I like to wear lipstick but not much else make-up-wise, and I like NBC news the best. I like *Survivor* and the *Amazing Race*. Can't stand the music shows or the dance ones. I prefer to wear blue jeans and although I think I might like shorts, I don't wear them because of the weight I've gained. I think I'm usually thin. It took a lot to gain this weight. And, oh! I love ice cream! Rocky Road's my favorite!'

Berta was smiling when she finished – the first smile I'd seen from her. And it was lovely. White, even teeth, the mouth full and generous, her eyes shining. I took that moment to really look at her eyes. 'Your eyes,' I said. 'They're violet! Like Elizabeth Taylor's!'

Berta pointed her finger at me. 'I know who that is! *Cleopatra*!'

Trisha grinned at me. 'She likes old movies!'

Both men had leaned forward and were studying Berta's eyes.

'Wow,' Tom said. 'They are violet!'

'Violet, like purple?' Ken said. ''Cause her eyes are purple!'

'Violet's a lighter shade of purple,' Trisha told Ken.

'Really pretty,' Ken said.

Berta's face was turning scarlet. 'And she blushes!' I said, adding that to my list that was growing longer.

'And I prefer baths over showers,' Berta said, 'and turkey over ham at the holidays.'

'What holidays have you had since your accident?' I asked.

'Ah,' Berta started, looking around, 'well, Kerry brought me leftovers from Thanksgiving last year and Christmas.'

'But we had ham at Thanksgiving,' Ken said, 'and leg of lamb at Christmas.'

'Then how do you know you prefer turkey?' I asked Berta.

The smile left her face and she stared at me. Finally she said, 'I don't know.'

'That's a memory!' Trisha said, jumping up and down in her seat.

'I'll be damned if it isn't!' I said, smiling.

'What if I have a family? What if I have kids? We've established that I'm in my mid-thirties – which is the age Kerry was – so I should have a family, right? The age of Kerry's twins or younger, right? What if I left them alone to come to Codderville and now they think I've abandoned them?' She began to cry. 'How selfish am I that it took me this long to even consider those I probably left behind? Oh my God, what if I'm married?' And the sobs began for real.

I grabbed her hand. 'Berta, we're going to find out. I swear to you, we will.'

SIX

L ater that afternoon we all met at the house to get ready for Graham's graduation. He had the highest GPA of his graduating class, but because of his antics with the cherry bombs, wasn't allowed to be valedictorian. Or to graduate with his class. I got the kids upstairs to get dressed, Willis in our room to actually put on a tie, and answered the door when the doorbell rang. Vera, Willis's mother, stood on the front porch.

'I brought a pie,' she said, thrusting said pie in my general direction as she moved around me into the house.

'Thanks,' I said. It was pecan. Vera Pugh's home-made pecan pie. My favorite. I took a deep whiff then hurried into the kitchen to hide it from myself.

'I hope that young man has learned his lesson,' Vera said, sitting at the kitchen table, tiny feet not touching the floor.

'I hope so, too,' I agreed.

'What was he thinking?' she said.

I shrugged. I could hear the pecan pie calling to me. It was a siren's song – so sweet.

Willis came out of the bedroom. On seeing me still in my robe, he said, 'Are you going to get dressed?'

I shot him a look. About this time he noticed his mother. 'Oh, hey, Ma. I didn't know you were here.'

'If you'd known, I hope you wouldn't have talked to your wife in that manner, young man!' she said. I didn't have the easiest of relationships with Vera Pugh, but right then I could have kissed her.

'I'm off to get dressed,' I said.

'About time,' Vera said.

I ignored her as best I could. This was certainly a dress-up occasion but I wasn't about to wear my little black dress again. This called for something festive. OK, I admit it, I'd gone wild when I bought the black dress. For a woman who heretofore had worn nothing but blue jeans and T-shirts everywhere but to church, I had a vastly different wardrobe to go with my new body. I picked one of the four dresses I'd bought – a white spaghetti-strapped sundress with a skirt with a graduating floral design that ended in a riot of color at the hem. I found a necklace that went well with it and stepped out of the bedroom into the kitchen.

Willis and Vera were still sitting at the kitchen table, and had been joined by three of my four children. Megan, of course, was the tardy one.

'Whoa!' my husband said on seeing me.

Vera beamed. 'I always said you should wear more dresses. You look very nice.'

'Thank you,' I said. I may have blushed. Or maybe not.

'Yeah, Mom,' Graham said, 'you're looking good.'

'Love the dress, E.J.,' Alicia said, and Bess just smiled at me.

Megan finally came down and, upon seeing me, said, 'Nice dress. Can I borrow it?' Her highest form of compliment.

We managed to get the entire crowd into the minivan and headed to the high school. The extra graduation ceremony (the one paid for by the parents of the four cherry-bombing bad boys) was to be held in the school's theatre. We dropped Graham off at the back and drove to the front. Since there were only four boys graduating, the parking spaces were plentiful. Willis parked the minivan in front and we trooped in.

One of the women from the committee was in the foyer, right at the doors leading into the theatre. She was handing out programs, which were quite small. We found seats near the front, next to the parents of Graham's partners in crime, and I glanced at the program. All this trouble and they'd misspelled Pugh. Graham's name was listed as 'Graham Pug.' Good thing this was the end of high school; if it had been the beginning, he would have been stuck with the moniker for four years.

It appears we didn't merit the principal, or even the vice principal. The diplomas were handed out by the school counselor, who appeared totally bored with the entire thing.

But that didn't matter. We got to stand up as a family when Graham appeared and cheer like he was a Beatle. After, we went out to dinner as a family at an Olive Garden that had just opened in Black Cat Ridge.

I sat back and watched my family, the kids picking on each other, Willis laughing at them, and even Vera with a smile on her face. I was happy. That never bodes well.

The next day Willis had taken a half day off work, which he occasionally does when he's not hip deep in it. Although things had gone well the night before, for some reason he seemed to no longer be speaking to me.

'I discovered a new restaurant in Codderville yesterday,' I said. He was sitting on the sofa in the family room, a *Popular Mechanics* magazine in front of him. He made no reply to my opening gambit.

'I only had iced tea and the menu was vegetarian, but it looked cool. Reminded me of college,' I said. 'Molly's Munchies. Have you heard of it?'

Direct question. Would he be childish and not answer? Or would he be adult and let this go? Or somewhere in the middle.

'Yes,' he said, taking the middle ground.

'You ever go there?' I asked.

'Yes,' he said.

'I loved the patchouli and Grateful Dead posters. Very retro.'

'Um,' he said.

'How was the food?' This would get him. No way could he answer with a yes or no!

'OK,' he said.

'I want to rip off your clothes, stick your junk in hummus and lick it off,' I said.

He put down his magazine and stared at me. 'You always think you can sway me with sex, don't you?'

'Yes,' I said.

'You always think no matter what you've done, I'll forgive you just for a romp in the hay.'

'Yes,' I said.

He stood up. 'You're mostly right,' he said, coming over and picking me up in his arms. 'Lose another ten pounds and this would be a lot easier,' he said. I forgave him as we headed into the bedroom.

Twenty minutes later we heard Megan coming in the front door and scrambled to get dressed.

'You promised me hummus,' Willis said.

'Next time,' I countered.

'I'm supposed to forgive you now, right?' he said.

I stopped, blue jeans halfway up. 'Forgive me? For what? Not *obeying* you? Remember I took that part out of our marriage ceremony!'

'Are we going to start this again?' he demanded.

'I believe you started it!' I shouted.

'Don't shout at me!' he shouted.

'You stop first!' I shouted.

He pulled me to him John Wayne-style and slapped a big, fat, sloppy kiss on me.

'I think we're going to have to stay in bed until this thing is over,' he whispered in my ear.

'Probably,' I whispered back.

'Mo-om!' Megan said, opening the door. Willis and I sprang away from each other.

'Oh, gross!' she said. 'Were y'all doing it in the middle of the afternoon?' she said, following that with a retching sound.

'We were taking a nap,' I said. 'Daddy came home because he wasn't feeling well.'

Megan shook her head. 'And then you lie to your innocent child. I'm not sure which is worse,' Megan said, still shaking her head as she turned and left the room. 'Azalea and D'Wanda's brother is taking us to the mall. I'll be back by curfew.'

I knew Trisha was actually paying Megan money to watch TV while she was gone (God knows and I know Megan wasn't actually watching Trisha's daughters). I could only hope that what Megan brought home from the mall was at least PG13 and not triple X. My daughter had inherited my chest, which is not a terrible thing for an adult woman to deal with, but a teenage girl has to deal with teenage boys and a thirty-two D cup is more than teenage boys can handle without an immediate cold shower. She had tried to leave the house with three buttons unbuttoned on a shirt, only to have me button them right back up again before she got out the door. Yes, I know, she just unbuttons them once out of my sight, but I do what I can. I buy two-size-too-big T-shirts, only to catch her washing them in hot water. I take them away and give them to her sisters. It's a battle I'll be waging until she goes off to college and/ or gets pregnant and they droop.

I left the bedroom and headed into the kitchen, opening the freezer. 'Graham's doing the night shift tonight, and Bess and Alicia are doing something at the church—'

'It's a sleepover,' Willis said. 'A lock-in. Why isn't Megan going?'

I shrugged. 'She said she was going to the mall.'

'You let that child run wild,' he said.

I looked inside the open freezer. 'Nothing in here worth defrosting,' I told Willis, while looking at a plentiful assortment of defrostable food. 'How about we go out to eat?' I slammed the freezer door and turned to look at my husband.

He was back on the couch, magazine back in his hands. 'You really think I'm going to take you out to dinner and ignore all of this?'

'All of what?' I said, my voice cold as ice.

He threw down the magazine and stood up. 'You know what! I don't want you involved in another goddam murder, E.J.! How many times and in how many ways do I have to say it?'

'Tell you what,' I said, straightening my jeans and grabbing my purse, 'I'll check and see if Trisha or Berta – oh, hell, both! – would like to go out to dinner! I'm a little tired of dealing with you!'

'You're tired? Put yourself in my shoes! Every time you walk out the door, I'm not sure if you're coming back! I feel like the husband of a cop or something, and I'm not! At least they get a paycheck! You're just doing this for . . . I don't know, what, E.J.? Why are you doing this? For kicks? Is that it? Is it fun for you? Because it certainly isn't fun for me! You're going to get yourself killed and I'm going to end up being a single dad to four kids, two of whom I never wanted!'

We both stopped. Neither of us spoke. His last words hung in the air like a guillotine.

Finally I put my purse down. 'You need to leave,' I said

quietly. 'The suitcases are in the hall closet. Get one and pack it. And leave. Right now.'

'I didn't mean—' he started, but I was out of there, upstairs to my children's rooms, sitting on Bess's bed, stroking her new comforter and wondering if my entire adult life has been a lie.

MEGAN

I know they were doing it. I can't believe my mother lied to me! Parents *should not* lie to their children! It's just rude! And to see my dad all flushed like that! So gross! I still feel like I could throw up a little, ya know?

Donzel, Azalea and D'Wanda's brother, picked me up with the twins in the back seat, me riding shotgun. He was always doing that. Donzel's, like, almost twenty but I was pretty sure he had a crush on me. Problem: he was a total dweeb. Glasses, zits, *and* he was, like, short! Way shorter than me. *What* was he thinking? Had he no shame? How embarrassing would that be for me? I mean really! So I put on my seat belt, but still turned all the way around to talk to Azalea and D'Wanda.

'So after I talked to y'all, I went in her closet,' I said, continuing the saga of Mrs McClure and her dirty laundry, 'and she has leather pants!'

'Gross!' Azalea said.

'She's so old!' D'Wanda said.

'I know!' I said. 'I can just imagine her in those pants,' and here I shielded my mouth and whispered so Donzel couldn't hear me and start thinking dirty thoughts about me – which I knew he did all the time – and said, 'and one of those nipple-less bras with some sheer top over it!'

'That's so gross I think I'm gonna puke!' D'Wanda said.

'What's she gonna show, anyway? Skinny-assed white chick!' Azalea said.

'I know! Right?' I said. 'It's not like she's got anything up there to brag about!'

'But ya know, there are guys out there who like skinny chicks!' D'Wanda said.

Being twins and all, both Azalea and D'Wanda had basically

the same body type – very big boobs and very big butts. And, well, big in the middle too, but in a very attractive way. They *are* my BFFs, you know.

'Y'all gonna buy something at the mall?' Donzel asked.

Azalea, the nice twin, said, 'Hush up, Donzel, nobody's talking to you!'

'Jeez,' I said and rolled my eyes, which started D'Wanda giggling, and when D'Wanda giggles, everybody giggles. It's called infectious laughter. It's like a medical condition or something.

After we calmed down, I put my hand up to shield my mouth again, and told Azalea and D'Wanda, 'My parents were *doing it* when I came in a while ago!'

Azalea covered her mouth with her hands, and D'Wanda said 'Gross!'

'I know!' I said. 'I thought I was gonna puke!'

The twins looked at each other then leaned forward and D'Wanda said, 'We saw our mom doing it with her boyfriend one night!'

'Y'all hush, now!' Donzel said. 'You never saw any such thing!'

'We did, too!' Azalea said. 'And it was disgusting!'

Boys just don't understand. We women are sensitive about these things. Parents shouldn't be doing that after they have all their children. It's like, you know, overkill.

I fell asleep on Bess's bed. When I woke up it was dark. I felt empty, like my life's blood had been drained from my body. How was I supposed to go on? For ten years Willis had been living a lie. Yes, I know I pushed Bess on him. But there was no other choice. None whatsoever. I had worried then that he might leave. I thought I didn't know if the man I married was strong enough to take on a damaged child like Bess. It was a hard time for all of us. But last year, with Alicia, I didn't even consider him – I just took her on. What was one more kid? When Willis's former sister-in-law had showed up and dropped her four-year-old in our laps, neither of us had hesitated to take him in, even though it hadn't lasted that long. And when a teenage girl I saved from committing suicide moved in with us, he seemed OK with that, although she hadn't stayed that long either. But Alicia was official – our official, government-sanctioned foster child. I guess we'd be responsible for her college education. Scratch that – Willis would be responsible for her college education. He's the one with the job, his own company. I write romance novels and, although I make a fairly good income, it was supplemental. Not something we could actually live on.

What had I done? Thrown my husband out because, in anger, he'd finally admitted something he'd held secret all these years? Something I'd never thought to ask him? I've been a knee-jerk, pinko, bra-burning liberal most of my life, and for the first time in that now rather long life, I had to ask myself, what kind of wife was I? I think the goal had been equality, a full partnership between a loving couple. I'd gone over my half, way over, leaving Willis at best a third. We had discussed bringing Bess into our home ad nauseum, but at the end, there was no choice. It had to be done. And I loved her like she had been yet another one to cause a fifth-degree episiotomy. I hadn't given two seconds' thought to bringing Alicia into our home. And maybe I should have. OK, I definitely should have.

Willis had brought up Graham's crush on Alicia as a reason not to legally adopt her – had that been the real reason? The only reason? Now I don't think so. What had my ridiculous and ill-advised generosity done to my family? Bess and Megan were hardly around each other anymore. Before Alicia they'd been real sisters – fighting and bickering but getting together to torment Graham. Now that dynamic was gone.

I sat down heavily at the breakfast-room table. Bess and Alicia were at the lock-in at the church, but Megan was at the mall with Azalea and D'Wanda. Twin girls who would always pick each other over Megan.

I began to tear up, and before I knew what was happening I was bawling like a baby.

How could I continue worrying about Berta Harris? How could I fulfill my promise to Ken Killian? My marriage was in trouble. I was in trouble. I dried my eyes and dialed Megan's cell phone number.

'What?' she said upon answering. Obviously my name had come up on her screen.

'Are you at the mall yet?' I asked.

'No,' she said, 'your husband met me there and drove me to the church! He's making me go to this lame lock-in!'

'Are you inside yet?' I asked.

'Mother! I'm walking in now!'

'When you get inside I want to speak to Lisa,' I said, mentioning the name of the youth minister.

'Jeez! OK, I'm inside. I'm looking for Lisa. Oh, there she is.'

'Hello?' came Lisa's voice.

'Hi, Lisa, it's E.J. Pugh. Sorry Megan's late getting there.'

'That's OK, we don't lock the doors for another hour,' she said.

'You might want to keep an eye on her, or tell her sisters to. Bess will rat her out in a New York minute. I'm afraid Megan might try to leave,' I said.

'I'll keep an eye on her for the next hour, then she'll have no chance to leave. When we say lock-in, we mean it!' Lisa said and laughed.

'Thanks, Lisa. See you in the morning.'

I hung up and considered where my husband might be. He didn't have any single friends to take him in, and his married friends had wives that were friends of mine, so that wouldn't be OK for him. Then I thought of the one place he'd go where he'd always be welcome. His mother's.

I got in the minivan and drove to Codderville, to the tiny two-bedroom house my husband had been raised in. Vera, his mom, and I weren't exactly friends, but we tolerated each other. She loved my kids, so therefore she had to accept me. This might be awkward, I thought. I knocked on her front door, and I could see through the glass in the door and the sheer curtain that Willis was coming to answer it.

When he opened the door, I said, 'Can you come out? So we can talk?'

He nodded and stepped out on the porch, closing the door behind him. We sat in wicker chairs, away from the porch swing we usually sat in when spending time on his mother's porch.

'I'm sorry,' I said. 'It was a gut reaction.'

He nodded his head but said nothing.

'Thanks for taking Megan to the lock-in. I was going to do it, but when I called her she was already at the church,' I said. Still he said nothing.

'Are you going to talk to me?' I asked.

My husband shook his head. 'I don't have anything to say,' he said.

'Why don't you come on home and we can talk about it later, or not at all. Your choice,' I said.

Willis shook his head again. 'No, I'm not coming home,' he said. 'I'm going to stay here.'

'For how long?' I asked, feeling bile rising.

'I'm not sure. I might get an apartment.'

I stood up. My only other option was to take to my knees and plead with him to come home. I couldn't do that. Looking at him, I figured it wouldn't work anyway.

'What do you want me to tell the kids?' I asked.

'You'll think of something. Tell them I have my cell if they want to call.' He stood too, turned his back on me, and walked back into his mother's house.

MEGAN

What can be lamer than a church lock-in? It's like a slumber party but with boys – and at our church, that meant a bunch of twelve-year-olds – and they literally lock you in! Me and Bess and Alicia were the only fifteen-year-olds there. None of the older kids ever came to these things, but Bess and Alicia came as volunteers to help Lisa with the younger kids. I bet my mom and dad didn't even know that! You can't force someone to be a volunteer, can you? I mean, isn't that, like, voluntary, for crying out loud?

'Hey,' Bess said when I found them. 'What are you doing here?'

'Mom and Dad made me come,' I said.

'Jeez,' she said. 'Why?'

'How do I know? They're acting weird. I caught them doing it,' I told her and Alicia.

Bess scrunched up her nose. 'Oh, gross!'

Alicia turned red. 'Y'all shouldn't talk about that.'

'Why not?' Bess and I said, almost in unison.

'It's not right. They're a married a couple. Of course they
. . . do it.'

'Well, duh,' I said. 'But do I have to watch?'

Bess covered her mouth with her hands and squealed. 'Oh,
I'm gonna puke!' she said, laughing.

Alicia, Miss Goodie-Two-Shoes, said, 'This is not a laughing
matter. Megan, you should always knock before you enter
someone's bedroom.'

Bess removed her hands from her face and pointed a finger
at Alicia. 'Sounds like someone's had this problem
themselves!'

I laughed. 'Uh oh, Alicia, which one of your foster moms
did you catch?'

Alicia walked off in a huff. 'Was it something I said?' I asked.

Bess laughed. 'Oh, don't mind her. She just gets uptight
about things. She's not like us.'

'You mean she's not totally weird?' I said.

'Exactly,' Bess replied.

SEVEN

I didn't sleep well that night. Tossed and turned, had weird dreams. I woke up around three a.m. with a knot the size of Dallas in my stomach. Got up, took some Pepcid, and tried to get back to sleep. That didn't work. I turned on the TV and stared at some cooking shows for an hour, then crawled back to bed. I woke up around five a.m. to pee, couldn't go back to sleep.

I got up and put on my robe and went in the kitchen to make coffee. There was a message on the answering machine and I raced to see what Willis had to say. It wasn't him. It was Graham. 'Mom, I'm staying at Brad's tonight. See you tomorrow.'

That was all. That meant I was alone in the house. I couldn't stand to think what Willis and I could have accomplished on a Sunday morning all alone like this. Reading the paper in bed, drinking a third cup of coffee, laughing. Oh my God, I thought. I felt panic slipping in. I hugged myself, arms tight around my body. He's gone, I thought, really gone. And it was my fault.

I went to the sink and turned on the cold water. It was still fairly cold – the heat of the day hadn't yet warmed it to mid-boil. I splashed the water on my face, then dried it on a kitchen towel. Poured myself another cup of coffee. Stared out the window. Saw Luna getting in her car next door.

I rapped on the window to get her attention. She looked over and started to wave, but I beckoned her over. She shook her head, obviously at my gall, but headed to my house anyway.

'What?' she said, popping her head in.

'What did Willis say to you the other night?' I asked.

'What do you mean?'

'What do you think I mean?' I all but shouted. 'It's a simple question!'

She glared at me, then her face softened. 'What's wrong?' she asked.

I took my still-full coffee cup and dropped into a chair at the kitchen table. 'He's left me,' I said.

Luna went to the cupboard and got a cup, filled it with coffee, used some sweetener, then came to the table and sat opposite me. 'When did this happen?' she asked.

'Last night,' I told her.

'I'm sorry.'

'Yeah, isn't everyone,' I said.

I felt Luna's hand on mine and my eyes began to fill with water. Don't cry, I told myself. Goddamit, don't cry!

'Why?' she asked.

I pulled my hand from beneath hers. 'Why what? Why did he leave? Jeez, Luna, you already know that! You probably know it better than I do! What did he say to you while you were waiting for Trisha and me to get back?'

'With Berta "I don't know who I am" Harris?'

I shook my head. 'Not in the mood for your idea of humor,' I said.

'Right,' she said. 'What did Willis say? Well, he called me in the middle of the night, woke me up, said, "She's at it again," and hung up. I, of course, got dressed and came right over. When I came in the back door, all he said was "coffee" with a question mark, I said yes, then we sat right here at this table for almost an hour before y'all showed up. He didn't say much of anything the entire time.'

'How mad was he?' I asked.

'On a scale of one to ten, I'd say about a twelve,' she said.

'More than usual?' I asked.

She shrugged. 'Hard to tell. Like I said, he didn't say much. But his knuckles were white where he held the coffee cup.'

I put my hands to my face. Why? I wondered. Was I trying to hide? I should be hiding, I thought. In the attic. In the basement, if we had one. Maybe I should find a cave somewhere, crawl in and pull ground vegetation in after me to cover me up. Stay there until I died of starvation.

'Where is he?' Luna asked, her voice surprisingly gentle.

'At his mother's.'

'In Codderville?'

'Yeah.' Luna knew Vera, Willis's mother. Knew where she

lived. Had been there a dozen times. I guess the question had just been something to say.

There was silence for a few minutes, minutes in which I did not take my hands from my face. Minutes where I remained as hidden as possible in my own kitchen.

'Do the kids know?' Luna asked.

I shook my head. 'They're not here. The girls are at a lock-in at the church and Graham spent the night with a friend.'

She pushed herself up from the table. 'Speaking of church, I'm off to the gym. You want me to bring you anything? Donuts? Chocolate? Booze?'

I shook my head, although I could certainly use some chocolate to ease the pain. But I'd worked so hard— 'Yeah,' I said. 'A couple of Mars bars— Hell, no!' I said, standing up. 'This is the worst thing that's happened to me since the Lesters died. And I'm not ruining my diet with a stinking Mars bar! Go to Lambs and get me some of those dark chocolate truffles, please, and two turtles, milk or dark, I don't care, and four dark chocolate-covered cherries! And then come right back! And buy a bottle of something alcoholic that goes with chocolate! Ask the liquor store guy! He'll know. And here!' I said, rushing to my purse. I grabbed a twenty and handed it to her. 'It's on me.'

'And you expect me to ruin my diet too, just to indulge your pity-party?' Luna asked, hands on hips.

'Yes!' I said.

She shrugged. 'OK,' she said and was out the door.

I was sitting at the kitchen table thinking only of the chocolate to come, when the phone rang. There's a wall extension in the kitchen so I picked it up. 'Hello?' I said, hoping my husband was calling to say it was all just a giant mistake and he was on his way home.

'E.J.?' a timid voice asked.

'Yes, who's this?'

'It's me. Berta Harris. I thought I'd call and see what we're going to do today to figure out who's trying to kill me?'

'Are you at Ken's?' I asked.

'Yes, they're being very nice to me. Kerry's boys are very sweet,' Berta said.

'Ah, something's come up here,' I told her. 'It might be later today before I can do anything.'

'Oh,' she said. Then, 'Well, OK. I guess I'll just stay here?'

'I think that would be best. May I speak to Ken for a moment?'

'Oh. Yes. Of course. Ken?'

'Hi, E.J.,' Ken's voice said.

'Ken, something's come up. Do you have a problem with Berta staying there a little longer?'

'Not at all. The boys and I are going to teach her some card games.'

'Great, Ken. Thanks. Bye,' I said and hung up just as the doorbell rang.

The door popped open before I had a chance to get there. 'Hey, E.J.,' Trisha said. 'So where to? Have you talked to Berta today? What's the plan, Stan?'

I flopped onto the living-room sofa. 'I have no plan,' I said.

'What's wrong?' Trisha said, a look of concern on her face. She floated gently down on the love seat opposite the sofa.

So I told her. But, unlike Luna, I gave her all the details, from the hurtful words he'd uttered, to the blatant truth of those words, to me kicking him out, then to me almost begging him to come back. Before I finished telling it, I was bawling. Trisha came over to the sofa and gathered my big head and shoulders to her tiny ones, patting me on the back and saying, 'Cry it out, honey. Just let it all out. But he'll be back! I promise you!' and words to that effect that I barely heard over my own noise.

Finally I pulled away and used tissues on the coffee table to clean myself up. Then I was in the kitchen and on the phone. Turning to Trisha, I asked, 'What kind of chocolate do you like?' I dialed Luna's cell phone.

Trisha wrinkled her little nose and patted her little tummy. 'I don't. It gives me gas.'

I put the phone back in the cradle and stared at her. 'How awful!' I finally said.

She waved away my words. 'Oh, it's no biggie. I'm not a big fan of chocolate anyway.'

I stared at her. What was *wrong* with this woman? Not a big fan of chocolate?

That's like not being a big fan of air! Air, earth, water, fire, and chocolate! Was she insane? I picked up the phone again and hit the redial button. When Luna picked up, she was grunting.

'What are you doing?' I demanded.

'I'm on the treadmill. I told you I was going to the gym.'

'And I said come right back! What part of that did you not understand?'

'Lambs doesn't open until ten and the liquor store doesn't open until after twelve on Sundays. The last vestiges of the Texas blue laws,' she said, panting away.

'Get extra liquor,' I said.

'You only gave me a twenty.'

'Are you going to eat some chocolate? Are you going to drink some liquor? Then pitch in, goddamit!' And I hung up. Did no one understand my grief? Jeez!

MEGAN

Since neither of our illustrious parents bothered to answer the house phone or either cell, me and Bess and Alicia got a ride home with Jarrell Hinsley's mom. Jarrell is like barely thirteen and five foot zero or something, but he has this mad crush on me. It works for getting rides and stuff, but other than that it's a pain in the you know what.

We thanked Jarrell and his mom profusely as we got out at our house, and I even gave Jarrell a little pity smile, then we headed inside. It was deathly quiet in the house. Me and Bess eyed each other, and even Alicia seemed a little freaked. Then we heard a scream. Followed by a high-pitched burst of what sounded like laughter.

'Mom?' Bess called out.

'Family room!' came back to us.

We dropped our stuff in the foyer and headed to the back of the house. Mom, Mrs Luna from next door, and my boss, Mrs McClure from across the street, were in the room. Mom was lying flat on her back on the couch, Mrs Luna was lying on her stomach on the coffee table, feet hanging way off it, and Mrs McClure was curled up in a ball on the throw rug between the coffee table and the couch.

'Y'all all right?' I asked.

Alicia grabbed my arm and Bess's and tried pulling us out of the room. 'We need to go upstairs,' she said.

'Oh, poo poo, Alicia!' my mom said, lifting her head to smile at us. 'My beautiful girls. All three of you. Wanna piece of chocolate?'

That's when we saw all the empty little brown paper cups the candies came in, the open box of Lambs chocolates, and the tipped over bottles of what I could only assume was alcohol. I don't believe in drinking. And I think grown-ups do it way too much, as was evidenced by the disgusting display in front of us. Church had been out for barely an hour, and here were these three women – one of them my *mother*! – drunk as . . . as . . . heck, I don't know. Drunk as whatever gets drunk a lot!

I brushed off Alicia's hand on my arm, poised myself with hands on hips and said sternly, 'Mother, you're drunk!'

My mom's head popped up again and, looking at me, she said, 'Ya think?' then burst into very childish giggles. Which started off Mrs McClure and Mrs Luna. Now Mrs McClure I could understand. Having sat for her children four times now, there was no wonder the woman wanted to drink. But Mrs Luna? She was a policeman, for gawd's sake! Police woman. Police person. Whatever. My point being: she shouldn't be drunk on a Sunday afternoon in a house where there were impressionable teenagers such as us three.

'Where's Daddy?' I demanded.

Mom's head came up again and she opened her mouth to speak, but Mrs Luna twirled around on the coffee table so that she was sideways, the top half of her actually over Mrs McClure, and shoved her hand over my mother's mouth. 'Shhhh . . .' she said. It was probably the most disgusting display of childishness I've ever seen, and I go to school with *boys*!

Bess touched my arm and said, 'Let's just go upstairs. And girls,' she said, looking sadly at Alicia then at me, 'let's never speak of this.'

*   *   *

OK, I thought. Three down and one to go. Or was it six down? I giggled again as I thought about how many children I had. 'I've got a bunch of kids!' I told my good buddies.

'You do,' Luna said. 'I've been saying that for years.'

'How many kids you got?' Trisha asked.

'Half dozen or more maybe,' I said.

Trisha stuck up an arm, thumb up. 'Yep,' she said. 'That's a lot of kids.'

Luna picked her head up off the table. 'You don't have that many kids,' she said.

'I don't?'

'Naw. I have two,' Luna said.

Trisha sat up, hitting the top of her head on Luna's chin. Luna said a bad word and Trisha's head fell back on the sofa and she covered her mouth as she giggled. 'Oops!' she said. Then she said, 'Why did I sit up? Oh! I know, I know!' she said, raising one arm. With the other arm she pointed an accusing finger at Luna. 'You don't have two kids! I've never seen them!'

Luna whirled around on the coffee table and sat up, lifting up her T-shirt. 'Hey, you wanna see my stretch marks? I do too have kids! Two boys.' Trisha stared at Luna's stretch marks.

'Wow,' Trisha said. 'Those are awesome!'

'Yeah,' Luna said proudly. 'Ernesto weighed twelve pounds! You should have seen the episiotomy!'

'Yuck!' Trisha said, and fell back. 'No, thanks! Hey!' Accusatory finger pointed at Luna yet again. 'If you got kids, where the heck are they?'

'Ernesto joined the Navy the second he graduated high school, and Roman's in his third year at A&M.'

Trisha made a face. 'Yuck, an Aggie!'

'Jesus,' Luna said, 'you're not another T-sipper, are you?'

'Four years and a stab at grad school,' she said. 'Go Longhorns!'

Trisha and I both did the Longhorn sign with both hands – index and pinky finger up, two middle fingers and thumb down – and made a 'woo-wooing' sound.

'Where'd you go?' Trisha asked.

'I'm a graduate of the School of Hard Knocks! And I have *many* advanced degrees!' Luna said.

We all thought that was the funniest thing we'd ever heard.

I'm not sure when we fell asleep, or passed out, or whatever, but we did.

I woke up around dinner time with a terrible headache. I was in my bedroom. There were normal house sounds going on outside my door. I could even smell something delicious coming from the kitchen. I got up and went to the bathroom, splashed water on my face and changed out of my wrinkled and booze-soaked clothing. Opening the door from my bedroom into the great room, I could see Megan and Graham in the kitchen with Bess and Alicia in the breakfast room, setting the table.

'Hey,' I said sheepishly.

They all turned around. 'Hey back,' Graham said. 'Are you feeling OK or do you need some O.J. or coffee or something?'

'Maybe a Coke?' I suggested. 'A little cold caffeine might be in order.'

Graham handed a canned Coke out of the fridge to Megan who, begrudgingly, brought it to me. She didn't say a word when she handed it to me. The other two girls kept their eyes on the table, as if putting the forks and knives in the correct position would win them points in some inner Miss Manners contest.

I opened the Coke and took a long pull on it. Nothing had ever tasted better. I took another long pull and realized that hadn't been a good idea. I made it to the hall bath in the nick of time.

By the time I'd cleaned myself up and returned to the great room, Megan was bringing the food to the table. We all sat down in our usual spots, the one chair conspicuously vacant.

'Where's Daddy?' Bess asked.

'We'll talk about it later,' Graham said. 'You want this food I just slaved over to get cold?'

Bess rolled her eyes. 'You're such a drama queen,' she said.

'That's drama *king* to you, my dear,' he said.

'What is this?' I asked as I gingerly took a forkful of chicken, cheese, green chilies and other wondrous things.

'My version of King Ranch chicken. What do you think?'

I took a bite and could have sworn I was in heaven. I stared at my son. 'When did you learn to cook?'

'Oh, I piddle around some. I enjoy it.'

'This is good,' Alicia said, actually taking a large bite. She usually just wet her fork a bit and pretended to eat.

'Not bad,' Megan said, halfway through what I assumed would be her *first* helping. 'But the salad's the best.'

I laughed. 'I assume you made the salad?'

No response from my daughter. After a minute, Graham said, 'Yeah, she made the salad, but it seems to have sapped her of all her strength.'

Bess never looked up from her plate. The realization began to dawn that possibly my girls had heard or seen something earlier in the day – possibly while I was inebriated – that had them concerned.

I decided not to pursue the issue until after dinner. Graham had gone to too much trouble for me to let my actions ruin his lovely meal. And then I got another brainstorm: Graham had quiet deftly maneuvered Bess away from her question of 'Where's Daddy?' He knew. He must have called Willis. He was doing all this because he knew.

I felt shame and embarrassment. My son felt so sorry for me he manipulated his sisters and fixed dinner because he knew I'd be a wreck. I couldn't help but wonder how Willis was doing. Maybe already dating, who knew? At least he was probably sober and not having giant pity-parties. He might even feel relieved. Relieved that he was finally out of this hell-hole called a marriage, relieved that he didn't have to deal with me anymore, put up with my crap, especially my penchant for sticking my nose in where it didn't belong.

I was beginning to feel a little nauseous. I took a drink of ice water, hoping it would quell my desire to puke. It did. I pushed my food gently around my plate, no longer able to eat Graham's perfectly wonderful offering. Finally, the meal was over and I got up, picked up my plate and started for the sink.

'That's OK, Mom,' Graham said. 'Bess and Alicia signed up to do the cleaning tonight.'

Both girls glared at him, but started clearing the table. Megan headed for the stairs.

Graham said, 'Why don't we go in the living room?'

The living room is where family members went when they wanted to have a discussion not overheard by others. Or to just get away from the blaring TV. Unfortunately the TV was turned off, so I had a feeling a discussion of sorts was in order. I followed him to the front of the house, feeling more like the child than the parent.

We sat, me in the love seat, Graham on the sofa. He leaned forward elbows on knees, hands clasped in front, shoulders slightly slumped. He looked so much like a man at that moment that I almost cried. My eighteen-year-old boy was all grown-up and heading off to college in a little more than a month. I cleared my mind of that thought.

'I called Dad today,' Graham said.

All I could do was nod.

'He said he was staying at Grandma Vera's for a while. That you were supposed to explain why.'

Again, I nodded.

'But I did get out of him that you asked him to leave, and that he agreed it was the best plan.'

Be the grown-up! my mind kept telling me, but my body kept replying, *Hide, hide!*

I took a deep breath and looked my son square in the eye. 'Some things came up. We decided it was time for a break. We've been together since college, over twenty years. We just need a little time apart.'

'I assume the girls don't know?' Graham said.

'No, they don't. But they need to. Would you mind gathering them up?'

It was Graham's turn to nod, which he did, then got up in search of his sisters. It took a good ten minutes for them to gather in the living room, ten minutes I took to gather my thoughts. When they were all seated, I said, 'First I want to apologize for whatever I did this afternoon when I was . . . ah . . . indisposed—'

'You mean drunk?' Megan said, arms crossed under her ample chest, her tone cold enough to fix our current weather problems.

I looked her in the eye. I was finally getting good at that. 'Yes, honey, drunk. I was drunk. It happens. Was it a wise decision to get drunk on a Sunday morning? No, not at all. But it happened and I think we need to all get past it. I hope I didn't do or say anything to embarrass any of you.'

'You only embarrassed yourself, Mother,' Megan said, not easing up a bit.

'Can it, Meg,' Graham said. 'Give her a break.'

Megan sighed heavily and looked away from both her brother and me.

'We have something more we need to talk about,' I said. 'Your father has temporarily moved to Grandma Vera's house.'

All three girls turned open-mouthed stares toward me. 'It wasn't something we planned, it just came up—'

'Is Grandma Vera sick?' Bess asked.

'No, honey, it's nothing like that.' I took a deep breath. 'Your father and I decided we needed a break—'

'He left?' Megan said jumping up. 'He just walked out on us?' Then she frowned. 'Or did you throw him out?'

'It was a mutual decision, Megan,' I said. 'We've been together a very long time, and we just need a little time apart—'

Megan turned and headed upstairs. I looked at my other three children.

'When is he coming back?' Bess asked.

'We don't know yet,' I answered. 'But you can reach him on his cell phone or his office phone, or even Grandma Vera's phone, whenever you want to talk to him.'

Bess looked at Graham. 'I've noticed you don't have any questions. That's because you already knew, didn't you?'

Graham shrugged. 'For just a few hours. I called Dad earlier today and he told me he was staying at Grandma's. He didn't give me any more information than she just gave us.' He looked at me. 'Which sure as hell wasn't much.'

'What is it you want to know?' I asked. I took a minute to look at each child for a brief instant.

'Is it because of me?' Alicia asked.

I felt the bile rising again in the back of my throat. No way was I going to lay this at that poor girl's feet. She had enough wounds, physical and emotional. She didn't need this one added to it.

'Absolutely not,' I said, and smiled.

'Then why?' Bess asked.

'These are private reasons,' I said. 'Things between a husband and wife.'

'Problems in the bedroom?' Graham asked. 'Get Dad some Viagra for crying out loud!'

I laughed. Maybe not appropriate, but I did. 'No, honey, not that. And that's not a question you put to your parents.'

'Yeah, Graham,' Bess said. 'Like, yuck!'

I heard a commotion on the stairs and we all turned to look. Megan was coming down the stairs with two large suitcases in her hands.

'Graham,' she said, as she hit the foyer, 'would you please drive me to Grandma's?'

EIGHT

MEGAN

Of course she wouldn't let me go. When you're fifteen you're no better than a slave! You have no rights. And your owner can do whatever she wants with you. Clean this, pick up that, take the trash out, clean the toilet, brush your hair, brush your teeth, set the table! I swear it goes on forever! I hate her. I really, really, honestly do! My dad is the only person in the world I can relate to and she threw him out! She denies it, says it was a mutual decision, but that's, excuse the expression, crap! She knows I love my dad and I don't love her, so she threw him out, just to hurt me!! I swear I think that's her entire goal in life, to ruin mine!

I sat in my room, my tears shed. I have no more in me. I'd cried them out. I might never cry again. She had ruined my life! If I weren't as stable as I am – very, very stable – I'd probably attempt suicide right now! A lesser woman would. Really.

At least I have my job with Mrs McClure. She's going to get her hair done tomorrow, and a mani-pedi, so I'll get at least two hours. I didn't get a chance to spend any money at the mall the other night since my dad kidnapped me and made me go to that stupid church thing, so I have, like, money saved! I'll add the pay tomorrow, add that to the money saved, and I'll have, like, close to one hundred dollars! I'm going to save a little more then I'm going to run off to New York City, or maybe Los Angeles. I see myself more as a model slash stage actress, but I'll do movies if I have to. I'm versatile.

Monday came in on great clumping feet, like a Clydesdale running through my head. But with that came the realization that I could do nothing about my husband and his decision of whether or not to come home or stay at his mother's and screw around with waitresses. That was his choice. Meanwhile, I'd made a commitment not only to Berta Harris, but also to Ken Killian. I made promises to find out who killed Kerry and who wanted to kill Berta. And since I had no one here to continuously tell me not to, it was time I got with it.

Berta had woken up knowing she was in trouble, just not what kind. She'd woken up knowing she liked Diet Coke, the color blue, and Mexican food. She knew she didn't like Chinese food or sandals, but liked NBC news and *Survivor*. She just didn't know who she was. And how did any of that get me any closer to who killed Kerry and who *wanted* to kill Berta?

OK, I thought. Why do people murder other people? Luna told me once it was variations on the twin themes of love or money. Although I wasn't sure if that followed with Kerry's murder. I was positive Kerry's death had something to do with Berta. The way Kerry acted when Trisha and I came to her real estate office proved – at least to me – that Kerry knew something bad, that she was already under some kind of duress.

And that something bad, the duress, had to be related to Berta. So why was someone trying to kill her? She was on a lonely road in Codderville when she was run over by a hit-and-run driver. I wondered what road she might have been on. I picked up the phone and called Berta.

'Good morning,' I said when she answered the phone. 'It's E.J.'

'I know,' Berta said, a smile in her voice. 'I recognized your voice. What's up?'

'Do you know what road you were hit on?'

'You mean with the hit-and-run driver?'

'Yes,' I said.

'No.'

'Who found you and where?'

'Hum,' she said. 'I don't know. Since I left the hospital so quickly and sneakily, I never had the chance to ask anyone about anything.'

'OK, thanks,' I said and hung up, immediately dialing Luna's number at the police department in Codderville. When she answered, I said, 'Hey, I need your help.'

'I'm not speaking to you,' she said and hung up.

I redialed. 'Don't hang up! It's important. Sorry about the booze yesterday. If it's any consolation, I have no memory of anything after the last truffle.'

'There were truffles?' She sighed. 'What do you want?'

'Anyway you can find the call or whatever for when Berta was picked up and taken to the hospital back whenever?'

'I know you think I'm a complete idiot, and this department can't do its job without your help, but we already did that. We checked with the hospital ER to find out when she was admitted, traced that back to a nine-one-one call and found out who came to the scene.'

'Great! So tell all!' I said, smiling.

'No,' she said and hung up.

I hit redial again. 'What?' she demanded on picking up the phone.

'Why are you doing this?' I said in as reasonable a voice as I could muster. 'You know and I know you're going to give me the information eventually. Why drag it out? Unless you enjoy having me call you every five minutes. Is that what this is? Do you have a girl crush on me—?'

A heartfelt sigh came from the other end of the line. 'She was admitted to the ER at eleven p.m. on October 3, 2010.' I stood up, stretching the kitchen phone cord across the room to open the junk drawer where I kept a tablet and pen. Why not keep it next to the phone? With teenagers in the house? Get real. 'The nine-one-one call came from the cell phone of an eighty-four-year-old man who was walking his dog and saw a woman in the middle of the road. That road being Burkley Road on the north side of the ball park in Codderville. He didn't know if she was dead or alive. I did an interview with him Friday and I don't suspect him of any foul play. The police officers who responded to the scene said she was alive but unconscious when they got there and they got a response from a bus in less than five minutes. She was rushed to Codderville Memorial. The rest you know.' And again she hung up on me. I didn't hit redial – not even to say thank you.

* * *

I sat in Kerry Killian's beautifully appointed living room, in one of the silk striped arm chairs. Berta sat on the couch, and Ken, who hadn't gone back to work yet, sat on the love seat. The boys were out.

'Does Burkley Road mean anything to you?' I asked Berta. She shook her head.

'The ball park?'

Again she shook her head.

'Maybe if she saw the place?' Ken suggested.

'Good idea,' I said. 'Berta, are you up to seeing the spot where you were hit?'

She looked from me to Ken and back again. She sighed heavily and said, 'Yes. I think it's something I need to do.'

'Thata girl!' Ken said, smiling, and stood up.

We all hopped in Ken's car, an SUV with lots of leg room in the back seat, where I was delegated, and drove from Black Cat Ridge to Codderville. It was another beautiful day, royal-blue sky, bright sun, brown grass and sagging trees. The temp as we left Black Cat Ridge at ten a.m. was ninety-four degrees. It was early July and if the temp went as high as predicted, today would mark the eighth day in a row of over one hundred degrees – the sixteenth day since official summer began. The lake levels were decreasing, creeks were disappearing, and there was no rain in sight. The short-lived storm of the other night was so strong that it just ran off topsoil, sending little more than muddy slime into the aquifer. Gotta love a Texas summer.

We crossed the bridge over the Colorado River (the Texas Colorado River, that is), the water running sluggishly along. We were seeing parts of the bank that hadn't seen daylight in one hundred years. Just looking at it depressed me. The sages on TV were declaring this the beginning of a ten-year drought, or a fifteen-year drought, or even a twenty-year drought, depending on which station you watched or listened to.

I directed Ken to the ball park and we found Burkley Road. Although it had been nine months since her hit-and-run, you could still see faint blood stains and less faint skid marks. We sat in the car for a few moments, just looking at the scene, each one of us, I suppose, playing a similar yet different scenario in our heads.

Berta walking down the side of Burkley Road, a car comes out of nowhere and – and this is where I noted the skid marks – swerves to hit her. Those skid marks didn't show that the car tried to avoid hitting her at all. They showed an attempt to hit her by swerving in her direction. Whoever was behind the hit-and-run was purposely trying to kill Berta. Or whoever she really was.

I got out of the car to take a closer look at the skid marks. Surely Luna had noticed this! Was she insane? Jeez! It was so obvious! Ken got out behind me, with Berta a slow third.

I turned to Ken. 'You notice anything about those skid marks?'

He looked at the side of the road where the faint stains of blood still proclaimed their presence. Then at the skid marks. And back again. Then he looked at me. 'Someone was intentionally trying to kill her,' he said.

'I've been telling y'all that all along!' Berta exclaimed. Then smiled. 'Oh, I'm southern! Did you hear the way I said "y'all"? It was very natural!'

'Better than that,' Ken said, again smiling at her, a hand on her back, 'I'd say you said "y'all" like a Texan.'

'Really?' Berta said eyes big. 'Oh, I hope so!'

'OK,' I said, 'Back to the skid marks—'

'Didn't you believe me when I said someone was trying to kill me?'

'Oh, no! Berta, we believed you! E.J., tell her!' Ken demanded.

I was getting a little tired of this . . . *thing*, for want of a better word, between Ken and Berta. His wife hadn't been buried yet and here Ken was treating Berta like a cub to his mama lion.

'No, Berta, we believed you, but there was no proof. Now we have proof!' I said.

'Oh!' Berta said, then smiled. 'That's a good thing, right?'

'Right!' Ken declared, putting his arm around Berta's shoulders.

I wanted to say, 'Oh no you don't!' and bitch slap somebody, just for Kerry's benefit, but I knew she didn't care anymore and it really wasn't any of my business. But still!

I sighed and pulled out my cell phone, speed-dialing Luna at the Codderville PD.

'Luna,' she said.

'Don't hang up!' I started. Seems like that's always the way I start a phone conversation with my next-door neighbor and as close to a best friend as I had any more.

'Why shouldn't I?' she asked.

'Because I think you forgot to tell me something this morning when we talked about where Berta got hit.'

'I was very forthcoming,' Luna said.

'How about the part regarding the skid marks?'

There was a small silence. Then she said, 'Skid marks?'

'You know, the ones that prove that Berta was an intentional murder victim and not just an accident gone wrong?'

'I'm not sure you can actually say they *prove* anything—'

'Oh, bullshit!' I said. 'They do and you damn well know it! This poor woman has been sitting around waiting to find out what's happening, and you're intentionally keeping information back!'

'Well, here's some information we're no longer keeping back. You need to bring your new friend in. We know who she is.'

We were a silent group as we headed to the police station, all three of us again, I'm sure, sharing a fantasy – this one regarding the true identity of Berta Harris. I'm sure Berta was the most anxious. I can hardly imagine what it must be like to have no memory of who you are, and then have someone say they know. What will Luna tell her? Will she let Ken and me in with Berta when she does tell her? Will it be something bad? Something good? Something innocuous?

Ken pulled up in front of the station and parked the car. None of us moved. We just stared ahead to the door that would take us to Berta's identity. I think I understood why Berta was afraid to find out, but I'm not sure I knew why Ken and I were anxious. Maybe he *was* having feelings for her, and now he'd find out if she was married, had six kids, or was a nun. And me? I'm not sure. Maybe it was the anxiety of it all being over. That my marriage had broken up over nothing. That if Willis had waited one more day, this wouldn't have happened.

Ken cleared his throat, bringing me out of my reverie. 'Guess we should go in,' he said.

I nodded my head, but no one could see me in the back seat. 'I'm scared,' Berta said, taking Ken's hand. I could see him squeeze it.

'Don't be,' he said. 'It won't change anything.'

I'm not sure what he meant by that, but I had a sneaking suspicion. I tried to send Ken a telepathic message: *Too soon, fella, way too soon!* I doubt he got it.

I opened the back door and Ken opened the driver's door. Slowly Berta opened hers and we headed inside. Luna was waiting for us and took us into a conference room where we all took seats.

'Ms Harris,' Luna said, 'we will be telling you some things you might wish to keep private, so it's up to you whether Mr Killian and Mrs Pugh stay here.'

'Oh, please,' Berta said, grabbing my hand on one side, and Ken's on the other. 'Please let them stay.'

Luna took a seat. 'That's entirely up to you.' She cleared her throat and shuffled some pages in a folder. 'OK,' she started, 'we sent your fingerprints out to be examined and it appears you were fingerprinted in high school for a law enforcement program you participated in. That's how we found out who you are.'

'OK,' Berta said.

'Your true name is Rosalee Bunch. And you're actually from right here – Codderville. You went to Codderville High School and would have graduated in 1995.'

'Would have?' Berta questioned. I felt her fingers tighten on mine.

Luna looked at the table not at Berta. 'You're mom's name was Sharon Bunch, dad unknown. As far as we can tell, your mom moved to Codderville when you were a baby. She had no living relatives that anyone could find.'

Berta looked at me, her grip on my fingers becoming painful. 'This doesn't sound good,' she said in a tiny voice.

'Just hold on,' I said, removing my hand from hers and stretching my arm across her shoulders.

'In June of 1993, the summer after your sophomore year, you and your mother were living in a trailer on the outskirts of town. There was a large propane tank attached to the trailer.

It blew up. Your mother's remains were identified. You were never found.'

Luna put down the folder and finally looked up at Berta. I mean, Rosalee. No, Berta. 'My mother's name was Sharon?' Berta asked.

'Yes,' Luna answered.

'Did they think I hurt her?'

'Yes.'

'Oh my God!' Berta said, covering her face with her hands. Ken and I held onto her from either side.

'How could she have hurt her?' I asked.

'According to the arson investigator the propane tank had a leak, and there were a bunch of stick matches around the area. Like someone was playing with it – an even stupider Russian roulette,' Luna said.

'And they just assumed it was Berta?' I demanded, already getting my defenses up.

Luna shrugged. 'Her trailer blows up with her mother in it and the next day she's gone. It was the logical assumption from a law enforcement perspective.'

I was unsure whether Berta was getting any of this. Her hands were still over her face and she wasn't responding. Ken still had his hands on her arm, whispering things in her ear, like 'hold on,' and 'it's OK,' and 'just breathe.'

It was my turn to take one of her arms. 'Berta, look at me,' I said, shaking her gently.

She finally looked up. 'I killed my own mother!' she wailed, her face wet and red.

'No!' I said sternly. 'We don't know that! That was just the assumption the police made because you weren't around. We don't know the truth yet, but we'll find out. Maybe you saw someone else do it and ran away because you were afraid. Maybe someone kidnapped you and set the trailer on fire as he left with you! We have no idea what really happened, but we'll find out.'

'Unfortunately, though,' Luna said, 'we already got a judge to sign off on an arrest warrant, so we'll have to take you into custody, Ms Bunch.'

*   *   *

I called Trisha who promised to call her husband immediately. I hoped Tom planned on doing this pro bono; I certainly couldn't afford to pay him. Which got me to thinking what I could pay. My writing career affords me lump sums of money throughout the year. Largish lump sums when they're advances on a new book, smallish lump sums when it's royalties. Come tax time it looks like a lot of money, but I've never tried to live off it. That would mean spreading it out, even knowing when it was coming. Which I don't. Ever. I have a vague idea when my main publisher does their yearly royalty statements, and an even vaguer idea when different parts of the advance will show up. But then there's what we in the biz call 'mailbox money.' Those unexplained little checks from foreign rights, audio rights, film (don't I wish) rights, etc. I know it sounds like a lot of money, and sometimes it is. But it's hard to pay the mortgage with mailbox money. Those pesky mortgage people, and the electric people, the bank who carries the car loans, the AmEx people, and Visa and Master Card, all want their money on a monthly basis. How can you do that when one month you get a check for $2,580, and two months later you get a check for $1.86?

In other words, to keep the house and the lifestyle our children were used to, I'd need some of Willis's money. No child support for Graham, he having just turned eighteen. Did that mean Willis could forego our son's college education? Surely not. Graham's college fund was intact, but then there would be all those incidentals that weren't budgeted into his college fund. We did OK on our two incomes and one house. But what was going to happen when we went to two incomes and two houses? How were we going to afford that? Was it going to go that far? Was he really leaving me? Was there another woman? Or was it really just about my strange dead-body-finding ability?

We needed to talk, Willis and I, but did I want to push it just yet? Would a premature 'talk' lead to rushed judgments? Or do I let him wallow in his anger and his mother's country cooking until he realized that he could do quite well without me? And what about me? Did I want *him* back? I was the one who originally threw him out. But I'd already worked through that. Albeit weakly. Did I let him keep the excuses I made up for him saying what he said? That he basically didn't want our two extra girls. There was no denying that I'd thrust Alicia on him. I'd just assumed that he'd think what I thought: what's one extra mouth with all we've got? But I guess he didn't think that. I guess he thought another college education, another girl who could get pregnant, take drugs, wind up selling her body on the streets, etc. I don't know what men think. Do they think like that? Pregnancy, yes. My father had four daughters and every time we came home from a date, he'd say, 'Did you get pregnant?' It didn't matter if it was a first date or the night before our weddings, he'd ask the same question. And, when each of us announced our first pregnancies, Daddy would say, 'Well, it's about time.'

We teased about Megan getting pregnant at fifteen when she was a newborn, about taking the car keys away from her if she didn't settle down in her bassinet, but we really hadn't talked about that sort of thing since. But did he think it?

Ken Killian brought me back to the present. 'Are you getting in the car?' he asked.

'Oh, sorry,' I said. 'I was thinking.'

'Yeah, me too,' he said, a worried look on his face. Under the circumstances, not an unexpected look. 'I have something you need to know. I'm not sure it means anything, but—'

'Ken, what?' I said, slightly irritated.

'Lieutenant Luna said Berta – or Rosalee, I guess – would have graduated in 1995, right?'

'Yes, that's what she said.'

'That's when Kerry graduated.'

I sighed. 'A lot of people graduated in 1995, Ken.'

'Actually, no – there were only one hundred and twelve in the 1995 graduating class of Codderville High School.'

'Codder—' I turned to look at Ken, my eyes bugging out. 'Kerry went to Codderville High?'

He nodded his head, his eyes never having left the road.

'So—' I started.

'Yeah,' he said, his lips tight. 'Chances are real good Kerry knew Berta. Or rather, Rosalee.'

'Before the hospital,' I said, stating the obvious.

'Yeah, and Kerry never told Berta that,' Ken said.

I stared ahead myself. 'Ken, I think we should keep this information under wraps for now. Do you agree?'

'Yes,' he said. 'I agree. We tell no one.'

I had a vague notion that I turned into an idea. I do that sometimes. It tends to get me into trouble. 'Ken, you up for a little road trip?' I asked.

He glanced at me. We hadn't gotten on the highway yet to take us over the bridge and into Black Cat Ridge. 'Tell me what you want to do,' he said.

He pulled over at a gas station while I called Luna. 'Hey,' I said, when she picked up. 'Where precisely was Rosalee's mother's trailer located?'

'Why would you want to know that?' she asked.

'Just curious,' I said.

'No, you're never just curious. You want to go by there, don't you? What in the hell do you think you'll find there after fifteen years?' she said.

'I need to get a feel for the place,' I told her.

'You're out of your mind,' she said. It wasn't the first time she'd uttered those words.

'Be that as it may,' I said, 'address, please.'

She laughed – not exactly in a humorous way – and read off directions to the old trailer.

I read them to Ken and we turned around and headed back toward Codderville.

The directions took us to the extreme eastern part of the county, down a farm to market road, then to a county road, and finally to a dirt road. We got to the end of the dirt road and found an abandoned metal building with nothing but weeds around it. We turned around and headed back down the dirt road, going much slower this time. Through the trees on the left I saw the relentless sun shining on a tiny bit of chrome. The trailer. Ken pulled his car in as far as possible on what used to be a driveway, and we got out. The entire place was grossly over grown with cedar.

This whole section of Texas has a problem with what are erroneously called cedar trees. They are a cedar-ish type of tree, but of another genus entirely. They were brought over from

Japan, I think, to help with erosion back in the day. Now people have to clear the land constantly of the damn things. I won't even get into the cedar fever problem – a Christmas-time allergy that can fell an entire city.

Ken went to the back of his car and opened the trunk. Inside was a set of golf clubs. He pulled out two, handed me one, took the other and led the way, using the club to move limbs and weeds. We circled around the cedar trees as best we could, and Ken made a lot of noise whacking at the bushes and making honking sounds.

'What are you doing?' I finally asked.

'Snakes are more afraid of us than we are of them,' he said. 'They hear a lot of noise, they hide.'

Great. I hadn't thought of snakes. Now that's all I would think of. I stared at the ground and walked carefully, hitting trees with my club and making raspberries with my mouth.

We finally made it to the trailer. Even after fifteen years it was still there. No one had cleared it away. It was a single wide that may have been yellow at one time. There were indications of that color in spots. Half the roof and wall were caved in at the back and the front door was swinging wide open.

'You don't want to go in, do you?' Ken asked dubiously.

I stared at it. Did I want to go in? What would I learn if I did? Anything germane to the problems at hand? Maybe just a peek, I told myself.

I moved closer to the trailer and looked inside the opened front door. Half of a rotten sofa, a floor lamp with no shade and a busted bulb, ashes and items so burnt they were unrecognizable, a stainless-steel kitchen sink and faucet still intact, although the cabinets around it were half burned away.

Moving to the back of the trailer, to the burned-away wall and roof, I found nothing but ash. But even so, it appeared that this trailer was small, only a one-bedroom. Where had Rosalee slept? On the sofa? Or had her mom taken that and given her daughter the bedroom? Or had they slept together in the one small room?

'Well?' Ken said.

I shrugged. 'I guess we can go home,' I said.

'Have you learned anything?' he asked.

'Maybe,' I said, only because I didn't want this mini-adventure to seem to be an entire waste of time – which it might have been.

We headed back to Black Cat Ridge and Ken dropped me off at my house. We agreed to meet Friday evening to discuss this whole mess in depth. I stared at my house for a while, then turned around and went over to Trisha's house, needing a friend more than I needed to face my children. My luck: Trisha was gone and my daughter Megan was babysitting. I swear I can't get a break.

MEGAN

I finally get the girls down for their nap, just in time for *All My Children*, my fave summertime soap, when the doorbell rang. Thinking it was probably Azalea or D'Wanda, or both, I ran to the front door and opened it, only to find my mother standing there. Imagine my disappointment.

With one hand on my hip, I asked, 'Yes, Mother?'

'You're still here?' she asked, rudely pushing by me into the house. 'Is Trisha here? When will she be back?'

'No, Mrs McClure is not here, and I don't expect her back for an hour or so,' I answered, showing her how one is supposed to converse properly.

My mother flopped down on the sofa as if she planned to stay a while. I planned to nix her plan. 'Where is she?' my mother asked.

'She went to the hairdresser,' I said.

My mother frowned. 'Didn't she do that just last week? Or is she changing the color this week?'

Standing stiffly at attention, I said, 'I really don't know. Mrs McClure does not confide in me on such personal matters.'

My mother pushed herself up from the sofa. 'You know, honey, you used to be fun.'

She twittled her fingers at me and went out the door.

Ha! I thought. I used to be fun! *She* used to be fun! Now she just acted stupid most of the time. I'm not saying that she is – she just acts that way. I think she thinks it's funny. I hate to tell her: it isn't.

But she did make me think: Mrs McClure did say she was going to the hairdresser last week. She didn't have one of those complicated do's that older women have that need a weekly re-do. She had the kind of cut and the kind of hair that needed a daily or at least every-other-daily shampoo. So why would she go to the hairdresser twice in two weeks? Mom said color. That made sense.

I turned on *All My Children*. Erica had barely started seducing the new guy before I heard Mrs McClure's key in the lock from the attached garage to the house.

'Hi, Megan,' she called as she strolled in. 'How are the girls?'

'Asleep,' I said, checking out her hair. A little mussed, but not professionally so, and not one blond hair brighter, darker, or more highlighted than before she'd left two hours ago. Mrs McClure had lied.

NINE

As I walked through my living room, I saw through the window as Trisha drove into her garage. Which meant Megan would be home in another ten to fifteen minutes. And what was I to do with her? I had three fifteen-year-old girls, and Megan was the only one inflicting classic teenaged girl behavior upon me. The other two smiled occasionally in my direction, answered direct questions, did an occasional chore and, rarely, started a conversation. But Megan? Megan has decided for some reason that she hates me. I think it's because I'm her mother. She doesn't have the angst the other two girls have of having lost a mother. Megan has the one she was born with, and I think that's pissing her off.

How do you tell a fifteen-year-old drama queen how lucky she is to have an intact family? Well, almost intact. Intact until two days ago. Well, you don't, that's how. She would totally deny that having an intact family was somehow better than having had your family all killed around you, like Bess, or having your mother drop you off on the nearest doorstep, like Alicia. Of the three girls, I worried about Megan the most. She was as smart as the other two, as pretty, and in some ways as nice, but she was less cautious, extremely so. She's the one who'd end up with an over-aged boyfriend, the one who was going to try a drug just because she never had, the one who'd worry if she hadn't lost her virginity by a certain age. Unfortunately Megan was a leader, not a follower. I didn't have to worry about her friends leading her astray. I had to worry about her sisters following her into hell.

The front door burst open and Megan was home.

'Mom!' she said, running into the family room where I'd finally come to light.

'Right here,' I said, turning the page in a book I was pretending to read.

'OK, Mom, look at me!' Megan said, grabbing my hands which made my book fall closed in my lap.

'What?' I said, half laughing.

'Mrs McClure just came home—'

'I saw—'

'And her hair wasn't done!' my daughter said, flinging my hands down and standing back in triumph, arms crossing her chest.

I shook my head in confusion. 'What?'

'No color either!' she said, clipping her words. 'What do you say to that?'

'I'm not sure—'

'It was all messed up like she'd been driving in a convertible or something, and Mom?'

'Yes, honey?'

'She. Doesn't. Have. A. Convertible.'

'That's true.' I took a deep breath. Somehow there was something here that could become a bonding moment between me and my oldest daughter. I didn't want to blow it. 'Could you possibly be more concise?' I finally said.

'Do you need me to spell it out?' Megan demanded.

I didn't want to say 'yes,' but that was the right answer. 'Just lay it out for me,' I said instead.

'OK,' Megan said, sitting down beside me. 'Mrs Mc leaves this morning saying she's going to the hairdresser. You and I both know she used that same excuse last week, and she doesn't have the kind of do that needs doing every week, right?'

'Right.'

'She's a definitely wash-your-hair-in-the-shower-every-morning kind of woman, right?'

'Right.'

'So you decide she must be getting it colored, right?'

Finally this very vague conversation at Trisha's house came back to me. 'Right,' I said.

'Except she just came home and her hair has NOT. BEEN. COLORED.'

'Highlights?'

'Nope.'

'Shine?'

'Nope.'

'Maybe she got waxed?'

Megan shook her head. 'Wasn't walking funny.'

'Her face?'

'Wasn't red. Still had on the same make-up.'

'Mani-pedi!' I declared loudly.

'Not unless she chewed it off on the way home.'

'Damn,' I said.

'You are echoing my sentiments.'

'So what are you saying?' I asked my daughter.

She was silent for a long moment, then finally turned her head away to stare at someplace other than my face. She shrugged her shoulders. 'I dunno.'

'She lied to both of us,' I said.

'Exactly!' Megan said, turning back around to face me. Then she touched a finger to her chin and frowned. 'But why?'

'Well,' I said, 'I can think of a couple of reasons to lie to the babysitter, but not so many to lie to a friend.'

'Why would you lie to a babysitter? When did you lie to a babysitter? What about? Which babysitter? Melissa? Did you lie to Melissa? What about?' Megan started.

'Yes, I lied to Melissa. I told her you were normal,' I said.

'Mother!'

'I'm thinking.'

So we sat there on the sofa thinking. I knew what it was, but I didn't want to say it in front of my daughter. This was something she was too young to get involved in.

Megan finally broke the silence. 'She's having an affair!' she said.

Well, so much for her being too young. 'I'm sure that's not it,' I lied. 'I'll talk to her.' I stood up and said, 'What would you like for lunch?'

MEGAN

'So Mom agrees with me,' I told Azalea. 'The woman is definitely having an affair. Next time I babysit for her, get Donzel—'

'Girl, he's working!' Azalea said.

'Then borrow his car!' I suggested.

'I can't borrow his car! I don't have a license!'

'What difference does that make?'

'About $200! That's the difference between me getting caught without a license and not driving AT ALL!'

'See if D'Wanda will do it!'

'Are you stupid? We're twins! D'Wanda's the same damn age I am!'

'So what are we gonna do?'

'Well, if your mom agrees with you, have her follow Mrs Mc!'

I thought about it for a moment. 'That's an idea worth contemplating,' I said and hung up. I sat there on my bed and thought about it. There's no way Mom would follow her on my say so. Besides, if she did follow her and find out Mrs Mc was diddling the butcher, or whatever, she'd never tell me. I swear, she was shocked when I used the word 'affair.' I mean, did she raise me under a rock? Have I not been exposed to television, the internet, movies, radio? Do I not READ? Be that as it may, there was no way she'd consider me her partner in this. But just look what all Bess and Graham and I accomplished last year when that crazy guy was stalking Bess! Well, it was mostly me and Bess. Of course, I did all the dangerous stuff.

I sat up in bed like there was a cartoon bubble on top of my head with a light bulb in it! (That's cartoon-speak for an idea, in case you live in Outer Mongolia and never saw a cartoon.) Bess! We could figure a way through this together. I'd grab her the minute she walked in!

That night I lay in bed, my mind going nuts. I do not condone extra-marital affairs. Neither does Willis. At least, that's what he told me. And I believed him. I knew he had a problem with me playing amateur sleuth, but let's face it, not that big a problem. Until now. So what made now different? Another woman, that's what. He seemed quite eager to move out of the house. Even more eager not to come back. Hell, if Trisha McClure, who seemed like the perfect little *hausfrau*, could be bonking someone on the side, why not my husband?

Then it hit me. It *was* my husband! Trisha and Willis were having an affair! How could this have happened? And how had I missed it? He always said he loved a big woman! Trisha's barely five foot two! Weighs less than a hundred pounds! He lied! Or his taste changed. Oh my God, his taste changed! My grandmother always said your taste changes every seven years. But she was talking about food – like you didn't like black-eyed peas when you were a child, then started liking them as an adult. That sort of taste. But I wondered if maybe it went for other kinds of taste, too? Maybe as he got older and, let's face it, weaker, he felt the need to feel more powerful and to be able to protect his woman. At five foot eleven and one hundred and eighty (which I no longer am – one hundred and forty-five now, thank you very much), I'm not necessarily the weaker sex and need little protecting. Maybe that was part of the whole sleuthing thing. He felt I was always putting myself in jeopardy and he was rarely needed to save my ass. Well, if what he wanted was some fluffy little Barbie doll, then he could have her. I had no intention of changing. How could I? My basic anatomy was what it was. And you know, I was almost beginning to think of Trisha as a friend. And then she goes and steals my husband! I thought about heading to our smallish liquor cabinet for solace, but decided a nap would probably be a better idea.

The phone woke me up an hour later. By the third ring, no one else in the house had answered so I picked it up. 'Hello?'

'Hey, it's me,' Willis said.

I couldn't catch my breath. The son-of-a-bitch! The nerve calling here when he was out bonking my almost-friend and neighbor. Then I remembered I had no proof of any of this. Just conjecture. So I said, 'What do you want?'

'I need to come by and get some of my stuff. I thought I'd call first and make arrangements.'

'What kind of arrangements?' I asked.

'If you don't want to see me, then you can set a time when you won't be home and I'll come then. Or whatever.'

A thought struck me: should I make him leave his key? I had no idea on the etiquette of separation.

'I have no problem seeing you, Willis. Come whenever you want. The kids aren't home right now, so that's up to you.'

'Maybe we'll get a chance to talk if I come over now,' he said.

Tears sprang to my eyes. He's going to tell me about his affair. 'Whenever,' I said hastily and hung up.

MEGAN

When I came downstairs after an awesome bath – with bubbles and oils and loofahs and a tray holding everything I needed for a self-inflicted mani-pedi, Mom was in her bathroom putting on make-up.

'Where you going?' I asked, sitting cross-legged on the commode.

'Nowhere,' she said while applying mascara.

'You never put on make-up unless you're going out,' I reasoned.

She put the mascara back with only one eye done. 'You're right. When you're right, you're right.' And then she grabbed her jar of cold cream and started removing the make-up. Sometimes I think I come from dangerously deranged stock.

'Mom, what are you doing now?'

'Removing the make-up,' she said in what sounded like a reasonable tone of voice.

'What's going—' I was stopped from giving her the talking to she so richly deserved by the doorbell chimes. 'I'll get it,' I said and headed in that direction.

I opened the door to see my father standing there. 'Daddy!' I said, jumping on to him. He held me and swung me around like he used to when I was a kid. I threw my head back and said, 'Wee,' all the way home.

And then it struck me: this was why Mom was putting make-up on. I felt bad for her, but what's a woman to do? I was sort of glad my mom still loved my dad, and sort of glad my dad still loved my mom. He was wearing an obnoxious cologne that I'd never smelled before, B.O. with a hint of tuna fish. I think that was some sort of pheromone for the older set, which made it obvious that, as my Grandma Pugh would say, 'he'd come acourtin'.' Sweet, sort of.

I decided to make myself scarce. There was a chance they

might end up doing it, and God knew I didn't want to be around again when *that* happened!

So I told my dad, 'I'm off. Tell Mom!' and was out the door like a shot. I'm versatile that way.

I heard Megan yelling 'Daddy' at the front door, so assumed Willis had somehow found his way home, however temporarily. What with his lady love living right across the street, it wasn't surprising he remembered where he used to live.

I wandered aimlessly into the living room. 'Oh, hi,' I said casually when I saw him standing in the open doorway. 'Either in or out,' I said, like I would to one of the kids. 'We're in the middle of a drought here.'

He closed the door behind him. 'How're the perennials in the backyard?' he asked.

'Have you been sneaking over here to water them?' I asked, heading into the kitchen.

'No,' he said, following me.

'Then they're dead, I guess,' I said. 'They're not on my agenda.'

'Excuse me,' he said, and headed out the back door. I heard the water faucet turn on and, glancing out the window, saw him watering his precious plants. Maybe he could transplant them across the street, I thought, if Trisha got her house in the divorce. Then I thought, oh, how great it would be to have the two of them living across the street! What if she got pregnant? I sank down on a kitchen chair. I'd kill him. Then I'd kill her. Then I'd kill Tom for being such an ineffectual husband as to let her slip off with a neighbor!

Oh, yeah, I thought, everybody's to blame except you. Ha! I'd been with Willis most of my life. I'd only had sex with that other one guy in high school, and I'm not even sure that counted. How was I supposed to go on? Would I start dating? I see all these ads on TV for dating services, where they do complete checks for compatibility and so forth. I had this sinking feeling they wouldn't be able to find anyone compatible with me. 'Large woman with three live-at-home children, who writes lurid romance novels and likes to catch killers on the weekends.' No, I couldn't see that working for me.

Willis came back in the house. 'They're OK,' he said, presumably speaking of the perennials. Like I cared.

I sighed. 'You said you wanted to talk. So sit down,' I said, indicating the kitchen table where I was already sitting. 'Did Megan leave?'

'Oh, sorry, yes. She told me to tell you she was taking off.'

'Did she say where she was going?' I asked.

Willis shook his head. I let it slide. We sat there, each looking off into space, hands on the table top, not saying anything. Finally, Willis spoke. 'I heard they arrested Berta Harris again.'

'Yes. For killing her mother when she was a teenager.'

'Did she do it?' he asked.

I shrugged. 'I have no idea,' I said.

'Are you going to find out?' he asked.

Ah ha! I thought. Here it is! Trying to find out if I'm still on the case. Looking for ammunition to use against me in court!

'Tom is looking into things. Ken and I intend to help him if he needs it.'

He nodded. After a moment he said, 'I worry about you.'

'Yes, that's the impression you left me with, when you, how should I say it? Left me. I guess it's easier to worry about me from a longer distance.'

'I didn't leave you. You threw me out.'

I took a deep breath. 'I'll admit I didn't discuss taking Alicia in with you before I did it. That was wrong. But Bess was different – we had no other choice. And as for Alicia now, well it's too late—'

I totally missed his signals until it was too late. I turned around to find Bess and Alicia standing at the opened back door.

MEGAN

I was right behind Bess and Alicia and heard what Mom said. I could have died of embarrassment. Alicia had lived with us for a year, and now Mom confesses she didn't really want her? What a way for Alicia to find out! I was devastated for her. And what was that about Bess? No other choice? I thought maybe it was time to rethink my entire life.

Both my parents stood up as Alicia rushed pass them, Bess hard on her heels. I stayed back long enough to say, 'You're a real role model, Mom. So cool.' I said it in my most sarcastic voice so I'm pretty sure she got the drift.

Then I slowly followed the invisible trail left by my sisters' tears. Once upstairs, I went into Alicia's room. She had her ugly gray duffel bag open on her bed, and was shoving her clothing into it.

'Where you gonna go?' I asked as I walked in.

'I'll be sixteen in a couple of months,' she said, 'and I'll apply for emancipation.'

I was confused. 'But you're not black,' I said.

Alicia actually rolled her eyes at me and I began to wonder how much of the real Alicia I'd been seeing for the past year. 'An emancipated minor, for God's sake! That means I can live on my own.' She stopped for a minute and turned to face me. 'I'm sorry, Megan. I looked it up last year when I was living with Mrs Butler. I didn't mean to snap at you.'

'It's OK,' I said graciously.

'Anyway, I think there are rules that you have to check in with some adult, but mostly it means I can get a job, go to school, and have an apartment.'

'Great,' I said. 'Bess and I will come with you.'

'I'm not going anywhere and neither should Alicia,' Bess said. 'We need to let Mom explain herself. I know she loves me, and I'd bet my allowance she loves you too, Alicia!'

'What about me?' I said indignantly.

Bess snorted. 'She has to love you – you're her biological child.'

'Well, she sure doesn't show it!' I muttered.

I looked at Willis as Megan stormed out of the room. 'Don't even think about leaving,' I said. 'You started this – you're gonna help end it!'

Willis's head was in his hands. 'I know, I know,' he said, his voice half hidden by his posture. Finally he looked up at me. 'How do I fix it?'

I shook my head. I had no idea. How do you un-ring a bell? How do you make night day? How do you turn a frown into a smile? My only answer, clichéd as it was, was love. Lots of it, applied unsparingly.

We both went upstairs and decided the girls were all in Alicia's room, as that was the only door closed. I knocked on it. There had been a lively conversation going on inside the room before the knock; after the knock, there was total silence.

'Alicia?' I called out. 'Honey, open the door.'

No answer.

I nodded at Willis, who called out, 'Bess, are you in there? We need to talk.'

Finally the door opened and Megan stuck her head out. 'No one wants to speak to y'all,' she said and slammed the door.

I knocked on it again. 'Alicia, please open the door,' I said. Then added, 'Now, young lady!'

Strangely enough, that worked. Alicia was used to following orders, poor darlin'.

Alicia herself opened the door to her room. It was a small room, the smallest upstairs – my former office. Being on the north-east side of the house, it had two windows on two walls, one of which had a window seat. With the girls' help, I'd bought material and borrowed my mother-in-law's sewing machine to make curtains and a matching cushion cover for the window seat. We'd painted the room a dark plum, and the material was white with plum-colored flowers on it. Very pretty and muted. We bought a white comforter and plum and white throw pillows, and made some covers for pillows out of the curtain material. The room held her twin-sized bed, an old dresser we'd antiqued white, a small desk and chair, and a purplish (as close to plum as we could find) beanbag chair.

At the moment, Bess was sitting in the chair by the desk, Megan slouched in the beanbag chair, and Alicia was standing at the bed, folding clothes into her duffel bag.

I picked up the shirt she'd just put in the bag and hung it in the closet. 'You're not going anywhere,' I told her.

'I can stay at a halfway house until my sixteenth birthday,' she said, 'then I'll get emancipated.'

'That means—' Megan started but her dad interrupted.

'We know what it means.' He looked at me and I sat down on the twin bed, moving the duffel bag to the floor. Willis sat on one side, and I pulled Alicia down to the other side.

'We all need to talk,' I said. All I got for this were two hard stares from Megan and Bess, and the back of Alicia's head. I pulled in a large breath. This was going to take some finesse. 'OK, look. Ten years ago we all know what happened. Bess's birth family was killed next door. They were our best friends and we were made executors of their will, and also guardians of Bess. There was no family to take Bess, only us.' I touched Alicia on the shoulder. 'And there were killers after her. We did what we could to help, and eventually ended up adopting her.' Turning Alicia around to face me, I said, 'But you were a whole 'nother kettle of fish. I thought what was one more fourteen-year-old girl, when we already had two of 'em? I didn't even bother to discuss it with Daddy. I just did it. And your dad comes home to another new child. I should have discussed it with him. Whether he knows it or not, I'm positive he would have said yes, but I didn't give him that chance, Alicia. I just took it upon myself to make that decision for the entire family.'

Alicia pulled away from me and stood up. 'An excellent reason for me to leave,' she said.

At that moment I heard the front door open and Graham shout, 'Hey, where is everybody?' Also at that very moment, Alicia burst into tears and ran out of the room, with both the other girls following her.

Willis looked at me and said, 'Well, I thought you did a good job. Although you did put it all on me.'

'I did not! I took the entire blame!'

'Let's see,' he said. 'You're the big-hearted mom taking in every stray around, while I'm the big fat ogre saying "no no no"! That about right?'

'That's not what I said!'

He stood up. 'Oh, yeah, E.J. That's what you said.'

He left the room and I heard as he passed Graham on the stairs.

'Hey, Dad—'

'Bye, son.'

'Where are you—'

And the front door slammed behind him.

A few minutes later, Graham wandered into Alicia's room. 'What's with Dad? You two at it again?'

I stood up. 'You could say that,' I said, heading out of the room and down the stairs.

Behind me, Graham said, 'Is it me? Do I smell bad?'

MEGAN

I'm not a consoling type, sorry to say. But thank God Bess is. We were all crammed in the hall bath, *the* smallest bathroom in the house, thank you very much, with Alicia crying her eyes out. I'm not sure what Mom said deserved this much crying – I mean, it all seemed fairly reasonable to me, although, of course, I would never tell my mom that.

Finally, after a good five minutes of this drivel, I said, 'Oh, for God's sake, stop! You too, Bess! Listen, Alicia, you know I'm not one to take Mom's side on a whim, but just listen a minute. What she said is something that should have been said the day they decided to be your foster parents. If my parents had any form of decent communication, it would have been said then! Think about it. A year ago, if Mom said that she was all gung-ho for it, but Dad had reservations but he got over them, you'd have been all, "I understand, Mr Pugh. And I'll try to live up to your trust," or some snarky crap like that. Isn't that the truth? Don't even consider this past year of being a family. Just think about what it was like that day.'

Alicia and Bess had both actually been listening to me. Finally, Alicia sighed real big, grabbed some toilet paper off the role, and cleaned up her face. Then she said, 'You're right. It's just hearing them say that now – after a year of calling them mom and dad.'

I shrugged. 'Maybe six months,' I said.

Bess slugged me in the arm. 'That's not the point!' she said.

Looking at Bess, Alicia asked, 'Do you ever feel like you're not part of the family?'

'I used to. But only occasionally. Like when I stopped

growing at five foot two and everybody else in the house towered over me. I thought, like on those kids' shows we used to watch, which of these things does not belong?'

Alicia laughed a little. 'Yeah. I feel that way. But it's usually when y'all start fooling around and laughing I've got to admit, I don't get your humor.'

'Practically no one does,' I assured her.

'I only get it because I've been in this house for ten years,' Bess said. 'After you've been with us that long, you'll get it too.'

I smiled. 'For sure,' I said.

The smile was gone from Alicia's face. 'I don't know if I can hold out for another nine years.'

'Just consider several of those years you'll be off to college and then of course you'll be a grown up and only get stuck here on holidays—' Bess started, then she began to cry, Alicia followed, and they fell into each other's arms, wailing away. I felt it an opportune time to leave. And I never did get a chance to discuss Mrs Mc's affair with Bess! It didn't seem to fit into the present situation.

TEN

Alicia agreed to stay. On Friday Ken called and asked me to drop by as we'd planned. He had managed to bail Berta out and she'd been released into his custody. He said he was taking the twins to their grandparents' house in Codderville for the night. This would be an opportunity to talk to Berta alone. I left some money for my kids to order a pizza.

Berta opened the door when I rang the bell. It took a moment to undo all the locks and turn off the alarm system. Once I was inside she fussed for a full minute to get it back on. Then we went in the kitchen where she set out a lovely tray of vegetables and ranch dip, and some cold cuts and breads. I made myself a small sandwich and ate some veggies, trying desperately to ignore the ranch dip, and wondering if this was really the kind of meeting that required crudité.

'Have you learnt anything more about your past?' I asked her.

'No, I just got here only moments before Ken took the kids to their grandparents. He said he's got Kerry's old high school yearbooks around somewhere. I'd look, but I don't want to invade Ken's space any more than I already have.' She stopped for a moment, then looked up at me. 'Do you think maybe I was a nice person? I mean, other than killing my mother. What I just said, which I didn't plan on saying or anything, seems like maybe I'm a nice enough person?'

I touched her hand with mine. 'You *are* a nice person. You've been nothing but polite and generous the entire time I've known you. I don't think you can be that way now, if you weren't already that way. *And*, we don't know that you killed your mother! Remember that!'

Berta sighed. 'I know, but I just feel really bad about it, so maybe I did do it?'

'Maybe you feel bad about it because she was your mother and you just found out she's dead.'

'Oh!' she said, looking up. She smiled. 'That could be it! I'm going through grief!'

'Exactly!' I said.

Ken came in the door from the garage. 'Found 'em!' he said, carrying in a box. 'I thought I knew where she kept her high school memorabilia.'

He set the box down on the coffee table and we all stood to look into it. There were four blue yearbooks with white trim, 'The Lion's Roar' imprinted in different ways on each book. I know the Codderville High School football team is called the Lions.

'Does that ring any bells? The Lions?' I asked her.

She shook her head. Ken pulled out all four books. 'If Berta, I mean Rosalee, stopped going to school in 1993, that would have been her and Kerry's sophomore year.' He opened the front flap of each book, and, although they had been autographed profusely, each book had 'Kerry Metcalf – Freshman,' or 'Sophomore' or 'Junior,' etc., carefully printed in the upper left-hand corner of the inside cover. Even at fourteen, Kerry had been meticulous. He pulled out the sophomore book and flipped to the photos of the sophomores. We found Rosalee Bunch fairly early, being a 'B' and all. She had very light blonde hair, a pixie face, big hazel eyes, and a smile full of braces. The picture had been signed, 'Rosie B.'

'That's me?' Berta said.

'That's what it says,' Ken said. He smiled at her. 'You were adorable.'

'Let's look at Kerry!' Berta said, grinning.

He flipped over to the 'M's'. Kerry Metcalf had the same dark hair, the same bangs, and the same ponytail. Strangely enough, she had a different nose. Ken's face turned pink. 'Ah, Kerry never told anyone about that. She was embarrassed she'd done it.'

'There's nothing wrong with her nose!' Berta said, touching the nose in the picture.

'I don't see anything wrong either, but she did it nonetheless,' Ken said.

Then we decided to read the autographs and on the back inside cover, we found Rosalee Bunch's inscription. 'Roses are red, violets are blue, you make me drink another beer and I'll puke all over you!' Signed, 'Rosie B.'

'Uh oh,' Berta said. 'We shouldn't have been drinking at that age!'

'Probably not,' I agreed, thinking of my three girls who'd just finished their sophomore year.

'I don't understand why she didn't tell you who you were,' Ken said. 'That's just not like Kerry to do something like that.'

'Because she knew about my mother, of course,' Berta/Rosalee said. 'She didn't think I could handle it right now. She was waiting for me to remember, probably.'

Of course, I thought to myself. Absolutely no ulterior motive on Kerry's part. Or maybe that was true.

We went through the freshman yearbook and found a much younger Rosalee and a much younger Kerry. And this younger Kerry had short dark hair and no bangs. But by sophomore year she'd found the do of her lifetime. Later on down the road, I'd like to get a look at Ken and Kerry's wedding picture. I just had to know if she wore her hair in a ponytail on her wedding day.

At the bottom of the box were a bunch of photos banded together with a scrunchy. 'Ooo, pictures!' Berta said, picking them up.

She took off the scrunchy, looked at a picture, and handed it to me. I looked at it, then passed it over to Ken, who sat on the other side of Berta. The first photo was of Kerry and a boy a few years younger, whom Ken identified as her younger brother, Mark. In this and some of the subsequent pics, her hair was not in a ponytail – thus, it appeared these were taken before her sophomore year of high school. There were several pictures of the two of them, and a few more of them with what appeared to be an older sister, and an older couple Ken identified as their parents.

'Where's Mark now?' I asked.

He shrugged. 'Last I heard he was somewhere in Central America. Belize, I think. Strangely enough, I've never met him.'

There were family Christmas photos, then, finally, pictures of Kerry and her friends, Rosalee Bunch always front and center. From freshman year (Kerry with short hair) through sophomore year (Rosalee present in the pictures), the pictures were all of the same people mostly. Kerry and Rosalee, three boys (one of them Mark, Kerry's brother), and a younger girl, apparently the same age as Mark. The other two boys were Kerry and Rosalee's age, and appeared to be romantically involved with the girls, at least if the pictures could be trusted. Kerry and a dark-haired boy kissing on the couch while the crowd apparently cheered them on, Rosalee on the lap of a red-headed boy.

Berta frowned. 'What's wrong?' I asked her.

'Well,' she said, still studying the picture of herself and the red-headed boy, 'I don't find red-headed men attractive.' She looked up at me. 'Would that change?'

I shrugged. 'I don't know,' I admitted. 'Ken?'

He shrugged too. 'I have no idea,' he said. 'He may not have been your boyfriend,' he added. 'He may have just been a friend and you were sitting on his lap as a joke or something.'

Berta was nodding before he had all his words out. 'Exactly!' she said. 'I was thinking the same thing.'

'Who's the boy with Kerry?' I asked.

'I never knew his name. Her big love, though,' Ken said. 'She rarely talked about him. I think they had a really bad break-up.'

We finished the batch of pictures and started going through papers at the bottom of the box. Surprise, surprise. Kerry Metcalf Killian was a straight-A student. There were report cards, tests, and book reports, each with a big red A on the front, and words like 'excellent,' 'very astute,' and even one that said 'masterful.'

'I'm not surprised Kerry was so smart!' Berta said. 'She struck me as super smart.'

'Oh, yes, she was,' Ken said. 'She should have gone to law school, but she decided I should go and she'd work to support me, then she'd start having babies and I could work to support her.' Ken beamed. 'And that's just what we did!'

Berta beamed back at him. I was beginning to understand the attraction between these two: they were co-presidents of the Kerry Killian Fan Club.

I needed someone to bounce ideas off. It certainly wasn't

these two. As far as they were concerned, Kerry Killian could do no wrong. I was beginning to think Kerry had a hidden agenda when it came to helping Berta/Rosalee. Why didn't Kerry tell Rosalee who she was? Why befriend her and hide her for all those months? My usual sounding board, Willis, was out of the question. I couldn't go to Luna to talk it out – she, of course, didn't want me involved in this. My former partner-in-crime, Trisha McClure, was having an affair with my husband—

Stop it, I told myself. Trisha's not having an affair with Willis. I just made that whole thing up. She and Tom seemed very happy. The only proof I have that Trisha's having an affair is that she didn't go to the hairdresser like she told Megan. And even that might not be true. Megan could have missed something. Maybe her salon has a tanning booth and she's doing it so slowly Megan didn't notice the darkening. Of course with the drought currently upon us, and so many days of one-hundred-plus degrees, all you had to do was stand outside for five minutes and you'd have a South Beach tan.

And to take this whole thing another step, what proof do I have that Willis is having an affair? Proof, hell, I don't even really have suspicion! He's done nothing to make me feel he's having an affair. This has all been my own paranoia. On the other hand, why leave me now? He's had plenty of opportunity to leave me. This certainly isn't the first time I've gotten involved in a murder.

Stop it! I told myself, more sternly this time. The question is: should I use Trisha as a sounding board?

I tuned back into Berta and Ken who were telling stories of the wondrousness of Kerry Killian. I said, 'Let's get off that subject for a minute. Let's try something: Berta, go sit in that chair opposite mine.' She did so. 'Sit up straight, hands in your lap, eyes closed.' She did so. 'Now, deep, even breaths. In and out, in and out. Slowly. OK, I'm going to ask you questions about Rosalee Bunch, and you're going to tell me everything you remember.'

Berta opened her eyes. 'How am I supposed to do that?' she asked.

Well, it was worth a shot.

MEGAN

Mrs Mc had called and said she needed me to babysit. Mom was gone so I left her a note on the refrigerator telling her where I was. Which was more polite than she was – she was gone and there was no note anywhere! She expects us to do all these things that she demands, and yet she does none of them! And we're supposed to respect that?

So anyway, I went over there, book in hand. I had no more plans of sneaking through Mrs Mc's bedroom, or anywhere else in her house. I was totally scandalized by her affair. I couldn't figure out who would have an affair with her, nor could I figure out why she would do it.

I mean, Mr Mc seemed nice enough, and he was certainly good-looking enough, so why would she be messing around on him? Maybe he beat her, I thought. Or gambled! Ooo, or maybe he was a secret drinker! I saw this made-for-Lifetime movie one time about this guy who was a secret drinker— Probably not a good time to go into that.

Anyway, I got to Mrs Mc's house, knocked and went in. The girls were on the floor playing with Barbies. Personally, I like Barbies. My mother wouldn't let Bess and me play with them because she thought they gave girls a poor body image (I don't understand why – I'd love to have a body like Barbie's!), so now both Bess and I play with them whenever we get the chance. I love her feet! Don't you wish you had feet built to go straight into high heels? That would be so cool!

I sat down with the girls and they loaned me a Barbie. I was only halfway finished taking her clothes off to change her into an evening gown, when Mrs Mc came out of her room heading for the front door.

'I'm off to the hairdresser,' she said, and was out the door.

Well, if this woman was having an affair, she was piss-poor at hiding it, that's all I can say. I was going to watch for Mom's car and call her as soon as she got home. No way was Mrs Mc *not* up to something!

*   *   *

After leaving Ken's house, having accomplished little more than finding out how long Kerry Killian had had her most recent hairstyle, I went straight to Trisha's house, going so far as to pull into her driveway instead of my own. I had no time to be crossing streets!

I rang the doorbell and opened the door at the same time. My daughter Megan was half-standing when I moved across the threshold.

'What are you doing here?' we said in unison.

Megan made it all the way up, jumped over the girls, and grabbed my arm, pulling me toward the kitchen. Trisha's kitchen was a standard issue builder's kitchen from the early 1980s. What they call a galley kitchen – longish, and so narrow two people would not be able to stand side by side in it.

Megan said, 'Guess where Mrs Mc is?'

'At the hairdressers,' I answered.

She put her index finger to her nose, a move we all learned watching a DVD of *The Sting*. 'On the money!' she said.

OK, maybe her second tan? Even I wasn't buying this, and I actually wanted to. I didn't want a friend with secrets. Not right now. Right now I needed an honest friend with no complications. I had enough complications for both of us. Again, as so often in the last ten or so years, I wished for Terry Lester, Bess's birth mom, my best friend. My God, we could have torn this place up, the two of us. People with murderous intentions would run screaming for the hills if Terry and I were on the case.

Funny, I thought, not in a 'ha ha' way but in an 'oh shit' way, Terry and her family were the first dead bodies I'd ever found. And even then Willis was reluctant to get involved. But he finally did, involved enough to save the lives of the kids and me.

I moved into Trisha's living room and sat down as far away from her daughters as possible. Megan sat down with the girls, occasionally looking over at me with a questioning look. I didn't know what to tell her. If Trisha was telling Tom the same thing she told Megan and me, then he was either very stupid or not listening. And not listening can get you cuckolded in a New York minute.

I sat there for two hours, going through everything I knew about Berta's case, and everything that had happened since the day Trisha and I went to Berta's 'memorial.'

I now understood the twelve-step programs. In a way it was a sort of wacky genius. If amnesia is caused by a knock on the head and an emotional trauma, go find out which emotional trauma caused it. The thing was, even with all the twelve-step programs, we still didn't know what the emotional trauma was. The knock on the head presumably came from the hit-and-run. But what was the trauma? What had happened to Rosalee Bunch that had caused her mind to retreat? If Berta was any indicator, Rosalee Bunch was a nice woman. Slightly timid, afraid of her own shadow, and loyal to her friends. Why would she kill her mother? I needed to talk to Luna – that was the only way I'd be able to get ahold of any history of child abuse or neglect. There had to be a reason Rosalee hurt her mother, if, in fact, she had. And what if she hadn't? Then someone else had set the fire – thrown those matches at the leaking propane tank. Was that what this was all about? Had Rosalee seen the person who caused the explosion and could identify him or her? Then why wait so long to do it? Rosalee had been gone since the night it happened. Luna had said there had been a search for her, thinking she might be hurt, but they found nothing – no sign of her. According to Rosalee's file, still in a box in evidence, they'd finally decided she was, as they say in police-speak, 'a person of interest.' Was that the reason? She finally comes home and the killer is afraid she's back for him, so he tries to kill her by running over her in a car? Then throwing an electric space heater in the tub with her? But it had been months between the two incidents.

Why? Rosalee escapes from the hospital. The killer has no idea where or how. He waits. How does he find out where Berta/Rosalee is? Because he does. He goes to the house she's living in – Kerry's flip house – and crashes an electric space heater through the bathroom window into the garden tub. But how stupid is this killer? I pondered. Not to figure out that the cord on the space heater was too short to reach into the tub from outside? I needed to get back over to Kerry's flip house and check out the outside plugs.

Did the killer know where Berta was now? How could he? OK, the police knew, my family knew, Kerry's family – of course – knew, and Tom and Trisha knew, and I guess Tom's secretary and anyone of them may have told. Way too many people. Should we hide her somewhere better? And by 'we,' I meant just Luna and me and no one else. Eliminate all the chances of someone telling someone. She'd only been at Ken's for under a week, but there'd been no attempts on her life. And Kerry's funeral was tomorrow – Saturday. Should she go? The church and cemetery would be crowded. Not only was Kerry a popular woman who belonged to just about anything one could belong to or volunteer for, and sold homes to at least half the people living in Black Cat Ridge, but there was also the murder factor. I've noticed, since my penchant for finding dead bodies started, that a murder victim's funeral was much more popular than your ordinary died-in-bed scenario.

All this basically meant that it was pretty much a given that the killer would be in attendance at the funeral. So should she go? Would she be safer at the funeral than left alone in Ken's house? Probably. If she were left alone, all the killer had to do was show up at the funeral and see that Berta/Rosalee was not there, leave and, by process of elimination, end up at Ken and Kerry Killian's house and *voila*! One dead Berta. Or Rosalee.

I heard Trisha's garage door opening and looked out the living-room window to see the rear end of Trisha's Lexus move into the garage. Two minutes later the door from the garage to the breakfast room opened and Trisha came in.

'Megan, how'd the— Oh, E.J.! What are you doing here?' Trisha said, confusion on her face.

'I came over to see you, but you weren't here. I thought I'd just hang out 'til you got home,' I said.

'Come on in the bedroom while I change clothes,' she said. 'Megan, you OK for a few more minutes?'

'Sure, no problem,' my daughter said, turning the page on her magazine while Trisha's two girls stared at the TV. I noticed they hadn't even said 'hi' to their mother. The few times I'd been gone when my kids were this age, when I got home they came running at me, throwing their arms around my legs and bursting into tears. Which of course made me go out less and less, until I became the brain-dead mother of small children they apparently longed for.

I sat down on Trisha's bed – an ornate gilded affair with a royal purple duvet and gold and royal purple throw pillows. The bedside tables and dresser were also gilded. I had to wonder where in the world one would go to buy something this awful, but I said nothing. What could one say?

'So what's up?' Trisha asked.

'Oh, I was just over at Ken's house, talking to him and Berta, Rosalee, whatever, and I swear to God, both of them are in this two-person Kerry Killian Fan Club! It's really weird. And anyway, we saw all these pictures that Kerry had from high school, with Rosalee in them, and some other kids, but all they wanted to talk about was Kerry! I just need to bounce this stuff off somebody, and,' I said grinning, 'I, of course, thought of you.'

'I don't know whether to be flattered or insulted.'

'Maybe a little of both?' I said, trying to help. Since I was being honest, I thought she might too. 'So, where are you really going when you tell Megan you're going to the hairdresser?'

'What?' she said, her head whipping around. Then she laughed self-consciously. 'I should have known I couldn't get that by you,' she said, and paused. 'OK, here's the truth. My big brother's in rehab.'

'OK,' I said, slightly confused.

Trisha sat down on the bed next to me. 'I didn't want to confuse Megan. I thought the hairdresser thing would be easier for her to process than going into the entire saga of my brother and his drug and alcohol problems.'

'Oh, right, you mentioned he had problems, because of your dad—'

She stood up. 'Right. Dad was a drunk and he started taking my brother to bars with him when he was, I don't know, twelve? Something like that. I'm not sure at what age he started drinking, but it wasn't much after that.'

'I'm so sorry, Trisha,' I said, feeling slightly guilty about my assumption at one point that she was having an affair with my husband. A good imagination is good for a writer, but sometimes it can wreak havoc in a real person's life.

'Seems like it's a no-brainer to go from alcohol to drugs. Kind of a combo thing. Do a little weed, wash it down with bourbon, snort a little coke, and do a shot of Jim Beam. The other day, drinking with you and Luna, that's the first booze I've had since my wedding. I stay away from the stuff.'

'I'm sorry,' I said.

'It's not your fault. You didn't know. Besides, you had your own issues that day. Now, let's forget about that and talk about why you came over. Something about Kerry Killian being perfect?'

'It's just that I found out some stuff and Ken and Berta didn't want to talk about anything, except the wonderfulness of Kerry.'

'So what did you find out?' she asked.

'Let's see. There were four kids. Kerry and Rosalee and two boys, one Kerry's boyfriend – Ken said the break-up was really bad between them – and the other was this red-headed guy Rosalee hung out with, but not necessarily her boyfriend.'

'Did Berta have any clue who the redhead was?'

'Not even a hint. Doesn't even find red-headed men attractive. Oh, and there were two other kids – younger. One was Kerry's younger brother, Mark, and the other was a dark-haired girl about his age. Maybe his girlfriend. But they were young. Like twelve, thirteen, something like that.'

'If we had pictures of those kids—' Trisha started.

'Ah ha! We do! Kerry's yearbooks! Maybe we can find out if these boys were in her class in school.' I jumped up. 'Let's go back over to Ken's!' I felt like an idiot for not looking for the boys while I'd been there earlier. But I'd been doing a lot of idiotic things of late – like kicking my husband out of the house.

As we went from the bedroom back into the living room, we found the girls were back to playing with Barbies. All three of them.

'Megan, a little longer?' Trisha asked. 'I'll pay you for this interlude, too, since I didn't come out of my room.'

'Sure. Y'all have fun!' Megan said, not taking her eyes of the sparkly dress she'd put on her Barbie doll. All my girls like things that sparkle, glitter or are otherwise shiny. They're like monkeys and cats.

We made it back over to Ken's house, with a stop at Thundercloud for subs, chips, and sodas. We were welcomed in, probably more to do with the food than just our general fellowship.

Ken and Berta were busily sorting pictures for a collage of Kerry's life to put on a giant poster board for the funeral.

'What's this?' I asked.

'A collage of Kerry's life,' Ken said, tears in his eyes. 'From baby to mother of teenage boys.'

I looked at the pictures spread out on the dining-room table in chronological order. A pretty blonde baby, a little girl in pigtails, blonde hair getting darker and darker as she aged, until she hit high school and adopted the dark brown ponytail and Betty Page bangs, her wedding (the ponytail had been pulled into a bun), the birth of the twins, and her first house sold.

I put an arm around Ken's shoulders and hugged him. 'This is great, Ken,' I said. 'Kerry would love it.'

He nodded. 'Yeah, I think she would. Her mom sent these early pictures.'

'She was adorable,' I said, looking at the baby pics.

Ken smiled. 'What's that old song, "You must have been a beautiful baby?"' He wiped the tears from his eyes. 'Anyway, I thought you'd bailed on us. Why are you back?'

'Trisha suggested we look up the boys in the yearbooks,' I told Ken and Berta.

Ken frowned. 'I'm not sure, but I think Kerry said her boyfriend didn't go to high school with her. Maybe the other boy didn't either. Was there another high school in Codderville back then? I know there are two now, Codderville High and the new one, Crestview High, but that was built, like, five years ago.'

We all looked at each other and shrugged. The only one who would know what schools had been around back then would be Berta but, of course, she didn't. My husband had gone to Codderville High and would know of any other schools back then, but I didn't think this would be an ideal time to ask him. Instead, I picked up Ken's phone and dialed my mother-in-law's number. Hopefully Willis would be at his office. Vera picked up on the second ring.

'Hello?'

'Vera. Hey, it's E.J.'

'Hello, dear, Willis isn't here right now.'

'I'm actually calling for you, Vera.'

'Oh. Well, certainly. What can I do for you?'

'Is there or was there at any time another high school in Codderville?'

'Yes, of course,' she said. 'Bishop Byne. The Catholic school. Kinder through to twelfth grade. They shut it down about ten years ago. No word on what they're going to do with the buildings.'

'Do you know anyone who has yearbooks from the nineties?'

'Well, now, Mrs Ramirez down the street had five children and they all went to Bishop Byne. I'm sure one of them must have gone during the nineties. Let me call her. What specific year are you looking for?' she asked.

'Between 'ninety-three and 'ninety-six,' I said.

'I'll call you back,' Vera said and rang off. That was one thing about my mother-in-law: unlike her son she loved my little capers, and she loved being involved. The first time I realized there was a possibility I could learn to love the old bat was right after the Lesters were killed and she came over to my house with mops and buckets and all things cleanable to clean up the mess left by the killers of the Lester family. She told me then she was raised learning to clean up poop, pee, vomit and blood. And it was my turn to learn. And, unfortunately, learn I did.

Ken, Berta, Trisha and I spent this downtime going through the yearbooks we had, looking for the red-headed boy. Even though the pictures were in color, we didn't find any redheads of the male variety, either the same year as the girls or on one year either side. The red-headed boy, as well as Kerry's boyfriend, must have gone to Bishop Byne.

We were interrupted several times by the door chimes, heralding another arrival of food for the reception after the funeral. Ken was opening his home for it, so all the food stuff was being brought to the house. Kerry being Kerry, there was an extra refrigerator in the laundry room that did duty as the boys' fridge – filled with sodas, juices, and snacks. This was cleaned out and we were able to fit all the stuff for the next day in.

After a large foil pan of home-made lasagna was fitted in, Ken came up behind us and peered inside. 'Do you think I need to call a caterer? Or maybe just get the grocery store to send over some trays?' he asked.

Berta, Trisha and I turned to look at him askance. 'Do you see this fridge?' I asked. 'Do you see that there's not a cubic inch left for anything?'

'So you're saying no? I don't need to get extra?'

We all nodded. Berta patted him on the arm and said, 'There will be plenty.'

We took a break, and Trisha called Megan to tell her what to fix the girls for lunch.

Sitting around Kerry's black lacquered kitchen table, Ken said, 'What's your theory, E.J.? Regarding these two boys, I mean.'

I shrugged. 'No theory, Ken. Just a vague idea. They seemed to hang around a lot, all these kids. Finding either of the boys, or Mark, Kerry's brother, would just tell us more about Rosalee and what was going on between her and her mother,' I said, not looking at Berta when I said it.

'I'm not sure I want to know the answer to that,' Berta said, head down. 'I just can't imagine doing such a thing, but,' she said, looking up, 'maybe she was abusive or something?'

I nodded and touched her hand. 'That's very possible,' I said. 'You could have been defending yourself.'

'By burning her alive?' Berta said, and burst into tears.

'Wait now,' Trisha said, grabbing Berta's other hand. 'Did you ever read *The Burning Bed*? They made a movie out of it with Farrah Fawcett. Remember? She burned up her husband but got off because he battered her!'

'Got off?' Berta said. 'I don't care about getting off! I care that I may have killed my own mother!' The sobs became harder and Ken took her in his arms. Trisha and I shared a look.

I decided to get things into perspective. 'Tomorrow is Kerry's funeral. Berta, I think it would be safer for you to go than to stay here alone.'

'Of course I'm going!' Berta said. 'Kerry was my oldest friend – that I'm aware of anyway – and I will be there for Ken and her boys come hell or high water!'

Ken grinned at her. 'See, I told you you were a Texan! Come hell or high water!'

Berta grinned back at him and I thought about asking for the restroom so I could puke in private. But my phone rang.

'Hello?' I said.

'Mrs Ramirez said she and her husband couldn't afford to buy yearbooks for their kids. But she did say she knew the school nurse who was there from the seventies until the school closed ten years ago: Carolyn Gable, and she goes to the senior center I drive the bus for. I've known her for years – just didn't know she worked at Bishop Byne.'

Not unlike Kerry Killian, my mother-in-law was big on giving back to her community. At seventy-six, she still drove the bus at the senior center, volunteered to serve lunch there twice a week, and had a weekly volunteer stint at the Codderville Memorial Hospital. She also coordinated a phone tree for volunteers at the animal shelter. I tried never to mention how tired I was or how busy. It just sounded foolish.

'So can you get ahold—'

'Already have,' she said. 'She doesn't have yearbooks, but she does have a memory like a steel trap. She said she'll be gone most of the weekend, but she'll meet us at the senior center on Monday at three o'clock. She does the lunch and they should be all cleaned up by then. You up for it?'

'I couldn't meet tomorrow anyway. Kerry's funeral is tomorrow—'

'What time? I want to pay my respects,' she said.

'It's at eleven with a reception after at Kerry's home.'

'Perfect,' Vera said. 'I'll meet you at the church – the funeral is in a church, right?'

'Hold on,' I said and turned to Ken. 'Where will the funeral be held?' I asked.

'McCarty's Funeral Home on the feeder road going into Codderville,' he said.

I was slightly surprised Kerry's family didn't have a church; everyone in Black Cat Ridge seemed to belong to one of the many churches – and the one synagogue – the township boasted. Hell, even Willis and I belonged to a church. Which made me stop and think: would that become a custody issue too? Who gets the kids, the friends, the church? I shook my head to loosen the thoughts of the death of my marriage, and got back to the phone.

'McCarty's Funeral home,' I told Vera.

'Well, I like 'em better when they're in a church and all, but McCarty's has some nice stained-glass windows,' Vera said. 'I'll meet you there about ten thirty. Should I bring Willis?'

Uh oh, I thought, he and Ken were friendly enough for Ken to come over here the night before Kerry died to talk about Kerry's behavior. 'It's up to him,' I finally told Vera, and we rang off.

ELEVEN

Trisha and her husband Tom picked me up the next morning a little after ten to drive to the funeral home. I was wearing the same little black dress I'd worn to Berta's 'memorial,' but Trisha was wearing a pant suit that screamed Armani. It also screamed 'I'm going to steam you to death' as it was already in the nineties at ten a.m., and summer weight wool is not something we Texans can actually get our minds around.

Graham and the girls were going to pick up Ken, Jr and Keith. Graham thought it might make it a little easier to have friends around, and besides, he said, 'they think me having a car is cool.' And he shrugged. Sometimes that kid is my hero.

We got to the funeral home right behind Ken and Berta. Ken's parents were also in his car and Kerry's parents and her sister had come in a separate car. The place was already getting crowded and we had almost an hour to go. Even though Ken had suggested donations to any of Kerry's charities be sent in lieu of flowers, the chapel was still flooded with blossoms – living plants in plentiful bloom, cut flower arrangements so big they had to stand on the floor, a spray of white roses covering half of the top of the casket, dried flower arrangements, and even some silk arrangements. It was a funeral bouquet at its finest, the smell bound to linger in my nostrils as least until next Wednesday.

Trisha and I helped Berta place the plants the way she wanted them. Strange as her relationship had been with Kerry, no one seemed to argue that she had every right to play the role she'd chosen. OK, maybe Kerry's sister and mother might have wanted to step in and do something, but then again, they both looked a little numb.

Vera showed up at 10:30 a.m. on the dot, as promised, carrying a three-tiered cake carrier. 'Didn't want to leave this in the car with the heat being what it is,' she said, handing me the carrier. 'See if they got a refrigerator in here without a dead person in it. If so, put in the top two tiers only, not the third one – wrap that in a towel to keep it warm, but it'll probably have to be warmed up anyway at the house.'

I did as I was told and the funeral director directed me to a young woman who took me to the employees' lounge where there was a refrigerator. 'Better put a sign or something on those things,' she said, 'or those guys down in hair and make-up will surely take off with it.' And then she left me alone.

OK, let's review: Kerry has been murdered by person or persons unknown, Berta, aka Rosalee Bunch, has twice been assaulted with an attempt, all feared, on her life. My husband had left me and it seemed that now, after twenty-three years of marriage, we were heading for divorce. And here I stood, in the industrially-decorated employee lounge of a funeral home, wondering whether I should risk putting Vera's food in the refrigerator and having it eaten by the hair and make-up guys, put in the car and having it ruined by the heat, or setting it beside me in the chapel and letting all three tiers become room temperature. *That* was, indeed, my most pressing problem.

Then I had an epiphany. I did not know who killed Kerry, who'd made the numerous attempts on Berta/Rosalee's life, or whether or not my marriage could be saved, but I did know one thing: limo drivers always had the air conditioning on high.

I made my way around to the back of the building where the hearse and several limos were waiting. An African-American man in his fifties was leaning against one of the limos and smoking an unfiltered cigarette.

'Is that an unfiltered Camel or a joint?' I asked.

'Neither, ma'am, it's a Pall-Mall, like my daddy used to smoke,' he said, giving me a big grin.

I introduced myself and told him my problem. 'John Cox,' he said, extending a hand to shake. 'I'm carrying precious cargo, the bereaved, and I don't like for them to find any discomfort they don't already got. So with this weather, what I'm saying is, that cake thingamabob can just ride up front with me. The a/c's already on and it's done cooled down a bit.'

'Thank you, Mr Cox. You saved me from the wrath of my mother-in-law!'

He shivered. 'Ma'am, I don't know yours, but mine'd beat me to death and tell God I died.'

I handed off the three-tiered cake holder and hurried into the building and into the chapel. Willis was already there, sitting on the same row with Vera and the kids. Ken and his extended family were behind a screen that had separate seating for the bereaved, but I saw Berta sitting by herself close to the front of the main part of the chapel. I passed my family and went to sit next to Berta. She had a full box of tissues in her lap, and several used ones beside her. I scooted next to her and took her hand.

'I don't know what I'd do without you, E.J.,' she said. 'You've taken up where Kerry left off.'

Somehow, her heartfelt sentiment made my stomach queasy. Had I bitten off more than I wanted to chew with befriending Berta? Would this be a retelling of *Single White Female*? Was she going to dye her hair red and buy a minivan?

Wait, I said, soothing myself. She didn't have bangs and a ponytail, did she? No, she did not. Which means she wasn't single-white-femaling Kerry, so why would she do that with me? Right? Right?

Then I realized she was waiting for a reply. 'Glad to do it,' I said half-heartedly as I patted her hand. And the thought finally – too late for me, actually – came to me: am I patting the hand of a con artist who never had amnesia but killed Kerry for some reason, and is now taking over Kerry's life – Ken and the twins – and was going to worm her way into becoming the volunteer queen of Black Cat Ridge? Or, now, wait a minute, Kerry had a thriving business. She'd sold more homes in Black Cat than any other realtor. You couldn't go around any block in the township and not find at least one Kerry Killian For Sale sign. Is that what she was after? Kerry had to be loaded. She could easily have been making more money than Ken, who was an attorney with a good practice in Austin.

Or, and this made my stomach turn over a little bit, had there been a little bit more to the history between Ken and

Berta than either had said? That one awkward meeting at Kerry's home when Ken came home early and found Berta there may not have been it. It may have been the start of something. Say Berta is a conniving con artist. Kerry's told her which three days per week Ken works, so she knows the two days a week he's home – with Kerry either at her office or showing a house. So Berta comes back to Ken and Kerry's home, seduces Ken, and they connive together to kill Kerry and take all her money. Ha, ha! I thought. Ken, you'll be in for a rude awakening when this so called Berta Harris, aka Rosalee Bunch, decides to slit your throat and take off with the money—

I was making myself sick. I decided to tune in to the eulogies now in progress.

There was a long line of realtors, both from Black Cat and Codderville, all there to make sure everyone else knew Kerry could be replaced, and quickly too. Members of her volunteer groups gave heartfelt reasons why Kerry Killian would be missed: no one on earth could replace her in cheer, will, determination, and tenacity. Inside my head I gave that a righteous hallelujah and an amen.

When the for-hire preacher got up to give his rote sermon – funeral, female – I ventured back to my speculations. I knew what I'd been thinking earlier was ludicrous. Besides the fact that I knew in my heart that both Berta and Ken were truly bereaved about the loss of Kerry, I couldn't fathom a con that would take so many months to transpire. I mean, really, the hit-and-run was in October of last year, which was when Kerry and Berta first got together. And Kerry hid Berta. The electric heater was thrown in Berta's bath two weeks ago. Why wait nine, almost ten months, if this was a con Berta was playing? Of course, if it was a con, then the whole electric heater in the bath story was bogus.

And what was Kerry's angle? She had to recognize Berta as Rosalee Bunch, but she didn't tell Berta that or anything about her past life. Why not? Well, it would be awkward for one. *Oh, hey, girlfriend, by the way, you're real name is Rosalee Bunch and the police are after you for killing your mother fifteen years ago. But other than that, how're you feeling?*

The hired preacher finished up and we waited while the family left the chapel. I got in line with Berta to leave the chapel, where there was the usual gridlock at the front where the family was lined up to have their hands shaken. The collage Ken and Berta had put together was on a table right outside the door and the receiving line gridlock was stymied by another gridlock of people admiring the pictures.

Once out and to our cars, I rode again with Trisha and Tom into Codderville where Kerry's family had a large plot in a very old graveyard there. The trees were huge and acted as a parasol, keeping the noontime heat somewhat at bay. But it was still in the high nineties, and the service was kept bless-edly short. Berta asked Tom for a ride with us back to Ken's house, as Ken and the other family members had to take the limo back to the funeral home to get their cars. The twins, who had ridden in the limo with their dad from the funeral home to the graveside, opted to hop back in Graham's car and go straight home.

I briefly excused myself and ran to the limo to get Vera's three-tiered cake carrier. 'Thanks so much, Mr Cox,' I said.

'You're more than welcome, and I gotta say, that's some nice smelling stuff you got there,' he said, looking longingly at the carrier. If it had been anyone else's home-made food, I would have lifted a lid and given him some of whatever it was, but it wasn't anyone's food. It was Vera's. I just wasn't woman enough to mess with Vera Pugh's food. And I didn't know a woman who was, frankly.

MEGAN

Funerals are sad. Really. This one especially because of, you know, Ken and Keith and all. Keith's really cute and nicer than he used to be. I knew him in middle school and he was pretty mean, but he seems to have mellowed with age. The party – or whatever you call it – after the funeral was at Keith and Ken's house, which I'd never been to before and it was really nice. I mean, my mom *tries* to decorate – like a throw pillow here or there – but Mrs Killian's house was beautiful and Keith said his mom did it all herself – no decorator!

Looking at it gave me a wonderful idea: I think maybe I'll become an interior decorator. I certainly have the style and taste. And I'd look really cute carrying swatches in high heels and a cashmere scarf, my hair tousled from being in my convertible.

Mom and some other ladies were setting out tons of food and we grabbed some plates and piled them high and all headed upstairs to the twin's suite. They actually have a *suite*, can you believe it? There was a big room with a pool table, a foosball table and couches and chairs, and doors on either side leading to a bedroom for each boy. Both bedrooms had separate baths. I would *kill* for my own bathroom! I mean it. Well, maybe not literally. I'm glad I kept that to myself, you know, because of what happened to Keith's mom? Über bad taste.

Even as big as the living-room area was, it was crowded with all of us in there – me, the twins, Graham, Bess, and Alicia. But we all sat around on the floor eating and talking. Both Keith and Ken seemed to be doing OK, under the circumstances. And Graham was keeping them entertained with tales of his exploits – none of which I believed AT ALL.

When the phone rang, Keith leaned over me to get it, his bare arm touching my bare arm. I got all goose-fleshy. I swear to God, when he moved back with the cordless phone, he did it again. The first time might have been an accident, the second time certainly was not! Then I caught Bess looking at me. She raised one eyebrow – which I easily interpreted as, *OMG, did he really just do that?* And I shrugged my shoulders just the slightest bit – which she knew meant, *Oh, yes he did!*

Graham, of course, had not stopped talking when Keith picked up the phone, so Keith had to wave his arm for quiet. To his brother, he said, 'It's Uncle Mark!'

Ken moved over next to Keith, sharing the phone with him. 'Hey, Uncle Mark! Missed you at the funeral. We were getting worried about you . . .' They both listened for a long moment, then Keith said, 'Why didn't you call earlier?' Silence. Then, 'Oh, right, no cells during the service. Hey, we'll come get you—' Silence. Then Keith looked at Graham and whispered, 'Will you drive us into Codderville?'

Graham nodded. 'No prob,' he said.

Ken said, 'Hey, we have a friend here who is actually licensed to drive and he'll bring us down there to get you. Grandpa's really pissed—' Ken stopped then laughed. '*I'm* not gonna tell him that!' Then silence, another laugh, then, 'We're on our way.'

Keith asked Ken, 'What'd he say about Grandpa?'

'Something about grandpa's attitude and a place where the sun don't shine,' Ken said.

'Where's he at?' Graham asked getting up.

'At the Best Western,' Keith said. Then he turned to me. 'You're coming, right?'

The gooseflesh was back. 'Sure,' I said.

'Hey, let's all go!' Ken said.

Alicia shook her head. 'Then there wouldn't be room for your uncle,' she said, as always practical. 'Besides, I want to go down and help. Y'all give me your plates and I'll take them downstairs.'

'You're going, right?' Ken asked Bess. So I gave Bess the raised eyebrow and she gave me one back. Interesting.

Alicia, the party-pooper, gathered up all the dishes with Graham, of all people, helping her to carry it all downstairs.

I'm weak. Mostly from hunger. OK, so my spirit, my flesh, my very soul is weak. I went back for seconds, but I didn't have dessert. Well, just some ambrosia and one brownie. Really, just one. I mean, I'd have to go to a funeral every day for a week or two to gain back the weight I lost just by over-indulging at a funeral feast, right? I slipped two chocolate chip cookies and a napkin-wrapped baklava in my purse for later.

'You're going to feel guilty later,' a voice said behind me.

I recognized the voice. I should, I've listened to it every day of my life for the past twenty-three years. 'I'll get over it,' I said, turning around to face him.

'How's your friend Berta doing?' Willis asked.

'She's fine,' I said.

I almost asked how his friend Trisha was doing, then remembered she been seeing her brother, not my husband. My brain tangents were going to get me into trouble one of these days.

'How are you faring at Vera's?' I asked.

'Fine,' he said.

We both looked off toward the living room where people were milling about, eating and drinking. So it's come to this, I thought. We don't have anything to say to each other. It's definitely over.

'I think we should talk,' Willis said.

'I thought that's what we were doing,' I said.

He sighed. Oh, I recognized that sigh. That was his 'E.J., you're being obtuse,' sigh. 'About us,' he said.

Whoa. Right to the nitty-gritty. 'Shall we make an appointment?' I asked, finally turning to look at him. He looked back at me and for a moment we just stared at each other. I'm not sure who the first one was to start it, but one of us smiled, and then we both ended up laughing. Inappropriate to where we were belly laughs. Holding each other's arms to keep from falling down laughs. Laughs so deep that even in the middle of it I knew it was going to turn to tears if I didn't get out of there. I let go and felt my way to the kitchen because my vision was blurred by tears of laughter. Once in the kitchen, which was blessedly unoccupied, I fell against a counter and felt my face, my jaw, my insides crumble and the tears to come. And then he was there, in the kitchen with me, his arms around me, holding me close. We fit so well. We always had. My head fit neatly in the crook of his neck, his arms encircled me like they had when we were younger and I was thinner. Everything fit.

'I'm so sorry—' he said, just as I said, 'I'm sorry—'

We just held each other. Maybe it wasn't over, I thought. Maybe there was still hope.

MEGAN

So we all got crammed in Graham's car, Graham in the driver's seat, the shotgun seat on hold for Uncle Mark, and Bess and me half-sitting on the laps of the appropriate twin. Wouldn't that be a hoot? I thought. Bess and me marrying twins?

'So what's going on with your uncle and your grandfather?' Graham asked from the front seat.

'Grandpa was dissing Uncle Mark all during the funeral,'

Keith said. 'Grandma got so mad she hit him with her program. Is that what you call that thing when it's a funeral?'

'I dunno,' Graham said. 'Why's he upset with him?'

'Uncle Mark hasn't lived in the States since forever,' Ken said. 'Mom said he went to Belize during spring break his junior year in college and never came back. Me and Keith only know him 'cause Mom took us down there two summers ago. Dad couldn't go because he had a couple of court dates, but we went and stayed a month. It was great. Belize is really cool. You ever been there?' he said, talking directly to Bess.

'What does he do down there?' Graham asked. Like twenty questions or something. Personally, I think Keith and I had other things to discuss. Graham could just shut up and drive, like a good chauffeur.

'He owns juice stands – about six of 'em, right, Ken?'

'Huh?' Ken said, raising his head from where he and Bess were having a private moment. I mean talking; don't go there.

'Uncle Mark's juice stands – he has about six, right?'

Ken shrugged. 'I didn't count.'

'Asshole,' Keith said.

'Retard,' Ken shot back.

I knew before she started that it was going to happen. I tried to get her attention, tried to stop her, but living over a decade with my mother has definitely rubbed off on Bess.

'I find that offensive,' she said.

'Huh?' Ken said. Believe me, I think I got the good twin.

'Calling someone a retard. That's offensive.'

'Ah, why? Are you retarded?' he said.

'No! But it's offensive to people who are and the people who care for those who are.'

'Well, my brother's not retarded either, so it's, like, ya know, just a word.'

'It's an offensive word,' Bess insisted.

And then we found out that the back seat of Graham's car would hold four people easily, without anyone have to sit on anyone's lap. Sometimes I really hate my crunchy granola family.

* * *

We were caught – by Alicia, of all people.

'Oh!' she said coming in with a pile of used paper plates and plastic cups.

Willis and I moved away from each other. 'It's OK, honey,' Willis said. 'We're not even smooching.'

Alicia turned red. 'Well, you can if you want. It's OK with me.' Then she abruptly turned and headed for the dining room.

'Where are the rest of the kids? They making you do all the work?' I asked.

'I volunteered. They all went to pick up the twins' uncle in Codderville. I figured if we all went, there wouldn't be room for the uncle.'

I laughed. 'Always the responsible one, that's our Alicia.'

She ducked her head, took a deep breath, and then raised her eyes to ours. 'I know your fight was about me, and E.J. explained it to me, Willis. I've been thinking about it and I'll be sixteen next year, which is the age to become an emancipated minor. If I can stay until then, that's what I'd like to do.'

Willis nodded his head. 'I understand that. And I understand the temptation of becoming an emancipated minor. Sounds glamorous, but it would be hard. We'd both rather you stayed until you graduate high school. Then we'll talk about whether you want to go to college, trade school, get a job, whatever it is you want to do with your life. It'll all be better if you graduate high school first.'

Alicia nodded her head. 'We can talk about it more later. Right now I think it's time you two went home to an empty house.' She grinned and rushed out of the room.

MEGAN

We found the Best Western in Codderville and, after driving around the whole thing twice, finally found the right room number.

'We'll be right back,' Keith said as both twins bailed out of the car.

Graham had parked right in front of the room, so it was only a few feet away. I saw Keith knock on the door and saw the door open at his touch. Just like in the movies. But I didn't think about that then. Keith stepped inside, immediately followed by Ken. Before Ken could even shut the door they were both outside again, Ken vomiting in the bushes. Graham hopped out of the car, followed by Bess and myself. Keith, leaning against the window of the motel room, grabbed my arm as I started past him into the room.

'Don't!' he said, his voice hoarse. His lips made movements like he was trying to say more, but he just shook his head and held on to me.

But I didn't need to go in to see what was in the room. Bess hurriedly backed out and went to Ken, helping him sit down on the curb. Graham was in the room, but I could see past him to the body on the floor. The overhead light was on, shining brightly on the blood that caked the carpet and stained Uncle Mark's funeral attire. I turned to Keith and led him to the curb where Ken and Bess sat, and encouraged him to do the same. He did, elbows on up raised knees, head in hands. I put my arm around his shoulders and patted him. I didn't know what else to do.

Graham was out and standing by his car. He had his cell phone to his ear. 911, I supposed. Then he hung up and hit one digit, which was probably his number for either Mom or Dad. He hung up and hit another one digit number, and hung up from that after a few seconds. 'Shit!' he said. Then he rummaged in the glove box of his car, found a business card and dialed again.

'Hey, Mrs Luna! Are you at home or at work? Home? Great. Look. Something's happened,' he said. 'The police are on their way.'

It wasn't one of our rip-your-clothes-off moments. It was different. Almost like the first time. A quiet exploration of each other's bodies, as if they were new to us. After we lay on the couch entangled in each other's arms, my head on his bare chest, his dress shirt from the funeral tossed over my bare back and buttocks due to the air conditioning. He was running his fingers through my hair and I was studying a gray hair on his chest. I'd never seen it before, but then again, he's blonde, so the gray ones are more easily hidden.

When the doorbell rang we both started, but when the pounding on the door ensued, we both jumped up. I pulled Willis's dress shirt on. It was long enough to cover my bottom and I went to the door as Willis grabbed the rest of his clothes and headed for the bedroom.

I peeked through the peep hole and saw Elena Luna standing there. I opened the door. 'Bad timing,' I said.

'I hope that was Willis you were rolling around with, 'cause I need to talk to both of you right now. Get dressed.'

I moved with her into the house. 'What's going on?' I said, finding my clothes still on the couch. I turned my back to Luna and pulled on panties, managed to get my bra on under the dress shirt, then took it off and slipped my dress on, and rammed my feet into my heels. I took the dress shirt to the bedroom and gave it to Willis.

'Luna's here. She needs us both. Something's up,' I said and left him there.

He followed me out, buttoning his shirt and stuffing it in his pants as he came in.

'Shoes and socks?' he said.

'By the back door,' I said.

'I'm glad you two made up. Now, listen: Graham just called me. If not already there, the police should be on the scene shortly—'

'Oh my God! What's happened?' I said, feeling panic about to consume me.

'The kids are OK. All the kids – including Mr Killian's kids. The thing is, and I know this is your trick, but you may have passed it down: they found a dead body.'

I snuck a look at Willis, whose arms were up in the air. 'Well, why the hell not?' he said to his own personal deity, or maybe he was talking to the devil himself.

MEGAN

It probably only took like a few minutes for the police to show up, but it seemed like forever. Keith started crying, his head on my shoulder, and I thought it was sweet at first, then the snot came and got on my dress and I thought maybe I wasn't cut out for this kind of stuff.

When the police got there it was regular police, in uniform, not Mrs Luna from next door. It was a Mexican man in his twenties or thirties – it's hard to tell with adults; I mean, after twenty they all look alike – and a woman who seemed older, but who knew.

The two went into the motel room, stayed for about a minute and a half, and then came out.

The woman talked to Graham who, of course, had taken over. When he indicated the twins, the woman came to talk to Keith while the man took Ken, Jr.

'Keith, right?' she said. 'I'm Officer Davis. You found the body?'

Keith sniffed and nodded his head.

'How do you know the deceased?' Officer Davis asked.

'He's my uncle,' Keith said.

She looked at the notes she'd taken when talking with Graham. 'Your last name is Killian?'

Keith nodded.

'Any kin to Kerry—'

'My mom,' he said and began to cry in earnest, hunched over his knees, his arms encircling his head. I patted his back. At least he wasn't snotting all over me.

Officer Davis waited for a moment for Keith to get over it. Finally she asked, 'Did you see anyone else in the room?'

Keith shook his head.

'Anyone loitering in the parking lot?'

Again he shook his head.

That's when a white car with lights flashing in the grill instead of on top, pulled up. Mrs Luna got out.

I ran up to her and hugged her. 'Boy, am I glad you're here!' I said.

I'd never hugged Mrs Luna before and she seemed a little taken aback. She patted my back like I was a dog.

'Davis,' she said, then jerked her head toward her car. To me, she said, 'Sit back down, Megan. I'll be with you in a minute.'

Then she and Officer Davis and the male officer conferred by Mrs Luna's car until another car pulled in. This one I recognized immediately. My mother's minivan. Bess and I both jumped up and even Graham left his perch by his car to rush to the minivan. Imagine our surprise at seeing Dad in the passenger seat.

Our parents grabbed on to us, everybody hugging at once. The back door of the minivan opened and Mr Killian got out. I saw the twins rush to their dad. I was glad he was there. My dress was ruined.

The male officer went to the motel office and came back with a key to one of the rooms He opened a door two down from Uncle Mark's room, went inside, and we heard him switch on the air conditioning.

Luna came up to the minivan where we had all collected. 'Let's let that room cool off a bit, then everyone can move in there. It's too hot out here for y'all to be standing around.'

'Thanks, Luna,' my dad said. My mom nodded but didn't let go of either me or Bess. Actually, she was beginning to hurt my neck a little.

Mr Killian hadn't said much to the boys, and they didn't say much to him, but he kept kissing them on the tops of their heads, which I thought was kind of sweet, although a little geeky. I know, my standards are high.

After a few minutes we were ushered into the extra motel room, which was a double, and the door was closed behind us. Bess and I crawled on one bed and the twins crawled on another, making room for Graham. Mom and Dad sat at the two chairs by this little table, and Mr Killian sat on a stool by the vanity. No one said anything for a long time, until, my mom, of course, broke the silence.

'How did y'all know to come here for your uncle?' she asked.

Neither boy answered, so Graham piped up. 'He called the house phone while we were upstairs eating. One of them –' he said, indicating the twins with a nod – 'answered the phone. I'm not sure what all he said, but the gist was he needed a ride so we came here to get him.'

'What did he say on the phone?' Mr Killian asked his

boys. When neither answered, he said, 'Keith, did you talk to him?'

Keith nodded his head. 'Yeah. We both did.' He gulped in air and shuttered a little. 'I told him Grandpa was pissed – oh, shit!' he said and began to cry. Ken, Jr put his arm around him and took up the tale. 'And Uncle Mark said something rude about Grandpa. Then said he was sorry he was late, but he couldn't get a ride to Black Cat Ridge. So we volunteered to come get him. Well, volunteered Graham to come get him.'

'Do you know what time the phone call was?' my mom asked.

Then Dad said, 'Why don't we let Luna ask the questions?' and Mom gave him an 'are you kidding me' look, and Dad gave her a 'enough is enough' look. So maybe they weren't back together after all. I thought with them coming together in the minivan that maybe . . . So much for wishes.

'Answer E.J.'s question,' Mr Killian said, which surprised me. Men usually stick together on these things. My dad shot him a look that shouted, *Betrayer!*

Keith shook his head. 'I have no idea. We hadn't been upstairs long and we were the first in line for the food, so when did y'all put out the food?'

Ooo, I thought, good detective work. I told you he was the smart one.

'We didn't put the food out until you and the family got back, Ken. Do you know what time that was?'

He nodded his head. 'Yes, I do because I looked at my watch. Wondering how much longer I was going to have to deal with Kerry's family.' He sighed. 'I guess it'll be a while yet.' When the boys looked at him aghast, he said, 'Sorry. It was twelve thirty-five.'

'It was one-oh-five by my car clock when we headed out,' Graham said.

'So the call came in somewhere between twelve thirty-five and one-oh-five. And you found him at what time?'

'We pulled up here at one twenty-three. I checked the clock because I wanted to see how long it took,' Graham said.

'That's a pretty short window of opportunity,' Dad said. 'We need to narrow down the phone call to a time less than the thirty minutes we have now. E.J., how soon after Ken arrived did y'all put out the food?'

'Actually, I was in the kitchen and saw Ken pull up. So we started a few minutes before they actually got in the door.'

Mr Killian said, 'I checked my watch while I was still in the car.'

'OK,' Dad said, 'so we're still at twelve thirty-five. E.J., how long did it take to put out all the food?'

'We already had some of it out, so maybe another ten minutes to get all the hot stuff out of the oven and onto hot pads and get the cold stuff out of the refrigerator.'

'OK, we're down to twenty minutes. Graham, how quickly did you kids grab your plates?'

'Now, wait,' Mom said. 'Y'all weren't the first in line! There were two moms there with younger kids and we had them fill the kids' plates before y'all started. That probably took another five minutes, because one of the kids kept trying to grab all the grapes off the fruit plate and the mother kept putting them back, and I'm thinking, well we have to throw those away!'

'OK, now we're down to fifteen minutes,' Dad said.

So I decided to join in. 'We all piled our plates pretty quick,' I said, 'and ran upstairs.'

Graham concurred.

'And I'd eaten a drumstick and some Jell-O salad and two macaroons when the phone rang,' Keith said. I'd have to do something about his eating habits. 'So maybe another five minutes or so?'

'So we're thinking the phone call came in five to one, and you found him at one twenty-three,' Dad said. 'So that's a window of twenty-eight minutes. Let's say thirty. So what does that mean, oh great detective E.J.?'

'You know,' Mom said, 'you're not as cute as you think you are.' They exchanged what I would call a less-than-friendly look. And all I could say to that would be a good grief, get over it! Then Mom said, 'At least we have a timeline for Luna.'

The door opened and Mrs Luna came in. 'Mr Killian, I'm going to drive you and your sons back to your house. Mark Metcalf's parents are at your house, right?'

Mr Killian nodded.

'I need to inform them.'

'Luna,' Mom said, 'we were able to narrow down the time of the phone call—'

'You mean Mark Metcalf's call to the Killian home? It came in at twelve fifty-three,' she said.

'Ha!' Dad said. 'I was pretty damn close!'

Mom shot him a look, then glared at Mrs Luna, who said, 'His phone was by the body. We checked his last outgoing call. It's called police work.' Turning her back on my mom, she said, 'Mr Killian, are you ready to go?'

My mom can be a pain in the butt, but she's *my* pain in the butt. I was a little pissed at both Mrs Luna and my dad. They had no right to treat her like that.

Graham drove Megan and Bess home in his car while I dropped Willis off at the Killians' house where his car was, picked up Alicia and drove home. I told her of the developments on our way.

'Oh, how awful!' she said. 'How are the twins?'

'OK, I guess. Pretty shook up.'

'They seemed to really like their uncle. They went to see him in Belize with their mother a couple of summers ago, they said. Gosh, this right on top of their mom's death. This is just awful!'

We agreed it was awful and got home to find Graham's car in the driveway and all three kids in the family room looking glum. Alicia rushed in and hugged both girls.

'I'm so sorry y'all had to see that!' she said. 'How awful!'

'It was horrible!' Megan said.

Bess just shook her head. I had to wonder if seeing all that blood brought back any painful memories for her. She'd been so little when I'd pulled her out of the house next door, her little body covered in her mother's blood and brain matter. We'd talked about what happened, but never about the details, never about the blood and gore.

I went to Bess and put my arm around her shoulder. She leaned her head against me. 'It's OK, Mom,' she said. 'I'm all right.'

'Graham, how about you?' I asked.

'Really gross,' he said. 'And the twins really lost it. But that's cool, ya know? I mean, if it was my uncle – well, if I had an uncle.'

'Luna said you handled yourself well,' I told him.

He shrugged, his blond good looks, so much like his father's, tended toward fair skin that blushed easily. He did so at the compliment. 'Well, you know, what else was I supposed to do? Scream like a little girl?'

'I did not scream!' Megan said, sitting up straight and almost sending Alicia to the floor.

Graham stared at her. 'No one said you did, numb nuts! You did good! Getting Keith to sit down and all. So did Bess. It was just a freeking expression, for crying out loud!'

'Well, OK then,' Megan said, sitting back on the couch, arms across her chest. 'But I didn't scream.'

Which led me to believe that somewhere inside my daughter's psyche she had definitely screamed, it just hadn't come out. And I didn't blame her for that. Dead bodies are a bitch to find, let me tell you!

On Sunday the house phone rang and I went in the kitchen to get it. 'Hello?' I said.

'Hey,' Willis said.

'Hey,' I said back.

'Would you like to invite me over for dinner?' he asked.

'Would you like me to invite you over for dinner?' I asked.

'Yes,' he said.

'OK,' I said. 'Would you like to come over for dinner?'

'Naw, I'm kinda busy—'

'Willis Pugh!'

He laughed. 'I'd love to come over for dinner. May I bring an overnight bag?' he asked.

I thought about it for a moment. Turning away from the kids, I said quietly, 'Wouldn't that just confuse the kids?'

'Yeah, I guess you're right. Just dinner. Then we'll see?' he said.

'Sounds like a plan,' I said. We said our goodbyes and I stood in the kitchen wondering what in the hell I could fix for dinner that could possibly entice my husband away from his mother's wonderful cooking? Other than take-out, of course.

I sent Graham to the store for a take-out roast chicken, a baguette and some dessert, opened a box of scalloped potatoes and a can of green beans – a little butter, lemon juice and garlic and they almost (*almost*) tasted like fresh – and I was almost ready to take Vera on. Of course, having been married to me for twenty-three years, Willis would know that the chicken was store-bought, the potatoes were boxed and the beans canned but, hey, I was making the effort, right?

While Graham was off to the store, the girls wandered off in different directions, leaving me alone in the kitchen. I sat at the kitchen table, thinking about what had transpired that day. The thought that Mark Metcalf's death had nothing to do with his sister's death had never entered my head. There was absolutely no way the two weren't related. But what did Mark have to do with Berta – I mean, Rosalee? Rosalee and Kerry were friends, and Mark was in the pictures of the six kids, so he obviously knew Rosalee. Is that what this was about? I thought. Was someone trying to get rid of people who knew Rosalee back when? If so, why try to kill Berta? I mean Rosalee? What could Mark, who'd been out of the country since high school, according to the twins, know that would put Rosalee or someone else in jeopardy? Whatever it was happened during high school or before, and it had to do with the night Rosalee Bunch's mother had been killed in the trailer fire, I knew it. I was anxious for tomorrow, when Vera and I were to meet up with the former nurse from Bishop Byne High School, the catholic high school in Codderville.

I suppose I should have been a little anxious about dinner, but I didn't feel anxious. I felt resigned. I wasn't going to change and he wasn't going to change. We either agreed to continue living with that, or not.

TWELVE

Last night had turned out OK. It was a little awkward at first, then Graham did something stupid, all attention turned to him, teasing became the name of the game, and we all fell back into our respective roles. A family counselor might have said that was a bad thing, but to me, at that moment, it felt good. Very good.

At nine, while we were all in the family room playing with the Wii, the doorbell rang. I went to answer it and found Berta on our doorstep.

'Hey!' I said.

'E.J., I'm sorry, I had a taxi bring me over here. Things are very tense at Ken's house, and I'm afraid my presence there may have precipitated that tension.' Tears sprang to her eyes. 'They think Ken and I are having an affair! Like I'd do something like that to Kerry!' She threw herself into my arms and bawled.

I brought her inside, more to close the door and keep the air conditioning in than as an act of kindness. You remember that old song, 'He ain't heavy, he's my brother'? Well, she wasn't my sister and she was getting mighty heavy.

'You can stay here tonight,' I told her, knowing that was what she expected, but unable to think of any alternative.

'Thank you,' she said, drying her eyes on a crumpled wad of tissues in her hand.

'You can have my room and I'll bunk with the girls,' I told her.

'Oh, I don't want to put you out, E.J. I can sleep on the couch!'

'It's no problem,' I said. Just in case there was even a shred of truth to my musing at the funeral home (the one about Berta/Rosalee being a con woman who killed Kerry – I know, there were so many, who can keep up?), I wanted to be upstairs with my children in case I need to protect them. Although with my kids, they might end up having to protect *me*.

We went into the family room. Willis, who had control of the Wii, turned it off when he saw Berta. 'Hi,' he said.

'Oh, you're back!' Berta said with a big smile. 'I'm so glad.'

There was a stone cold silence. I could see all four kids exchanging glances. Willis looked at me and I shrugged. He said, 'Not yet. But probably this week.'

The kids fell on the couch and began nudging each other furiously.

'But it's getting late,' Willis said, 'and I should be getting back. I'm staying at my mother's house,' he explained to Berta, 'and she gets antsy if I come in too late. She likes to have all her locks on just so and she can't do it if I'm out.'

'And I'm sure she worries,' Berta said.

'Well, it was nice seeing you again,' Willis said, then, 'kids, give me hugs.' They obliged and then I walked him to the front door. We stepped outside, away from prying eyes and ears, and he kissed me. 'I want to come home. I want to get clear of all that happened. I guess we've both – and Alicia – come to terms with the horrible thing I said—'

'It wasn't that horrible. I was just being sensitive—'

'No, it was pretty damn bad. I've loved Bess every moment of the past ten years, and maybe before that. She was the adorable daughter of my best friend. My baby girl's little playmate. How could I not already love her? Taking her in was never really an issue, hon, and I don't know why I made it one. The only thing we could do, and the only thing we wanted to do was make her part of the family.' He sighed. 'But Alicia was different—'

'I know,' I said. 'I messed up.'

'Yeah. And I messed up not telling you that you messed up right off the bat. We should have discussed it at the time. I know I would have said yes, but, sometimes, babe, I need to be part of the decision making around here.'

I nodded my head. 'I know, I know.'

'The rest of it,' he said, waving his arm to encompass the yard, the street, the township, maybe the world, 'I don't know. We might need to set some ground rules,' he said.

I nodded. 'That's a possibility,' I said.

He kissed me again. 'Gotta go,' he said, and headed for his giant pick-up truck.

Back inside, I said to the girls, 'Y'all need to pick a room and have a slumber party. I'm going to take one of y'alls rooms, so just let me know which.'

MEGAN

No way was she getting my room. I have privacy issues: like I like having some! Alicia – of course, Miss Goody-Two-Shoes – gave up hers and Bess, second in line for the title, said we could all sleep in her room. I'd rather stay in my bed, but Mom and Dad both were trying to be all 'we're a loving family,' so I figured I better go with the flow. I'm a morning showerer, but Alicia and Bess both shower at night, so I stayed in my room while they took turns.

I called Azalea and D'Wanda on my cell phone to tell them about Keith – oh, and the new murder, of course.

'He touched your arm?' D'Wanda said.

'Twice,' I said.

'Ooo, girl, he wants you!' Azalea said.

I made a face they obviously couldn't see. 'I don't know,' I said. 'He's kinda, well, not as strong as I want in a man.'

'Oh, 'cause he snotted on you?' D'Wanda said.

'And because he cried like a little girl.'

'Girl, that was his uncle!' Azalea said. 'You'd cry if you saw your uncle lying dead and bloody on a motel room floor! That's disgusting!'

'Ken vomited. I think that's more manly.'

'Hum,' one of the twins said. I can't tell them apart if they don't actually talk.

'You may be right,' D'Wanda said. 'It does seem a bit more manly. Disgusting, but manly.'

'That's all I'm saying,' I said.

Then there was a knock on my door. 'Hey, you coming to the slumber party?' Bess called.

'Be right there,' I said. To D'Wanda and Azalea I said, 'I gotta go.'

'What's this about a slumber party, and we weren't invited?' D'Wanda asked, her mad voice on.

'It's not a slumber party. Me, Bess and Alicia all have to sleep in the same room because we have company. My mom thinks calling it a slumber party will make it seem less torturous.'

'Huh. Well, glad I wasn't invited then,' D'Wanda said.

'Yeah, consider yourselves lucky,' I said. 'Bye.' I hung up and sat there staring at the door. Then I thought, well, Bess and I can dissect the twins and what happened today. That would be cool. I jumped off the bed and headed to Bess's room.

The next morning I tried getting to Luna before she headed to work. I caught her as she attempted to get in her car. We have side-by-side driveways, so it's sort of hard for her to sneak out.

'A moment, Lieutenant Luna,' I said.

'Jesus,' she said, and sighed. 'What?' Her hand was on the driver's-side door handle of the car. She didn't move it as I spoke.

'I would assume it's a given that Mark Metcalf's murder is somehow connected to Kerry's. Have you found anything to connect them, other than the fact that they were siblings?'

'And I would tell you this because . . .'

I smiled. 'Because we're best buds and you love me like a sister?'

'I don't think that's it,' she said.

'Because I've helped you on numerous occasions with murders and you owe me?'

'That *can't* be it,' she said.

'Because I asked "pretty please?"'

She actually had the gall to laugh. 'Pugh, if Mark Metcalf's murderer was sneaking up behind you with a ball peen hammer, I'm afraid I might not tell you. So why would I tell you confidential police information?'

'I just think there has to be a connection. And, in case you don't know it, Mark hung around with Rosalee and the others that summer that the trailer caught on fire.'

'Hum,' she said. 'Thanks for the information,' and with that, she opened the door of her car, got in, and drove off. And I was left standing in our connecting driveways with absolutely no new information – with less than no new information – she'd actually gotten what little info I had.

I went back in the house, poured a cup of coffee and turned the air conditioning up. Five minutes outside at eight in the morning with the temperature at ninety degrees already had me sweating. I vaguely wondered if we had enough money – or credit – to put a pool in the backyard?

I sat down at the kitchen table and thought. Mark was one of the kids we'd seen in the pictures Kerry had kept. We had identified Kerry, Rosalee, and Mark. Hopefully, this afternoon, when we saw Vera's friend, the school nurse at the now defunct Catholic school in Codderville, we'd find out who the other boys and the younger girl were. That could start us in a new direction, with any luck.

I heard my bedroom door open and Berta came out, hair mussed, wearing the clothes she'd had on the night before, all wrinkled from sleep.

'Hey,' I said. 'Good morning. You should have told me and I could have loaned you something to sleep in.'

'That's OK. I'm used to sleeping like this. When I was at Kerry's flip house, I never took off street clothes except to shower. You know, always ready to run, if necessary.'

'Well, let me loan you something to wear today. You can't stay in those wrinkled clothes.'

'Oh, E.J., I could never get into any clothes of yours! You're too small!'

OK, so she wasn't so bad after all. 'I think I can find something,' I said, knowing I'd stashed some of my 'fat' clothes, just in case.

I got her some fresh towels, and while she took a shower I found a pair of jeans and a T-shirt that I thought would fit, then went into the kitchen to see about breakfast.

By the time breakfast was ready to serve, Berta was out and wearing the clothes I set out. The jeans were too long, but they fit her well everywhere else. She'd rolled the legs up so they weren't dragging the ground. The kids came down in their classic stampede.

Graham ran for the back door. 'Wait!' I said. 'Eat!'

'Mom, I don't have time. I'm supposed to meet that guy in Austin today who's gonna be my roommate, remember?'

Bad Mother, I told myself. I'd totally forgotten. Graham was off to the University of Texas (the alma mater of both Willis and myself) in the fall, and he and his assigned dorm roommate were supposed to meet for lunch and then tour the campus together. He'd signed up for Dobie Hall, the same dorm I'd lived in for two of my four years at UT.

'I forgot, honey, with all that's going on.' I grabbed a granola bar out of the pantry and a small bottle of orange juice out of the fridge. 'Here,' I said. 'Your breakfast.'

He kissed me on the cheek. 'Bye,' he said as he headed once again for the back door.

'Drive carefully and have fun!' I called to his retreating back. 'And call me when you get there!' I'm not sure if he heard that, but I'd be calling him fairly often anyway. I do that. I'm a mother.

'Where's he going?' Bess asked, yawning.

'He has that meeting with his college roommate,' I reminded her.

'Oh, right,' she said. 'Cool.'

'Who does what?' Megan asked, sitting down and grabbing some bacon.

'Graham's on his way to Austin to meet his roommate,' Bess told her.

Alicia was totally silent on the subject.

When Berta came in I introduced her to the girls, who she'd never formally met, and we all sat down to breakfast.

After, Bess's co-worker from the dress shop in the mall picked her up and Alicia insisted on walking to the bus stop two blocks away to catch the bus into Codderville for her intern job with the D.A.'s office. Megan retreated to her room for whatever it is she does. I was cleaning the kitchen when the phone rang. I picked it up on the second ring.

'Hello?' I said.

'E.J., it's Vera,' my mother-in-law said, as if I wouldn't recognize her voice after twenty-three years.

'Hi,' I said. 'Are we still on for this afternoon?'

'That's why I'm calling. Just wanted to make sure you remembered.'

'I'll pick you up at two forty-five,' I suggested.

'That should work,' she said. 'See you then,' and she hung up.

The phone rang a second time before I'd put it back. I clicked on. 'Hello?'

'Hey, E.J. Can you send Megan over here so I can come over there? I'm up to my ears in motherhood,' Trisha said.

'No problem. Berta's over here too. So we can discuss some stuff, see what we can come up with. Did you hear about Kerry's brother?'

'No. He's the younger one in that picture?'

'Right. He came back from Belize for the funeral. And he got shot in his motel room.'

'Oh my God, are you serious? That's awful! Send Megan over right now!' And she hung up.

I called upstairs. 'Megan!' It took two screams, each progressively louder, before she budged from her room. The alternative, of course, was climbing the stairs to get her. I prefer my stair climbing to be in the gym, thank you very much.

'What?' she said, standing at the top of the stairs, hands on hips.

'Mrs McClure wants you to babysit. Right now.'

'Jeez, will this never end?' she whined.

'Money, remember?'

'Oh. Right. Be right there,' my daughter said, ran to her room, and came back with flip-flops on her feet and pounded down the stairs. 'I think I'll charge her more for these impromptu baby sittings. I mean, I need a little warning!'

'What else do you have to do? Just go!'

'I'm going to the pool this afternoon, so y'all don't stay out all day!'

'Go!'

'I'm going!'

Five minutes later there was a knock on the door and it opened, with Trisha sticking her head in. 'It's me!'

'In the family room!' I called back.

She came in, looking adorable in a pink terry playsuit with

spaghetti straps and short shorts. I could learn to hate this woman easily.

'So dish! Is he dead? The brother?'

'Very,' I said.

'Y'all shouldn't treat this so lightly!' Berta said, a new wad of tissue in her hand.

Trisha patted Berta's hand. 'I'm sorry. I didn't know him and I'm being callous. How are you holding up?'

'Well, I didn't know him either – well, not in this life, anyway – maybe when I was Rosalee I knew him, but Kerry's family is really torn up about this. The twins found him.'

'Oh, how awful!' Trisha said.

It was a consensus: this whole thing was awful.

'They were both very shaken. And E.J.'s kids were there too,' she said, shooting me a look that I easily interpreted as, *How can you be so callous when your own children witnessed this?* OK, when she's right, she's right.

The phone rang yet again. I went to the kitchen to pick it up. 'Hello?'

'Hey, E.J., it's Ken,' he said.

'Hi! How's it going over there?' I asked.

He sighed. 'Kerry's family left. Not without, however, threatening to sue me for custody of the boys!'

'Oh, for God's sake! They can't be serious!'

'Probably not. The boys assured them that Berta spent her nights in the guest room upstairs, and I think they'll believe that eventually, but right now, with losing two of their children at once, they're just not being terribly reasonable.' He sighed again. 'And who can blame them? I know it probably looks bad, me letting Berta stay here. I thought I was doing it for Kerry, but I have to admit, the boys and I liked having a woman around. It . . . helped, I guess.'

'I can see that,' I told him.

'I'm sorry, but can Berta stay with you for a while? I'm going to get some real furniture to go in the flip house. Let Berta stay there until all this mess about her mother's death is cleared up. But it could take a couple of days to get it ready. Is that OK?'

Then I heard myself saying, 'Ken, take all the time you need. Berta's fine here.'

Shit, I told myself. Willis wants to move back in! Shit!

'You're going to see that woman from the Catholic school today?' he asked.

'Yes,' I said.

'Did you get those pictures of the kids?'

'Oh, no! I think I left them on the coffee table—'

'Berta cleaned that up. She'll know where they are. Come on over and get them, OK? And bring Berta. I need to talk to her.'

'OK,' I said, 'we'll be there in a little while.'

I was becoming so immersed in this family's business I was beginning to know more about them than my own siblings. It was one of the drawbacks of my penchant for finding dead bodies – although I didn't find any dead bodies in this case! However, I did wonder, late at night, if my obsession with finding out what Berta Harris was doing in all those twelve-step groups had led in any way to Kerry's death. Was I seen by the killer when I went to Kerry's office? Did that set this whole thing in motion?

I moved back into the family room. 'That was Ken. We need to go by there and pick up those pictures before I go see the nurse. Berta, do you remember where you put those year-books and snapshots when you cleaned off the coffee table?'

'Of course,' she said. 'Right back where Ken got them. I'm an excellent housekeeper,' she said, in a way that reminded me too much of Dustin Hoffman in the movie *Rain Man*. Again, the woman was giving me the wigglies.

'I want to come!' Trisha said.

'Well, duh,' I said. 'Of course.'

I was wearing jean shorts and a T-shirt. The shorts were snug, the T-shirt loose. I thought about changing into a cute shorts outfit to match Trisha, but unfortunately I don't own any cute shorts outfits.

I called Megan to tell her where we were going, then called Graham quickly to see how his trip was going.

'I'm fine, Mom,' he said, using that tone they use.

'Just checking,' I said. 'Where are you?'

'Almost to Bastrop. Maybe another forty-five minutes,' he said.

'Make that an hour. Don't speed,' I said.

'The only law I'm breaking at the moment is talking on the cell phone,' he said.

'Well, use the speaker button!'

'Bye, Mom,' he said and actually hung up on me.

I gathered my Scooby gang and we got in the minivan and headed for Ken's.

The pictures were right where Berta said they would be, and we quickly found the one with the clearest shots of the three unidentified kids.

'We'll take this one,' I said.

'Here,' Ken said, pushing the whole stack toward me. 'Take them all, just to be on the safe side.'

Berta found a large manila envelope and we put the pictures inside.

One of the boys wandered downstairs. I had no idea which one he was.

'Hey, Mrs Pugh,' he said. 'How's Megan?'

Ah ha, I thought. It was Keith. I don't eavesdrop, but I do hear things.

'She's fine, Keith. She's babysitting right now for Mrs McClure's little girls,' I said, and Trisha gave him a finger wave to indicate that she was, indeed, Mrs McClure. 'How are you doing?'

He shook his head. 'This really sucks,' he said, coming in the room and flopping down on one of Kerry's beautiful tuxedo sofas.

I moved into the room and sat down on the same sofa. The others milled around in the dining room, where the yearbooks and snapshots had been stored.

'I'm so sorry you and Ken had to witness that. I'm so sorry it *happened* at all.'

'I don't know if I could have gotten through it without Megan,' he said.

Ah oh, I thought. Megan thought he wasn't manly enough. Was she going to break this poor boy's heart?

'I'm sorry my kids had to be there to see it, too, but I'm happy Megan could help you.'

'Graham was awesome,' he said.

'I heard your grandparents were pretty upset,' I said.

He shook his head. 'My grandpa has problems. A bad temper and control issues. He's the one who decided he was going to sue Dad for custody of us, but I think we're too old. Wouldn't any judge in his right mind let us decide where we wanted to go?'

I shrugged. 'I don't know, but we can certainly find out.'

All of a sudden he leaned over and hugged me. 'I don't know what Dad and us would have done without you, Mrs Pugh,' he said, then got up and headed back upstairs.

Good Lord, I hadn't been hugged this much since my last time at Weigh In!

With Keith upstairs, the others wandered back into the living room.

'Should I fix everyone some lunch?' Berta asked.

'Why don't I take everyone out for lunch?' Ken suggested. 'But first, Berta, can I see you in the kitchen for just a moment?'

They left and Trisha turned to me. 'OK, dish.'

'He's going to tell her that she has to stay with me for a while.'

'In your house?' Trisha asked, aghast.

I laughed. 'Yes. She spent the night last night, and it was OK.'

'But I thought Willis was coming home.'

'Yeah, I know.' I sighed. 'I haven't got a clue what I'm going to do.'

A red-faced Ken and a sullen Berta came back into the room. 'How about O'Brian's?' he suggested, naming a Black Cat watering hole that made terrific sandwiches and soups. We all agreed and headed there in the minivan.

Seeing Berta in my old jeans was good for me. I had the soup and salad combo, instead of the Monte Cristo sandwich I really wanted. Afterwards, I drove Ken back to his house.

'I'm going to Codderville to meet that nurse at three today. Anybody want to go with me?' I asked.

'I need to check in with my office,' Ken said. 'I better not.'

'And I need to get home before my girls start calling Megan mommy,' Trisha said.

'Can I go?' Berta asked.

'Of course,' I said, not seeing a way around it.

Once we got to my street, I pulled into Trisha's driveway, took the house key off my key chain and handed it to Berta.

'Why don't you go on in my house while I gather up my wayward daughter?'

'OK,' she said, still dejected, I suppose, from Ken's talk with her. She got out and started across the street.

'Send Megan out, please,' I said to Trisha as she opened the door. But instead of getting out, Trisha shut the door and turned to me. 'You're having a problem with Berta, aren't you?'

I leaned my head back against the headrest. 'Oh, God, is it that obvious?'

'To me,' she said. 'Not to Berta, though. It would take a Mac truck to get anything negative through to her.'

'She's just so needy!' I said.

'I know, I see that,' Trisha said. 'Do we really want to do this? All this bother, for what? Maybe she did kill her mother—'

I shook my head. 'I don't think so,' I said, surprised by Trisha's doubt. 'I really don't. That's why I'm doing this, Trish. She gets on my nerves, but that's no reason for her to go to prison for a crime she didn't commit. If that were the case, every committee chairperson of every committee at both the church and the kids' schools would be in prison.'

Trisha laughed. 'You're right. I guess I'm just getting tired of this. I don't see your fascination with these kinds of puzzles.'

I turned off the engine. 'I'll come in with you,' I said, and went in search of my darling daughter.

MEGAN

Jeez, I thought, I didn't take these girls to raise! I came over here at nine this morning, and here it was after one o'clock in the afternoon! The little one, Tamara, finally went down for a nap, which only meant Tabitha wanted my entire attention. I mean, the entire time I was on the phone, all she did was pester me. And I had so much to tell Azalea and D'Wanda! Little brat.

Finally I heard a car in the driveway and it was Mom's

minivan. Thank God for small favors! I told Azalea and D'Wanda, 'Finally, my mom's home which means the mother of the year' (which is what I call Mrs Mc now) 'is also finally home. Y'all get Donzel and come get me! I absolutely *have* to get to the pool today or I will *die!*'

I hung up the phone before Mrs Mc and my mom came in the front door. 'Mommy!' Tabitha said and ran to Mrs Mc and threw her arms around Mrs Mc's legs. I was glad she wasn't into full sentences yet or she would rat me out for being on the phone.

'Hi, sweetie,' Mrs Mc said, hugging Tabitha to her. And I thought, don't try to prove what a wonderful mother you are now, lady, while I'm standing here waiting for my cash!

Speaking of which she said, 'Megan, I'm so sorry I don't have enough cash to pay you right now. Will you take a check?'

I was ready to say a bad word. I really was. Then Mom did something actually mom-like and said, 'Trisha, make it out to me and I'll go cash it and give it to her.'

'Great idea!' Mrs Mc said and wrote a check, which she gave *to my mother*! I wouldn't even know if it was the right amount until my mother either let me see it or gave me the cash! And then even my *own mother* could stiff me by not letting me see the check and just give me any old amount of cash and say that's all the check was for! I'd have no way of proving her wrong! And Mrs Mc would totally take her side! Gawd, I hate being cheated and robbed! How are you supposed to 'look up to' and 'respect' these people when all they did was take your money and lie to you?

We got to the minivan and I got in, fuming. Then Mom handed me the check. It was for double the amount I should have gotten. And in the memo section it said, 'For above and beyond.' That was nice.

I drove Megan to the bank, got the cash, gave it to her and headed back to the house. On the way, I told my daughter, 'Mrs McClure is not having an affair.'

She actually turned her head to look at me. 'Then what is she doing? And please don't tell me she's going to the hairdresser!'

'I'm going to tell you, but this is not something you tell your siblings, or discuss with Mrs McClure or really anyone, OK?'

'I'll tell Azalea and D'Wanda. They're my best friends and they already know something fishy is going on!'

I sighed but tried to remember what it was like when I was fifteen going on thirty. 'Just them, OK?'

'Got it!' she said. 'Now dish!'

'Megan, this is serious. Please don't treat it lightly,' I said. She nodded.

I decided to condense the story. 'Mrs McClure's brother has had a hard time with alcohol and is now in a rehab facility not too far from here. That's where she's going when she says she's going to the hairdresser. She didn't tell you the truth because she was afraid you'd need some lengthy explanation. I told her you were mature enough to understand and not judge.' Good one, E.J., I told myself.

My daughter fairly preened next to me. 'I understand,' she said, her voice serious. 'And maybe it *is* something I should keep strictly to myself,' she said.

I nodded my head. 'I think that's a wise choice, honey.'

When we got to the house, D'Wanda and Azalea's brother's car was parked in front. Megan said, 'Oh! I forgot to tell you! I'm going swimming with Azalea and D'Wanda. Donzel is taking us. I'll be home by dinner,' she said, jumping out of the car before I'd fully parked.

She ran inside before me and, while I was still putting my stuff down and wondering where Berta was, Megan came running down stairs in her bathing suit.

'Where's your cover-up?' I asked.

'Couldn't find it,' she said, heading for the front door.

'Get a towel!'

'I'll use one of theirs!' she said, and was gone.

I found Berta in my bedroom, lying on the bed, her eyes open.

'Trying to take a nap?' I asked.

'No,' she said. 'Just trying not to give up all hope.'

I sighed inwardly. I tried to sympathize. It had to be hard, not knowing who you were, not knowing anything of your past, wondering if it was possible you'd killed your own mother.

And I guess, in her eyes, her one friend, Ken, had rejected her. But there was something about Berta that was beginning to chap my ass. I just couldn't put my finger on what it was.

'You still want to go with me to see that nurse?' I asked her.

She sat up and rubbed her eyes. 'Yes. It'll keep my mind off everything, I hope.'

I patted her arm. 'It should. Go wash your face and we'll take off, OK?'

She nodded and I went into the kitchen and grabbed two bottles of water for the trip.

We pulled into Vera's driveway twenty minutes later.

'Y'all come on in,' Vera said, leaning her head out of her back door. 'We're a little early and I got coffee and some cinnamon rolls fresh out of the oven.'

Berta got out and I sat behind the wheel for a moment, groaning. Vera makes cinnamon rolls that could make an angel weep. If I ate one I'd weep too because of the actual poundage that would immediately adhere to my hips. I slid out of the van and ran up Vera's back steps, hoping the running motion would negate the cinnamon roll poundage.

Vera's kitchen smelled like heaven. There was the delicious smell of her freshly brewed afternoon coffee, and the spice of cinnamon and nutmeg and the undeniable scent of baked bread and sugar.

I blame Vera for most of the weight I gained the first few years after we moved here from Houston. Since Vera and I rarely spoke to one another, when we were at her house, I spent most of the time eating her food, which ran to country, fried, and wonderful. Mashed potatoes with real butter and heavy cream, gravy, chicken fried steak, handmade macaroni and cheese and thick-cut pork chops rolled in cracker crumbs and deep fried, fried chicken and corn on the cob slathered in real butter, chicken and rice with whole chicken pieces still on the bone, and a gravy so thick your fork could stand up in it. And, oh my God, the desserts! Red velvet cake with cream cheese frosting, fresh-picked blackberries in a cobbler with a crust so lovely it melted in your mouth, pecan pie with half pecans not pieces, and a filling that slid down your throat like a sweet song fills your ears.

I'd avoided eating at Vera's house since I went on my diet. We'd shared meals together, but mostly at restaurants, 'My treat, Vera!' but here I was, in her kitchen, with cups of coffee set out on placemats, and a plate of still steaming cinnamon rolls, and to add insult to injury, a dish of dairy butter, in case there weren't already enough fat and calories in the rolls. I sat down next to Berta and stared at the rolls. Tearing my eyes away, I watched while Vera poured herself a cup of coffee.

'Vera, this is Berta Harris—'

'She introduced herself, honey, while you were still in the minivan.' Vera looked at Berta with her evil eye she usually reserved for my transgressions. 'But she *said* her name was Rosalee.'

'So she didn't tell you what's going on?' I asked.

Vera sat down quickly. 'No, she did not, and I can't get a word out of Willis. So tell me!'

So I explained how I originally met Berta, how Trisha and I ended up at Berta's 'memorial,' and how I'd visited Kerry the afternoon of her death.

I got that much out, talking fast and looking into Vera's eyes to avoid looking at Berta next to me, who had gone for straight out gluttony and buttered her cinnamon roll, or Vera's hands in front of me, picking small pieces of cinnamon roll off and putting them on the plate in front of her (Vera is five foot even and weighs maybe eighty pounds – she cooks, she doesn't eat). I explained about finding Berta and finding out about her amnesia and finding out from Luna who Berta really was, which led us to the boys, which led us to why we were going to see Carolyn Gable, the former Bishop Byne High School nurse. Which I followed up with the explanation of the two names.

Vera smiled and patted Berta/Rosalee's hand. 'That's OK, then,' she said.

The Codderville Senior Center is located in a defunct church's former fellowship hall. The entire church complex had been taken over by the city and included a thrift shop, classrooms for seniors and the unemployed where they taught everything from arts and crafts to computer and tech skills, secretarial skills, medical assistance training, etc. There was also an office to help people fill out the paperwork for unemployment, WIC, welfare, and food stamps, a gym for seniors, and a food bank. In this economy, the place was hopping.

Vera told me they were using the two senior center buses to pick up the elderly, both city and rural, who had no air conditioning, and bringing them to spend the worst hours of the day in the cool of the senior center. So far this summer we'd already had one death attributed to the heat, and several hospitalizations of elderly citizens of the county. The fan drive (people buying new fans and bringing them to the center for seniors without air conditioners) usually started running the beginning of August and lasted through mid-September. This year it started at the beginning of July.

When you walked in the senior center, you went directly into one large room divided into sections. The fellowship hall had an attached kitchen, which was now used to prepare hot lunches for the seniors who came there. For some, it was their only hot meal of the day; for others, it was their *only* meal of the day. It was also out of this kitchen that Meals on Wheels operated.

The area closest to the kitchen had long tables set out for lunch; there was another area of round tables stacked with games and puzzles. When we walked in that afternoon, there was a round table with five women who appeared to be closing in on the century mark in age playing canasta, and another round table with two very old men playing something that required them to beat the table with their fists a lot. In this area was a Ping Pong table with an elderly man playing Ping Pong with a teenage boy. Toward the back of the large room, bringing together the two sides, was an area of couches and easy chairs facing a stage with a large-screen TV. Volunteers were still clearing the lunch tables and we could see more volunteers in the kitchen cleaning up.

'Carolyn will be in the kitchen. She's a volunteer.' Of course she was. As far as I could tell, no one under ninety actually used the facility. All the volunteers looked to be in their seventies or eighties. And seemed as fit if not more fit than either Berta or myself. Well, maybe me six months ago.

The kitchen was separated from the fellowship hall by a wall with a cut out for coffee service, and a doorway with only a saloon-style swinging door. Each was topped with a valance of western-style material – horses and cowboys and cows. We went through the swinging doors and into the kitchen.

A large woman was at the sink. She was wearing a short-sleeved shirt and knee-length shorts with very sensible shoes on her feet. She turned when she heard the swinging door, whose hinges definitely needed a few minutes alone with some WD40. She had steel-gray hair and a beautiful face. Being on the chubby side, her face was mostly devoid of wrinkles. If she lost a few pounds, believe me, they'd come rushing back. She had big blue eyes, a cherub nose, and a smile that made you want to smile back. This smile was now aimed at Vera.

'Vera Pugh, how you doing?' she said. She started to reach for my mother-in-law, but then said, 'Now wait, I want a hug, but I've gotta dry off!' She dried her hands while Vera laughed, and then the two hugged. 'How come we never see each other anymore?' she asked Vera.

'You're usually doing lunch and I don't usually drive the bus anywhere 'til late afternoon or evening,' Vera said.

'Well, that's the truth of it. This your daughter-in-law?' she asked, showing me her hand. I shook hands with her and she said, 'I know it's you 'cause Vera's mentioned your pretty red hair.' She leaned in as if to whisper in my ear and said, 'I love your smutty books! They remind me of my youth!'

'It's nice to meet you, ma'am,' I said. Indicating Berta, I said, 'This is my friend, Berta Harris.'

'Y'all just call me Carolyn. Why don't we go in the dining room so we can sit down.' She turned her head and said, 'Alice Ann, I'm taking a break.'

Alice Ann called back and said, 'I'll finish up. You go on.'

Carolyn Gable waved and ushered us out to the dining area. We took chairs on either side of the long table, Berta and me on one side, the older two on the other.

'Now what can I do for y'all?' Carolyn Gable asked.

'I understand you used to be the nurse at Bishop Byne High School, is that right?' I asked.

She grinned. 'Yep. From 1965, straight out of nursing school, until the place closed ten years ago this past June.'

'And I understand you're one of those people with an incredible memory.'

She frowned. 'More like total recall. You wanna tell me what's going on?'

I pulled out the pictures of the four teenagers and younger kids. 'Could you tell us the names of these two boys and the younger girl?'

She looked at the pictures, then up at me. 'I could, but I won't necessarily do so. Not until you tell me what this is about.'

I looked at Berta and she nodded her head. So for the second time in less than an hour, I was telling Berta's story. 'So we're hoping to find one of these boys to find out what kind of relationship Berta here – or Rosalee, if you prefer – had with her mother.'

Carolyn reached out a hand to Berta. 'I'm so sorry, honey. What a terrible burden.' She pulled back and said, 'The dark-haired boy is Ray Thornton. A real piece of work. Don't know the girl he's with,' she said, pointing at Kerry. 'Ray was in trouble a lot, drinking, wrecking cars, that sort of thing. Don't know if any of his people are still around. His daddy died before I knew Ray, and his mama liked hanging out in bars and bringing men home, leastwise that's what I heard. The younger girl there, that's Ray's little sister, I'm pretty sure. She went to Bishop Byne, too, but I didn't know her much. What was her name? Betsy? Patty? Patsy? Something like that. The red-headed boy is Timothy Quartermyer. He was a very good student until his junior year when he met up with Ray and started hanging out with him. I don't know this girl either,' she said, pointing at Rosalee.

'That's me,' Berta said.

'Well, weren't you the pretty thing?' Carolyn said. 'Now, Timothy did have a girlfriend at Bishop Byne – Cynthia Douglas.' Carolyn Gable frowned. 'Now that I think of it, maybe Cynthia became a nun.' Then you could tell a light went on behind her eyes. 'Oh my God! I just now put it together! I went with my daughter last week to her church in Black Cat Ridge! They just got a new priest! Last name

Quartermyer! How many could there be? I think that's why Timothy and Cynthia probably went together: both knowing they were joining the church and neither, you know, trying to, um, tempt each other? Know what I mean?'

We all knew what she meant.

'So the red-headed boy may be the new priest at the Catholic church in Black Cat Ridge?' I summed up.

'That's what I'm saying,' Carolyn said. 'Although I gotta say I don't remember the priest having red hair.'

'Red fades some when people get older,' Vera said. 'Except for this one,' she said, pointing at me.

I sighed. 'OK, Vera, I colored it. Are you satisfied?'

'I knew it!'

'What happened to the dark-haired boy?' Berta asked, getting us back on track and again trying to take care of Kerry.

Carolyn shook her head. 'He didn't even graduate. Left school close to the end, just left town, no one, not even Tim, I believe, knew why or where.'

I looked at Berta. 'Think we have time to stop by the church in Black Cat Ridge?'

She nodded and opened her mouth to speak, but Vera beat her to it. 'I'm going with y'all,' she said, and by her tone there would be no arguing.

'Well, y'all are gonna need me for introductions,' Carolyn said. 'After all, I'm the only one who knows him – except maybe Rosalee here?'

Berta shrugged. 'I guess,' she said, her voice timid.

I invited Carolyn and Vera to ride with me, but Carolyn said, 'Ah hell, you'd just have to bring us all the way back to Codderville, when y'all will practically be home.' She and Vera headed to an antique Shelby Mustang convertible, got in and peeled out. I could only hope to catch up.

I called Vera on her cell phone. 'When you get to the church, don't go in. I want to see Tim's reaction to seeing Rosalee. I don't want y'all telling him beforehand.'

'OK,' she said, 'but I don't think it's fair!'

'Vera—'

'OK, OK! Jeez!' she said and hung up.

Luckily I knew where the Catholic church was in Black

Cat Ridge. Our Lady of the Vines was toward the back of Black Cat Ridge, well into the woods, and had the same funky parking lot as the Episcopal Church where Berta's 'memorial' had been held. There were very few cars in the lot so it was easy to find the Shelby Mustang in front of a part of the complex that had a sign over it proclaiming 'office.' I parked next to the two old ladies and we all got out.

I moved in front as the two older women barreled toward the door. 'Now, listen, ladies,' I said, hands up like a traffic cop, stopping them in their tracts. 'Please let me do the talking. Carolyn, you start by reminding him who you are, then introduce me.'

Hands on hips, head cocked, the formerly sweet lady from the senior center said, 'And just who would that be?'

'Someone investigating the death of Kerry Killian,' I said.

'Should she say Kerry Metcalf? He'd have known her by that name,' Berta said.

I shook my head. 'No, Kerry Killian.'

The three women looked at each other and I thought I was going to have a mutiny on my hands. Finally, Carolyn nodded. 'OK, let's do it.'

And we headed into the office, not unlike the Americans lining up to meet the German tank officer toward the end of Willis's favorite movie, *Kelly's Heroes*. I could hear the strains of the theme song to *The Good, The Bad, and the Ugly* in my mind.

MEGAN

I swear Donzel wouldn't leave me alone. He told me a thousand times how good I looked in my swimsuit (and it's not even a bikini, which is what I wanted, but my *mother* said no, I was too young! I have breasts! They need to be seen, for gawd's sake!), and followed me around like a puppy dog. Actually I did look really good in this dumb one-piece. It shows off all the good parts, like my beautiful breasts, and my nice butt. And when I wear my hair down, guys do get a little weird, if you know what I mean. I can't help it. It's fun to make guys weird.

Then my phone rang. I made the mistake of not checking the caller ID before answering.

'Oh my God, Megan?'

'Yes?' I said, stretching out the word because, really, who was this person calling me at the *pool*?

'It's Trisha McClure! I need you to come over immediately! I have an emergency!'

If I hadn't been trained from *birth* to be 'respectful' of my elders, I would have said something like, 'You need to wax your eyebrows?' or something equally catty. Instead I said, 'Mrs McClure, I'm not at home. I'm at the pool.'

'The one on Taylor?'

I frowned. I didn't like where this was going. 'Yes, ma'am.'

'I'm on my way to pick you up. You and the girls can come with me and you can watch them in the clinic lobby—'

'But Mrs McClure—'

'I'll pay you a hundred dollars!' she screeched.

'Well, you better hurry up then.' Now I sorta wished I had something to put on over my bathing suit.

We hadn't made an appointment, so it was just luck that when I asked to see Father Quartermyer that the secretary said, 'Have a seat.'

When he came out of his office to greet us, I could see the red in his hair. It had faded even from the old pictures we had of him, but you could still see red under the fluorescent lights of the office. He had freckled skin – face neck and hands – eyes as green as an Irish valley, and was tall and lanky. On seeing him, I felt like I do whenever I see a very appealing gay guy: girls, we lost another one.

'Hi,' he said, holding out his hand to Carolyn Gable, who shook it and said, 'Father, may we speak privately?'

'Certainly,' he said and led us into his office. He pointed to his two visitor chairs, and Berta and I insisted the older ladies take them, then Carolyn spoke up.

'Father, you may not remember me, but I was the nurse at Bishop Byne when you attended. Carolyn Gable.'

A smile broke out on the priest's face. 'Mrs Gable! I'm surprised I didn't recognize you! You haven't changed a bit!

How nice to see you!' he stood up from his desk and walked around it. 'I've got to have a hug!' he said. Carolyn obliged by standing and hugging back. Now more casual, the priest leaned a hip against his desk and crossed his arms. 'To what do I owe this honor?' he asked.

Pointing at me, Carolyn said, 'This is my friend, E.J. Pugh. She's investigating the death of Kerry Killian on behalf of her husband.'

Tim Quartermyer stood and again held out his hand, which I shook. 'I heard about that tragedy, although I never knew Mrs Killian or her family,' he said.

'Oh, but you did, Father,' I said. 'You knew her as Kerry Metcalf.'

He was very still for a long moment, his face a blank. Then he frowned. 'What is this? I haven't seen Kerry Metcalf in fifteen years!'

'Does this face ring any bells?' I asked, indicating Berta.

The priest bent down and looked into Berta's face. 'Rosie?' he said, incredulous. 'Rosie Bunch?'

Berta raised her hand and fluttered her fingers. 'Guilty as charged,' she said, then grimaced. 'Maybe I shouldn't say that?'

'Maybe not right now,' I said. To the priest, I said, 'Rosie has been charged with killing her mother the night before she disappeared. I have a feeling that you all were together that night, as it seems y'all were together a lot. Can you recall?'

'What night was that? Rosie, do you remember?' he asked.

'That's the problem, Father,' she said. 'I don't remember anything.'

I then went into Berta's story yet another time.

'My God,' he said, going back around his desk to sink into his chair. 'You have no idea what happened to your mother?'

'I have no idea what I had for breakfast the day I was run over,' Berta said. 'You seem to be the only one left around out of the old group. I was hoping you could tell me something about my relationship with my mother.'

His face turned red again and he looked to his desktop, his hands busy with a rosary sitting there. 'Why hash up that old stuff now, Rosie? Let it lie—'

'I can't, Father—'

Timothy Quartermyer looked up at Berta/Rosie. '*Please* don't call me Father.' He smiled. 'You used to call me Timmy. You're the only one who ever did. You knew it piss— Sorry, made me angry.'

'So we were friends?' Berta asked.

'Good friends. Not boyfriend-girlfriend, just friends. Sometimes that's stronger – at least, it can last longer.'

'Do you remember anything about the night Rosie's trailer blew up with her mom in it?' I asked.

He looked back at his desktop, his face turning red. 'No, I sure can't recall that. I found out through the grapevine that Mrs Bunch was dead and Rosie had taken off.'

I wasn't a Catholic, didn't know a lot about them, to tell you the truth, but the one thing I was pretty sure about was that, just like Protestant ministers and Jewish rabbis, priests weren't supposed to lie. But it was pretty evident that Father Timothy Quartermyer was lying his ass off.

MEGAN

We got to the clinic where Mrs Mc's big brother was drying out (I sure hope Graham never makes me come see him when he dries out), and she made us sit in the lobby and wait. There were some patients in the lobby – some not that old, like maybe late teens, early twenties – and most of them were guys. And boy, were they looking. For the first time I was a little bit grateful Mom didn't let me buy that bikini – but don't tell her I said that.

I got the girls situated with coloring books and colors and went up to the woman at the reception counter. 'Do y'all have like a robe or something I can put on? Mrs McClure picked me up at the pool to watch her kids, and it's kind of cold in here.'

'Sure, honey, just a second,' she said and left her station.

I looked around me, waiting for the great escape. Nothing happened. The reception lady came back with a terry cloth robe. It was puke gray. I put it on and cinched it up tight. Then I glanced at the inmates. I was wearing the same thing they were. 'Ah, y'all aren't going to confuse me with them, are you? And put me in a rubber room?'

The woman looked serious. 'You better stay with the little girls, then we'll know you don't go back. Otherwise . . .' As her voice trailed off, she shrugged her shoulders. Then she said, 'Oh, by the way, you said you were with Mrs McClure, right?'

'Uh huh,' I said.

'I just saw her going out the side door. She was moving pretty fast.'

'What?'

'Maybe you can catch her in the parking lot?' she said as I ran into the lobby to get the girls, then dragged them out to the parking lot, only to see their mother turn the corner onto Birch. Birch only headed one way. Back to Black Cat Ridge.

I figured I wasn't going to get much more out of Timothy Quartermyer with this whole gang with me, so we said 'thanks so much' and 'see ya' and headed back to our cars.

I hugged Carolyn Gable. 'Thanks for the help, Carolyn,' I said. 'I really appreciate it.'

'You're welcome,' she said. She reached out a hand to touch Berta's shoulder. 'Honey,' she said, 'I have a feeling this is going to work out. I know I'm gonna pray for you, and I'll get my church prayer line on it. We've been able to pull out a few miracles.'

Berta moved in for a hug. 'It may take a miracle,' she said. 'And thank you.'

Holding out her hand to Vera, she said, 'And you too, Mrs Pugh. I don't know what we'd of done without you.'

'Just found another way, that's all,' Vera said in her pragmatic way.

I waved goodbye to my mother-in-law and she said, 'Any message for Willis?'

It seemed my husband hadn't yet told his mother he was moving back. I said, 'No, not really,' and we headed to separate towns in separate cars.

Alone in the car with Berta, I asked her, 'Did that bring up any memories? Seeing Tim, talking with him?'

Berta shook her head. 'No, nothing. I thought it would, E.J., I really did,' she said, turning in her seat towards me. I looked away from the road for a second to see her face all red and splotchy, her eyes filling with tears. 'What if I never remember?'

I reached out a hand to her. 'OK,' I said. 'What if? Worst-case scenario: what if you don't remember?'

'Then I may be locked up for killing my mother!' she said, the tears released.

I waved that away. 'I *meant* once we find your mother's real killer. That, my dear, is a given. We will find out who killed your mother, and I can guaran-damn-tee you it wasn't you.'

'Why do you say that? The trailer I lived in with my mom blows up and I run away. Sure seems to make me guilty!'

'No, it makes you *look* guilty. So if you killed your mother, who ran you down? And who killed Kerry? You? Like I said before, there are definitely other scenarios that could explain what happened to your mother. One, you were terrified that whoever did it – presumably someone you knew – would come back to kill you; two, you were kidnapped by someone who blew up the trailer to cover his tracks; three, when the trailer blew up, you were thrown clear, hit your head, had amnesia, and wandered off—'

Berta laughed. 'OK, I have amnesia *on top of* amnesia? Now that's going to be hard to cure!'

'It's just a theory!' I said defensively. 'And four—' I was silent for a moment. 'I'm still working on four. But we have three pretty good ones.'

'I'll give you two *fairly* good ones,' Berta said.

'Back to my point—'

'You had a point?' Berta said. I smiled at her. She was actually teasing me, which was a good sign. The timid, obedient Berta might be taking a back seat to the more spunky (I hoped) Rosie.

'Yes, I had a point! Worst-case scenario if you don't recover your memory: you run into people you should know and embarrass yourself by not recognizing them. There. That's it.'

Berta shook her head. 'I wish it was going to be that simple.'

'Well, it may not even be that bad. If you keep the name Berta Harris, and stay in Black Cat Ridge, added to the fact that you left Codderville fifteen or so years ago and as far as we know, didn't come back until around the time you were run down, I doubt if you *would* run into anyone you knew.'

'Wouldn't there be a legal problem with me keeping an alias? Because that's what Berta Harris is, right? An alias?'

'People have their names legally changed all the time. You could do that.'

Berta nodded her head. 'Yes, I suppose so.'

Unless, of course, I thought to myself, she and Ken decide to change it another way. And that would be such a *bad* idea!

MEGAN

Mom's phone wasn't answering. She must have had it on vibrate *again*! So I called my grandma Vera, since I was in Codderville. Both Tabitha and Tamara were crying and the little one kept trying to walk into the street, and I had to keep chasing her, and a hundred bucks was *not* going to cut it! Not by a longshot! Grandma Vera answered the phone on the second ring.

'Megan?' she said.

So Grandma Vera had caller ID. I also heard she has a Twitter account. 'Grandma, listen! I'm babysitting for this lady, and she took us to the rehab center out on the highway? And then she ran off and left us here!'

'You said "us," honey. Who all?'

'Me and her two little girls!'

I heard Grandma Vera talking to someone, then she said, 'We're on our way!' and she hung up.

I took the girls back into the lobby, but the big one kept crying, and everybody was giving me dirty looks – like it was *my* fault – so I took them back outside and kept them busy singing songs. Then this really cool car, red and low slung and, well, sexy, pulled into the circle drive and stopped right in front of me. The tinted window rolled down and – believe it or not! – my grandma Vera's head poked out.

'Is this a nifty car or what?' Grandma said, grinning.

'Rad,' I said, and immediately regretted it. That was some-thing Graham would say. Ewww!

The driver's-side door opened and a big lady got out – a lady much too big to have fit in that low-slung car, but she did nonetheless. (Don't you just love that word? Nonetheless.

Three words but you can put them together and then they're
one word! You gotta love the English language.)

'Now you tell me what's going on here, young lady!' the
big lady said. Like she was the boss of me or something.
'The lady who brought you here: was she supposed to be
going into rehab?'

'Oh, no, ma'am. She comes here to visit her big brother,
and for some reason she just ran out of a side door and left
us here.'

'Did the nurse's aide at the reception desk call her?'

I shrugged. 'I dunno.'

'Did anyone call her?'

Again I shrugged. 'I dunno.'

'Where did her brother say she was going?'

I was getting a crick in my neck, so I just said, 'I dunno.'

Turning to the open passenger window of the red car, she
said, 'Vera, you told me this girl was smart.'

It was Grandma's turn to shrug. 'She used to be.'

Grandma got out of the car and looked up at me. (Grandma's
very short and I'm very tall. You do the math.) 'Girl, did you
do *anything*?'

I was getting a little p.o.'d. 'I ran after the car! And I took
care of these kids! They've been crying and running around, and
trying to get in the street, and you try taking care of two little
girls who are spoiled rotten and see how you do!' My hands
were on my hips and I was breathing hard. Uh oh. Not good.

'Little lady, are you getting snippy with me?' Grandma said,
hands on her own hips and a frown on her face.

I sighed. 'Yes, ma'am, I did get snippy, and I apologize.
I'm just upset.'

The big lady said, 'Well, Vera, she's not that stupid. She
knew to apologize to you.'

Grandma Vera patted me on the back. 'She's a good girl,'
she said.

Then the big lady said, 'Let's go kick some nurse's aide
butt,' and opened the door for us to go in.

She went right up to the reception desk and said, 'I want
to see the nurse in charge.'

'In regards to?' the girl behind the counter said.

'In regards to you keeping your minimum-wage job, young lady. Where is she? I'll find her myself!' She walked purposely away with the receptionist following.

'No, ma'am! You can't go back there without an escort!' The older lady kept walking. 'Ma'am! Come back! Please come back!'

A door along the hall opened, and a woman in blue scrubs with Mickey and Minnie Mouse on them, stepped into the hall. 'Sherry, what is going on?'

The girl, Sherry, I guess, said, 'I tried to stop her, Nurse. But she just barged through—'

'Go back to reception, Sherry. And don't leave your station again. You know that red button under the counter? When this sort of thing happens, you push that button and big, burly men come to your rescue. Can you remember that, Sherry?'

The girl turned all sorts of red – who could blame her? That nurse lady was mean! – said, 'Yes, ma'am,' and ran back to the reception desk.

'And you are?' she said to the big lady.

'Carolyn Gable, R.N., UT class of 'fifty-five,' she said.

'Judy Pearce, R.N., UT class of 'sixty-five,' she said, smiling at our nurse lady. 'Please come in my office. I certainly hope you're not applying for a job. That would be a bad first impression.'

'Hardly,' Mrs Gable said, turning back around and waving the rest of us forward.

We went into Nurse Pearce's office and sat down, Grandma taking both girls and sitting them on her tiny knees. They were perfectly content.

'This young lady,' Mrs Gable said to the head nurse, 'is my friend's granddaughter. She came here with the woman she babysits for, as I understand it, and then, Megan, please tell her what happened.'

'Yes, ma'am,' I said. Looking at the head nurse, I said, 'I was at the pool when Mrs McClure called me with an emergency so that's why I'm in my bathing suit,' I said, opening the robe so all could see I wasn't a patient. 'The receptionist gave me the robe to cover up.'

'Are you on point, dear?' Mrs Gable asked.

'Ah, maybe not. Anyway, Mrs McClure comes here to see her big brother, and she left me and her girls in the lobby, and went back and then we saw her leave through the side door and when I got outside, she was driving away.'

'Hum, well, I guess I've been a little slow in putting two and two together,' Nurse Pearce said. 'I saw you in the lobby but had no idea you were involved with Ray Thornton.'

Mrs Gable stood up and Grandma almost dropped the girls. They seemed really surprised. 'What has Ray Thornton to do with this?' Mrs Gable asked.

'Mrs McClure is his sister. Mr Thornton has been with us on mandatory drug and alcohol rehab due to DUIs, to reduce his sentence, but he escaped tonight. That's why we called his sister.'

Grandma and Mrs Gable looked at each other. Turning to me, Mrs Gable said, 'Which way did you say she was going?'

I pointed in the general direction of Black Cat Ridge. 'Home,' I said.

Mrs Gable pushed us all out of the room. Over her shoulder she yelled at Nurse Pearce, 'Call the sister! Find out where she is!'

'The younger girl in the photo?' I heard Grandma say.

Mrs Gable said, 'Got to be,' and we all headed outside.

Mrs Gable stuffed me and the little girls into the back seat of her very small sports car. I mean, there *was* a back seat, but not much of one. 'I had seat belts installed in the back for my grandkids,' she said to my grandma. 'Help Megan figure them out.'

We spent quality time pulling out the bottom seat cushion to find the various parts of the seat belts, then Grandma helped me clip the girls in. 'They really should be in car seats,' I told Mrs Gable.

'Thanks for the information dear, but do you *see* any car seats?'

I swear that woman could be as sarcastic as, well, me.

We got everyone settled and Mrs Gable headed out of Codderville and over the river to Black Cat Ridge. It was already getting dark and the perfect day was turning into a perfect night. I'd left the robe at the reception desk and was in just my bathing suit, and with such a small car, the air conditioning worked really, *really* well. I was freezing.

'What are you thinking?' Grandma asked Mrs Gable.

'Ray's family was Catholic. Which means his sister probably is, which means, since she lives in Black Cat Ridge—'

'That it's possible she goes to Our Lady of whatever in Black Cat Ridge, which means—'

'That she knows Timothy Quartermyer is the priest there, which—'

'Means that maybe Ray might be headed there—'

'Or at least his sister thinks he is—'

'So we go straight to the church.'

'Exactly,' Mrs Gable said and stepped harder on the gas. The two little girls looked up at me with wide eyes and big smiles. Hey, who doesn't like speed?

Grandma kept calling and recalling someone on her cell phone, so I finally asked, 'You calling my mom?'

'It's going to voice mail,' Grandma said.

'She has a bad habit of putting it on vibrate then forgetting about it,' I told her.

She hit another number and I heard her say, 'Willis? This is your mother. Things are heating up.' She listened for what seemed a long time and then said, 'Well, I have Megan with me, and have no idea where the other three are. Your wife and her friend Berta are God only knows where and E.J.'s cell phone just goes to voice—' A shorter silence, then, 'Yes, I know – vibrate. Maybe she likes it. Which means you really should move home. Anyway, I just thought I'd let you know we think we know who the killer is –' silence, then '– my friend Carolyn Gable and I.' Silence. 'Yes, you know her—'

'Vera, cut to the chase!' Mrs Gable said.

'Cutting to the chase here, Willis. Meet us at the Catholic church in Black Cat. We don't want to try to take this guy down with Megan and her two wards in tow.' Silence. 'She's babysitting, Willis.' Silence. 'Yes, I'm serious.' Silence. 'Hush! Carolyn and I have to stop this guy before he kills again!' Then she hung up on my dad. And I thought, what the hell is going on?

'Grandma?' I said.

She turned around and patted my hand. 'It's OK, honey. Your dad will show up and take care of you and the girls.'

'But who killed who and what has a priest got to do with it and where's Mom? Is she OK or is she in trouble?' I asked, sitting forward in my seat, my hands in a white-knuckled grip on the back of Grandma's seat.

Just leave it to my mother to get killed when I hadn't been nice to her lately. I swear she hates me.

I dropped Berta off at my house and drove to the pool to pick up Megan. I found D'Wanda, Azalea, and Donzel, but was told Megan had been picked up by Trisha and was going to the rehab center.

'In her bathing suit?' I asked, eyebrows arched.

'Yes, ma'am, she didn't have her cover-up with her,' Azalea (I think) said.

'OK, kids, thanks,' I said and headed out to my car. I picked up my cell phone to call Megan and saw I had eight calls and that my phone was on vibrate yet again. I put it on ring tone and checked the messages, thinking one had to be from Megan.

> Message 1: Megan: 'Mom, where are you? Did you leave your phone on vibrate? You need to call me immediately—'
> Message 2: Megan: 'Mom! Call me! It's like an emergency! This is Megan.'
> Message 3: Megan: 'Mother, if you *ever* get this message just know you forced me to call Grandma.'
> Message 4: Vera: 'E.J., it's Vera your mother-in-law. Where are you? Call me on my cell phone immediately!'
> Message 5: Vera: 'E.J., it's Vera again. Where are you? Call—'
> Message 6: Vera: 'E.J., it's Vera – on vibrate? Whatever for? Oh, for God's sake—'
> Message 7: Unknown: 'Hi, neighbor, this is Jim Jacobs asking for your vote—'
> Message 8: Willis: 'E.J., it's Willis. All hell appears to be breaking loose. My mother has Megan and Megan's babysitting charges and wants me to meet

them at the Catholic church in Black Cat. Something about how they know who the killer is. Once again you've managed to ensnare the entire family—'

I hung up, did a 180 in the middle of Black Cat Drive, and headed for the church of Timothy Quartermyer.

MEGAN

We got to Black Cat Ridge faster than you'd think. And then we were at the church. 'There's her car!' I said, seeing Mrs McClure's Toyota hybrid right in front of the sanctuary. Mrs Gable made a quick, fast turn and slammed on her breaks, sliding in right beside the Prius.

'Ah,' I said. 'Grandma, shouldn't we call the police?'

'No time!' Mrs Gable said, baling from the car. 'You call them while we go in!'

Grandma baled with her, leaving me and the girls in the back seat. I got my cell phone from the leg of my swimsuit – it fits very nicely there, what with the elastic and all – and just as I was about to call 911, the phone rang. I saw it was my mother.

'Well, you're alive, at least!' I said upon answering.

'What the hell is going on?' Mom asked.

'We're at the church. The Catholic one. Grandma and Mrs Gable have gone inside to confront Mrs McClure—'

'Trisha? What on earth for?' Mom asked.

'I don't know. Something about her brother,' I said.

'You've got Trisha's girls?' Mom asked.

'Yes, they're with me and they're getting antsy, Mom. I think they're hungry.' One of them, the little one, was beginning to cry. This entire experience has convinced me that children are not in my future!'

'I'm almost there, honey. Just hold on!'

'Dad's on his way too,' I told her.

'I know, he left me a message,' she said.

We hung up and I considered whether or not I should call 911 as Mrs Gable had instructed. I mean, both Mom and Dad were on their way. Wasn't that enough?

*   *   *

I saw Willis's pick-up in my rear-view mirror as I turned into the church parking lot. In front of me, I saw Carolyn Gable's Shelby Mustang, and pulled alongside it. I noticed Trisha's Prius on the other side. The passenger side door of the Mustang opened and my daughter's butt emerged.

'Thank God you're here!' she said as Willis pulled in on the other side of me.

'Help me get these girls out, Mom!'

I could hear them both crying. I helped unbuckle them and set them on the ground. One stopped crying, but the younger one continued to emit screeching howls. 'Put them in the minivan—' I started, but my daughter broke in.

'No! Mom, I'm going in there! I'm worried about Grandma!'

'No, young lady, you're getting in the minivan now,' Willis said from behind us, 'and taking these girls with you. Here,' he said, handing the younger one his keys. 'See how fun?'

For some reason the little one did see how fun and moved obediently into the minivan, along with her sister and a pissed off Megan.

Willis and I headed for the giant double doors of the church. 'Maybe we should try a side door,' I suggested, 'just in case.'

He nodded and we moved to the nearest side, and found a door that led into the lobby in front of the sanctuary. The door opened and closed silently as we made our way through. We could hear voices coming from inside the sanctuary.

Mrs Gable was saying, 'Trisha, dear, you really need to let me look at Timothy. I'm a nurse and he's hurt—'

An exasperated Trisha said, 'That was the point, for God's sake! He's supposed to be dead!'

'God, Patti, what're you doing?'

I peeked around the door jamb to see who was speaking. The man talking bore only a slight resemblance to the boy in the pictures, the first love of Kerry Metcalf Killian. Where Ray Thornton the boy had been broodingly handsome, the man was but a shadow of his former self. His hair prematurely graying, his skin sallow and loose, his stomach protruding over his belt buckle, he was barely recognizable. Unfortunately, Trisha was holding a gun, and I could see two black-clad feet sticking out beyond her. From what I'd heard Carolyn say, I could only assume that was Father Quartermyer.

I moved back into the lobby, over to a corner and called Luna. 'Catholic church – Black Cat. Trisha's got a gun!' I hissed and hung up.

'Still cleaning up your mess!' the woman I knew as Trisha shot back. 'The same thing I've been doing for fifteen years!'

'Patti, I forgive you—'

'Oh, shut up, Tim! I do *not* recognize you as God's emissary, OK? You're just Tim, and you've got to go!'

She aimed the gun at Tim, and before I knew what was happening, a large figure pounced from amongst the pews, knocking Trisha sideways, sending her gun flying. I looked around me where Willis had been. He wasn't there. Instead, he was in the sanctuary, lying on top of little Trisha McClure, or should I say Patti Thornton McClure?

The gun landed near Ray Thornton. He bent and picked it up, holding it loosely in his hand.

I went further into the sanctuary. 'Ray, why don't you give the gun to Nurse Gable?' I suggested.

He looked up and saw me, and shook his head. 'No. God, I'm sorry, Tim. Has somebody called an ambulance?' he asked.

'I did,' I told him. 'And the police.'

He nodded. 'That's good.'

Willis had gotten up off Trisha and had her sitting on the front pew, holding on to her arm.

'Patti, you shouldn't have done these things—'

'Shut up, Ray!' she spat. 'Just aim the gun at this asshole and let's get out of here!'

'Too much running, Patti. That's all I've done for the last fifteen years,' Ray said. He looked at Carolyn Gable. 'You never did like me, did you?' he said.

'Like had nothing to do with it, Ray. You just had a wild streak and I was hoping you'd grow out of it.' She shook her head. 'Instead, looks like you just let it take you over.'

'No, it wasn't like that,' he said, shaking his head, his hand gripping the gun harder. 'Me and Kerry – we could have made it, ya know? She was helping me, calming me down. I just needed to get out of that house. Away from my dad—'

'Shut up, Ray!' Trisha yelled.

'And you, too, Patti. I needed to get you away from Dad. So he'd stop—'

Trisha pulled away from Willis and ran at Ray. 'Shut up! Shut up! Shut up!' She flung herself on him, Willis right behind her. He grabbed her as she grabbed Ray. And the sanctity of the sanctuary was broken by the echoing sound of a gunshot.

MEGAN

I heard this loud noise come from the church, and since I figured there wasn't a car inside backfiring – like they always say they think it is on TV – I figured it had to be gunshot. I told the girls to stay put, rolled the windows up high enough so they couldn't fall out, but low enough for them to get some of the cooler night air, and ran inside.

At first all I could see was Mrs Gable holding a gun. Then Grandma sitting on Mrs McClure. Then I saw Mom on the floor with my dad, and blood all around.

'Daddy!' I screamed and ran over to them.

We all heard sirens coming into the parking lot.

'Oh my God!' I said, and started crying.

'Go to the door and lead the cops and paramedics in here!' Mrs Gable said. 'Now, girl!'

I jumped up and ran outside. I was waving my arms for the emergency vehicles when I noticed the minivan was gone. Yes, I said gone. I got a head rush and sort of fell down. When I opened my eyes my future husband, the father of my children, was leaning over me. 'How are you doing?' he said, taking this plastic mask off my face.

'OK?' I said. 'Oh! My dad—'

'We've got him in the ambulance now. Were you missing something?' he asked, grinning at me, and even though I was lying down, my knees got weak. I looked past him at Mrs McClure's little girls. 'Oh, God! I thought they'd been kidnapped!' I said, sitting up.

The big one said, 'Me drive, Meggie!'

That's when I noticed my mom's minivan on the other side of the parking lot wrapped around a tree.

'Seems she moved the gear shift out of park into neutral,' the man of my dreams said. 'The natural incline moved the car.'

'I shouldn't have left them—'

'You're damn right you shouldn't have!' my mother said from behind me. 'What were you thinking?'

'I was thinking I heard a gunshot and that maybe you or Dad were hurt! And I guess I was thinking right!' I said.

Then my mom hugged me. Well, that shook me up. 'Is Dad OK?' I asked her, peering around for my future husband who seemed to have deserted me.

'Good thing he doesn't wear earrings,' Mom said.

'Huh?'

'She shot off his earlobe.'

'Ewww!'

THIRTEEN

We were gathered at Ken Killian's house. Chairs had been pulled in from the dining-room table and the kitchen table to accommodate the crowd: Ken and his boys, Berta, Luna, Vera and Carolyn Gable, all four of my kids, and Willis – with a sporty bandage covering his ear – and me.

When Luna started to talk, Willis said, 'Speak up!' and pointed to the bandage. She rolled her eyes and spoke up.

'OK, to start from the beginning: this is what I've pieced together. I've interviewed Ray Thornton and he confessed to throwing the matches at the butane tank at the trailer that night, Berta – or should I call you Rosalee now?'

'I think I'll go with Rosie,' she said, smiling at Ken and his boys. 'That's what Kerry used to call me at school. I remember now.'

'OK, then, Rosie. He said he didn't think there was a leak. He said Rosie told him there was, but he didn't believe her. According to Ray, Kerry got pissed at him and left with Tim, who was also mad that he was throwing matches around. Kerry's brother went with them. Which means only you, Rosie, and Ray and his sister Patti, who we now know as Trisha McClure, were there when the trailer blew up. Ray said he was so drunk he just ran, and he didn't stop running until he passed out. He woke up the next day in the woods and made his way home, not remembering what he'd done until he heard about Rosie's mom dying in the trailer and Rosie missing. He had no idea why she ran away. But in talking to Trisha – or Patti – jeez, everybody involved with this has too many names! – anyway, Trisha said she told Rosie that if she ever breathed a word of this—'

'She was going to do horrible things to me,' Rosie/Berta whispered. 'She said she'd do anything to protect Ray, that he was the only person she could turn to, and she wasn't going to let some trailer trash like me get in the way. The things she said – I can't even say out loud what she was going to do. It was so horrible.'

'You're remembering?' I asked, grabbing her hand.

She nodded her head. 'Some of it,' she said.

'You may get it all back,' Carolyn Gable said. 'It'll just take some time.'

Berta looked up, tears in her eyes. 'I don't know if I want it all back,' she said.

'So you ran away?' Luna said.

Berta shrugged. 'Yes,' she said, not too sure of herself. 'To a city.' She looked at me. 'A big city. But not in Texas.'

'It'll come,' Carolyn said.

Luna nodded, and continued. 'Trisha said Rosie called her last year, said she needed money, and if Trisha wanted her to continue to keep quiet about what Ray did she was going to have to pay her $30,000.'

'Oh my God! I did that?' Rosie cried. 'How awful!'

'That's a weird amount,' I said. '$30,000. I mean, why not $50,000? Or $25,000?'

As if mesmerized, Rosie said, '$27,592.53.'

'Pardon?' I said.

Rosie looked up. 'That's the amount I needed,' she said.

'For what?' Luna asked.

Rosie shook her head. 'I'm not sure.'

'OK,' Luna said, sighing. 'Anyway. Trisha said she agreed to meet her late that night by the old ball park in Codderville. When she got there, she saw Rosie walking along the road and says she couldn't help herself. She professes she, excuse the expression, "just went nuts," and ran her down, then zoomed off for home. Where I supposed she kissed her daughters and tucked them into bed.'

Luna doesn't have much use for excuses. I can kind of see her point.

'So,' I said, taking up the story, 'we know what happened after that. Did Trisha think Rosie was dead?'

'She said she kept looking in the papers and never saw anything about a dead body, but just hoped she'd missed it,' Luna sad. 'Although, really, a dead body in Codderville? Front-page news.'

'So how did she find out I was alive?' Rosie asked.

'The twelve-step groups,' I said. 'You showed up in her MADD group and, even though you'd colored your hair, wore glasses, and gained weight, she must have recognized you.'

Rosie nodded. 'Not at first though. I'd been to, like, maybe two or three MADD meetings before the electric space heater in the bathtub incident,' she said.

'And what about that stupid attempt?' I asked Luna. 'What does Trisha have to say about that?'

'She claims she had an extension cord and had it all plugged in nicely. She claims it's all Rosie's fault. Says she's a witch and she can't be killed.'

Rosie laughed and covered her mouth with her hands. Bringing them down, she said, 'Well, that explains so much!'

We all had a nice laugh to relieve the tension, then I asked, 'But why kill Kerry?'

'She said Kerry called her at home the afternoon after you and Trisha visited her. She recognized Trisha as Patti then – whose full name by the way is Patricia Rene Thornton McClure. The first time she met Trisha when you called at her office she couldn't see past her changed appearance – eighteen years is a long time. Anyway, Kerry asked her if she was Patti, then accused her of running down Rosie. Asked her what she wanted and why she was doing this. Trisha said she told Kerry she'd explain everything if Kerry would meet her at Kerry's office late that afternoon. She said when she got there, Kerry was pacing up and down, wringing her hands, and she knew she was about to blow – her words, Ken,' Luna said to Kerry's husband, 'and knew she wouldn't keep her mouth shut. So, anyway—'

'So she shot her,' one of the twins said.

Ken put his arm around the boy's shoulders. 'At least we know now,' he told his boys. 'Your mom was trying to save a friend.'

'Why would she trust her? I mean, jeez, Mom, you already thought she tried to kill Rosie!' the boy said, raising his head as if to speak to the ceiling.

'Your mom was a good woman,' Rosie said. 'If I'd known what she planned to do, Keith, I would have stopped her.'

'No one's blaming you, Berta – I mean, Rosie,' Ken, Sr said.

'Really, Rosie,' Keith said, 'none of this is your fault. Let's be pragmatic,' the boy said. 'All this is that bitch Mrs McClure's fault.'

'Language!' Ken, Sr said automatically.

Keith looked askance at his dad. 'Really, Dad? *Really?*'

Ken shrugged. Ken, Jr, said, 'But what about Uncle Mark? That was her, wasn't it?'

'She denies it,' Luna said, 'but her brother Ray said she knew he was coming to town because Ray told her. Mark had called him, thinking they could get together for drinks while he was in town for the funeral, and he mentioned it to Trisha – or Patti, or whatever. He said Patti had the hots for Mark back in the day, but Mark wasn't into her. According to Ray, she confessed on the phone to him last night that she'd killed both Mark and Kerry. So,' Luna said, 'maybe she killed him because she thought that he, too, would recognize her, or because she'd waited a long time to get revenge for the rejection, or both.'

'Trisha seemed so normal,' I said. 'I liked her.'

'Me, too,' Rosie said and touched my hand. 'I'm sorry you lost a friend.'

'Hey, Lieutenant Luna,' one of the boys said, 'could you give me and Ken here maybe fifteen minutes alone with this bitch?'

'Almost wish I could,' Luna said, giving Keith a sad smile. 'The state would save a lot of money if I could just turn murderers over to their victims' families.'

'Then you'd get these serious church types who'd forgive them and let them go,' Carolyn Gable said.

'You've got a point,' Luna said. 'Anyway, although Codderville and Black Cat Ridge are only a few miles apart geographically, they're a thousand miles apart economically. Maybe Trisha thought coming back to the area, but living in Black Cat Ridge, no one would recognize her. Bottle blonde-haired beauty married to a rich man – who would suspect the little girl whose Daddy drank himself to death? Who did she recognize first? No one until Rosie showed up out of the blue? Once Rosie came out in the open, it was almost impossible for Trisha to get to her, but since she came to believe that maybe Rosie really did have amnesia after she'd run her over, everything was OK. Then there's Kerry and, the cherry on the top, Timothy Quartermyer was given the Black Cat Ridge parish and she began to believe again that it was all going to come out – that he would also recognize either her or Rosie, so she felt she had to kill him as well. When Trisha confessed to Ray last night, he knew it would only be a matter of time before she tried to do the same to Tim. He called her this afternoon to say it had to stop and that he wasn't going to let her hurt anyone else. That's when she rang Megan about her 'emergency,' picking her and the girls up on her way to the clinic to speak to Ray. But she was too late – he had already left to warn Tim.'

'So we're saying she's a little nutso,' Vera said.

'No, now, don't start with that defense!' Luna said. 'She's as sane as you and me.'

'What was Ray talking about with their dad?' I asked.

'I asked him about that,' Luna said. 'Ray said his dad was a heavy drinker, used to get Ray drunk when he was just a kid because he thought it was funny. And he sexually abused Trisha, according to Ray. She denies it, but it would explain why she was so determined to protect Ray. No one else knew about her past. As she said to Rosie, he was the only person she could really confide in.'

'Maybe if she admitted it, it could help in her defense,' I said.

'Whose side are you on?' Luna said.

'On the side of truth and justice, always,' I said.

MEGAN

I never did get that hundred dollars Mrs McClure promised me. I suppose she'll need it for her defense. Her husband got her a lawyer, saying he couldn't defend her because she was his wife. I thought only doctors had that rule. Anyway, he moved his kids to Austin where his practice is, so I'm not babysitting any more. Their house is on the market and there's a Kerry Killian sign on it. Mr Killian gave up his part-time law practice and is now taking over Mrs Killian's real estate company. Keith said he had to become a licensed realtor, but he passed the test with flying colors. Keith and I talk on the phone a lot, and we've met a couple of times at the pool. I think he approves of my swimsuit, if you know what I mean.

I never did see my fireman again. He was kind of old, I guess, but that's all relative. I mean, say I'm fifteen now and he's like thirty. When I'm thirty, he'll be forty-five, which isn't that much older, know what I mean? Once you hit thirty, you're old no matter what, so what's the difference?

Bess and Ken have been hanging out some and we've talked about maybe double dating, but nobody drives and it's so gross to have somebody's parents drop you off somewhere. We've been thinking about maybe getting Graham to do it. Then Alicia can come along and it'll be like a triple date. I mean, after all, it's totally obvious to both me and Bess that she has a thing for big bro. She won't admit it, but we know she does!

This whole thing with Mrs McClure has taught me a lesson: go with my first instinct. I knew something was up with her and that hairdresser business! Obviously, if a woman will lie about something as basic as beauty treatments, then she'd could do just about anything! Am I right?

My minivan was totaled. Oh, gee. What a shame. The insurance payout was a nice hefty down payment on an Audi A5 Cabriolet. Not a two-seater, but I love it. Totally and completely! I want to marry it. Willis says I can. Oh, and Willis. He's home. He looks sort of rakish with only one earlobe. Vera is knitting him a pale pink ear cozy, but I doubt if he'll ever wear it.

Good news on the Berta/Rosie front. She remembered that the '$27,592.53' was how much she needed to keep the bank from foreclosing on her home. She just didn't remember where her home was. So we ran some ads in the major papers of several large cities – not in Texas – with Rosie's picture but no name. I put my cell phone number in the ads.

While we waited for responses, I drove Rosie out to where Ken and I had gone that day – to the location of the trailer Rosie had shared with her mother. I brought hedge clippers and a rake. When we got to the trailer, a funny thing happened.

A smile appeared on Rosie's face. 'Mama,' she whispered.

'What do you see?' I asked her, my voice barely above a whisper.

'We're making Christmas decorations. We just wandered

around outside and found stuff that would look pretty, and Mama bought some red construction paper. And we're making wreaths and stuff.' She laughed. 'Mama was very talented. Very artistic. She worked at the dry cleaners in town. And when someone left something more than sixty days, she would bring it home and make me something – even if it was a man's suit, she could turn it into something really pretty.'

'This is a one-bedroom—' I started. I guess, me being a woman who has plenty, that one bedroom had gotten to me.

'We had twin beds and shared it, like sisters, Mama used to say. She was fourteen when she had me, so we were pretty close in age.' Rosie looked at me. 'I remember her,' she said. She came to me and put her arms around me and hugged me close. 'Thank you.'

The next week I got a call from a man named Ed Flushing. His wife Rosie had left back in November to come to Texas to get an inheritance, she said, that might be able to save their home. He didn't know where in Texas because she never talked about her past, but he recognized her picture.

He and their kids came down from Chicago a couple of weeks after we put the ad in the paper, and everything began to fall in place for Rosie. And this was the kicker: Ed Flushing and both her son and daughter were redheads!

At one point she turned to me and whispered, 'Don't ever tell him I thought I wasn't attracted to red-headed men, OK?'

I mimed locking my lips and throwing away the key.

Ed hadn't been able to save their home, but did find another job – having been laid off led to the foreclosure – in a small town in southern Illinois.

'I think you'll like it,' he said. 'It's kind of laid-back, and the schools are great. And there are three beauty shops there always looking for beauticians.'

'Oh!' Rosie said. 'I'm a beautician?'

Ed laughed. 'Yeah, you are.'

'Mom, did you forget me?' her daughter asked.

Rosie put her hands on either side of her daughter's face. 'For only a minute, darlin'. Only a minute.'

Rosie went back to Illinois with her family, but will have to come back to testify at Trisha's trial. Trisha's brother Ray pled guilty to manslaughter in the death of Rosie's mother and has already gone to Huntsville, where the state prison is. I hear they have a good AA program there; I hope he takes advantage of it.

It's going to be an interesting trial, as Trisha and her lawyer are pleading insanity, but with as many people as the district attorney will be calling – everybody involved – I don't see how she can keep a straight face on that one.

We'll see.